The Infinite Within

By

Michael Drakich

Traanu Enterprises
Amazon Edition

Copyright © Michael Drakich
ISBN-13: 9780987770639

First Edition Traanu Enterprises, July 2013

Editor Kate Richards
Cover Rachel Charron

Dedication

To my family, who have, without their knowledge,
provided many of the names of the characters in this novel,
especially the villains.

PROLOGUE

The blackness of space had entombed the Voyager 1 for some time. The ship turned its camera to view from whence it came. In looking back, the home star appeared no different from all the others, a small bright dot amongst billions, the home planet, no longer even visible.

No warmth from any star permeated its sheathed exterior. Despite the frigid cold of space, its equipment continued to operate. Sensors still recorded data and communications continued to send scheduled reports. But with energy at a premium, orders had been received to shut down some functions to extend the life of its power source.

The end would come in the next twenty years, somewhere out in the cold dark reaches of the galaxy. Its forward momentum would ensure the dead hulk's arrival at a distant star.

Though not as tightly packed, the particles of the solar wind from the home star still pushed against its framework, urging the spaceship in its headlong mission. But its speed had slowed considerably. In time, sensors indicated this push had waned to the point where more particles were travelling sideways than out.

The simple analysis was the device neared the Heliosheath boundary of the home star. Soon, the stellar wind of the galaxy would interfere with its progress and the last vestiges of home would be left behind.

A sensation not felt in a long time began to envelop it—warmth. The conflicting waves of solar wind from the star against the incoming waves from the rest of the galaxy heated the surrounding particles. Hot charged protons and electrons bounced off the ship's sheathing, transferring their energy into its framework.

1

As it neared the juxtaposition point, the photons around it roiled in the wake of the craft, forming a kind of slipstream. Others slipped off to head in the reverse direction, no different from the ripples in a pond when a motorized toy boat floated across. Eddies, in the waves of particles, allowed some of them to skip forward, others to slip past.

A sudden displacement of the solar wind near its port side gave the low-energy charged particle instrument pause. In an instant, the readings fell off the chart to zero. As if, for a brief moment, there was nothing there. Whatever phenomenon caused it was undetectable. Power limitations had already resulted in the termination of the plasma subsystem, the planetary radio astronomy experiment, the scan platform, and most recently, the ultraviolet spectrometer. Whether any of those devices could have analyzed the anomaly became a moot point. In the following instant, the readings returned to normal and the spacecraft Voyager 1 continued on its mission.

CHAPTER 1

Brooke lay on her back, staring through the skylight at the full moon above. "Look at it, Robert. Just hanging there, calling to me."

Her lover, sighed heavily, then propped himself up on one elbow. "Your turn will come someday, Brooke. They can't deny you forever."

She looked over at him and played a hand across his chest. "Easy for you to say, Mr. First Mission since Apollo. For six months you got to go there. Six months! It's not bad enough you've already had three other extended missions in space."

He grabbed at her fingers. "Hey, it wasn't all fun and games. That first mission to the moon nearly killed us. No matter how hard we tried, we couldn't keep the regolith out of the air system. In the end, Trevor lost a lung."

The recent image of one of Robert's crew mates surfaced in her mind. He had been so big and strong but now was only a shell of his former self. "Yeah, that was too bad. I understand he never recovered his bone mass either. How long has it been?"

Robert fell back onto his pillow. "It'll be four years next month. I've seen him a number of times since then. He looks terrible. I don't think he's getting any better."

"Still, they have a revolving crew of six up there now. And the new scrubbers have kept the system clean for some time. I've been training, for seven years. I can appreciate not being part of the original team with you. NASA's decision to send only males to set up the first base was probably based on concern with how it would look if someone died more than anything else. The American public wouldn't have been too happy if a woman got killed up there. Look at all the noise when those shuttles went down. But men can die heroes. It's not fair. I think I deserve my chance."

Robert chuckled. "So you want to die a hero?"

She rolled over and tapped him with the bottom of her fist. "No, silly. You *know* what I mean. Ever since I was a little girl, I've wanted to go into space, to be an astronaut, to visit the moon, the planets, the stars. Now that I'm so close, it seems further away than ever. With each rotation, they're sending females, but not me. Not even Americans. Girls from Canada, Russia, Europe, and Japan! Girls from…from Timbuktu, for all I know!"

"Hey! Easy on the hitting. I thought you were taking those classes for self-defense, not offense." Robert grabbed her arm and pulled her close. "I think you're the best girl in the world."

She wrestled away. "You're just saying that so I won't be mad at you."

"Maybe. Or maybe I just want to make sure I get quality time with you."

A nagging thought surged in her mind. Rumor on the base had Robert in the next moon rotation. "So when are you shipping out?"

He gaped, blinking. "When did you hear?"

"I have my sources, and a girl has to keep some secrets. Besides, how long do you think you could have held out not telling me…a week…a month?"

"I didn't want to upset you. I planned on telling you, once they made it official."

Brooke felt a sudden pang of disappointment. *Passed over again.* She stood up, yanked on a robe, and headed for the bedroom door.

Robert scrambled to catch up. "Hey, where're you going?"

"The kitchen. I hear a glass of wine calling my name."

4

Brooke pulled a bottle of white wine from the fridge. She grabbed one of her favorite fluted glasses and filled it to the brim. Her anger at Robert passed quickly. It wasn't his fault. She walked into the living room and stared out the window at the quiet street. The evening dark filled with scattered streetlights reminded her of the night sky.

A solitary car rolled past, its headlights briefly illuminating where she stood. It continued on, leaving her behind in the darkness. *My chance is passing me by.*

Soft footsteps told of Robert's approach, and his arms encircled her waist from behind, his mouth by her ear. "Come back to bed, Brooke. We can talk about it in the morning."

She pulled free and turned to face him. "That's just it, Robert. Another morning, another day without a mission. I'm forty-two. I'm not getting any younger. I've yet to go and they're already recycling you. It seems I'll never get my turn."

Robert then slumped into the sofa. "Do we have to go through this every time? Your turn will come."

"There must be a reason they're not sending me."

"Why don't you ask administration?"

"I did."

Robert rocked backward. "You did?"

"Yeah, for all the good it did me. Bart gave me the old 'good things come to those who wait' speech."

"At least he didn't shut you down. Maybe he's got something big planned for you."

Robert wrapped an arm over her shoulder as she sat down. "God, I hope you're right. I've completed all the training. In the simulators, the diving wells, and all the other shit they run us through. Hell, I even spent four months in that mock ship in Northern Canada, and another

5

month in the underwater lab in the Gulf of Mexico. I'm ready."

Robert hugged her tight and kissed her. "They wouldn't waste all that training on you, if they weren't going to use you. Come on, let's go back to bed."

Robert rose, but she didn't move. "You go ahead. I'll be along in a bit. I want to finish this glass of wine."

"Suit yourself." He left the room, and Brooke could hear the sheets rustle as he climbed back into bed. She ran every training exercise through her mind once again while sipping her wine.

Whatever they get for me, it better be good.

CHAPTER 2

"The numbers don't look good, Mr. President."

President Samuel "Sammy" Davidson chuckled, poured a drink, and looked to Janice, his chief of staff. "Jay baby, you have the ornate gift of stating the obvious. What numbers are left to look good? We still have a massive debt load. Unemployment won't drop. The dollar is getting hammered, and 2033 will be remembered as the year China passed us in total GDP. We no longer control either the House or the Senate, and my approval rating is dropping like a stone."

Janice sighed. "Honestly Sammy, I don't know whether to join you in a cocktail or admonish you on drinking so early in the day. After all, there are still several meetings scheduled, and appearances are important. You aren't always going to get by on your charm and your football career."

He took a large sip then smacked his lips. "Ah! Are you kidding? The American public never tires of watching reruns of my days of glory, both in college and in the NFL."

"That's the trouble. Too many of your detractors treat you like the jock you portray. Your political acumen is too sharp for that. The way you maneuvered into office despite trailing almost the entire way was proof enough of your ability to manipulate things to your advantage. But not even a year into your first term, the wheels are falling off. You already have a couple of small scandals nagging at you. It's just without the House or the Senate's backing, and without public approval, it's going to be hard to get anything done, let alone a run at a second term."

"Three years is a long time, Jay, a long time." He took another sip of his drink.

"Yes, Sammy. But without either house, I doubt we can swing things. It's going to take a lot of small steps to put any of your measures in place."

Sammy sat down and crossed his feet on the Resolute Desk. "Don't think in small steps. Think in giant leaps, just like Armstrong."

She watched him lounge there. Thoughts of how she had tried to rid him of the habit years ago fleeted through his mind. There was no changing him.

"Just what do you have in mind, Sammy?

The president took another swallow of his drink then gave her a knowing look from under his eyebrows. "Honestly, Jay baby, do I have to do all the thinking around here? Look, it's quite simple. I need to give the people something to cheer about, something to keep their minds off their troubles. I'm thinking heroes doing heroic things in the name of the good ol' USA. The guys before me employed the tactic of using an enemy abroad, a righteous war to strike down the evildoers of the world."

"Trouble is, there's no money to fight a war. You'll never get Senate approval."

"Exactly! So I can't go the road my predecessors trod. Too bad. It's tried and true. Besides, all the old bad guys are gone. North Korea gave up the ghost because they were starving to death. All those Muslim countries who hated us are too busy fighting their own countrymen. The political turmoil in their homelands is placing new people in power almost daily. Sheesh! If I pointed out one baddie, he'd be out of power before I could say boo. Outside of a couple of small countries with no real influence, there's nothing worth chasing."

She stepped near and looped a hand under his legs to pull them off

8

the desk. "Honestly, you're like a kid sometimes. So what's your plan?"

He grabbed his comp pad, pulled up the image of the crew who set up Moon Base Alpha, then showed it to Janice. "Homegrown heroes like Robert Tangler. When we beat the Chinese back to the moon, we showed the people we're still number one. But we made a big mistake. We brought our partners, the Russians and Europeans, along for the ride."

"And don't forget, along with the Drumdat Corporation. We needed their financial investment. They paid for the pair of base habitats. One went with the initial mission and the second is due to go up in a few weeks. Setting up Moon Base Alpha will cost a trillion dollars over the next decade. Where were we going to get the money on our own?"

Sammy poked one finger into his chest. "That's one of the reasons *I'm* in office, not the other guy. He surrendered a great American institution to foreigners."

"What institution was that?"

He shook his head in dismay. *When's this girl going to get it?* "The control of outer space, of course. It's no longer an American domain."

"Al…right. But the genie is out of the bottle, and you can't take it back."

He stood up and wrapped an arm across her shoulder, gave her a quick shake, then let her go. "Here's how it goes, Jay baby. We need a big play, a Hail Mary pass, something that's going to be remembered for a generation."

"Okay, Sammy, enough sports talk. What do you want me to do?"

The president stopped to refill his glass. "Okay, here's the plan.

9

We've done the moon thing, plenty of times. It's old hat. We even did the asteroid landing but no one paid attention. No, it's time to go big time. I'm thinking Mars. Let's put some people up on the Red Planet before my term is over. I've got it all worked out. Higgy, the NASA Administrator, is onboard and has been doing a little book juggling to help make it happen. All we need to do is appropriate that habitat that's ready to go and —"

She put up a hand to stop him. "Hold on, Sammy. Before you go any further, there's something I gotta do."

Disappointed at her interruption, he let it go. "What?"

"Pour myself a drink."

CHAPTER 3

It only took a few days for Brooke to receive the official announcement of Robert's return mission to the moon. Despite feeling jilted once again, she attended the press conference. A crew of three would be going up to the moon base to set up a second Helium 3 extractor. The joint mission was funded by Drumdat Energy, a new player in the fusion reactor business. As the cameras flashed away, a pang of jealousy struck her as Robert and two other astronauts, one a woman, waved to the reporters. *That should have been me.*

She held her anger in check as NASA Administrator Bartholomew "Bart" Higginbottom addressed the gathering. "As you are aware, recent developments in nuclear fusion have made the use of such energy economically viable, provided we can maintain a steady source of Helium 3. Therefore, we have designed a new extractor for installation at Moon Base Alpha. I have the utmost faith Captain Tangler and his team can get this equipment up and running with all expediency."

A number of reporters raised hands. Bart pointed one out. "Question?"

"Yes. With recent budget cuts to your program, how do you intend to continue to fund missions to the moon?"

"A good question. First, Moon Base Alpha is funded and teamed by not just the United States, but all of our partners in this venture: the European Space Agency, the Japanese, the Canadians, and of course, Russia. In fact, we will be using the Rus rocket system, developed by our counterparts in Russia and Europe, to fly this mission and many of the ones to come. And of course, a major funding component is being supplied by the Drumdat Energy Corporation."

"With those other countries involved, won't we be required to share the Helium 3?"

"True, and to a small extent, we will. But until the full development of nuclear fusion as an energy source around the world for us to market to, it is still not economically feasible to rely on it to fund our program. That's why we've taken Drumdat on as a business partner in this venture. Right now, they get the Helium 3 for free in exchange for funding."

Another reporter raised a hand. "Excuse me, Administrator Higginbottom, but isn't there pressure from Washington to cut the moon program altogether? Word has it the current administration is under siege by the Senate to cut your budget even further. Even with the funding from Drumdat, there are those in Washington who want your program gone to save money."

The administrator took hold of the podium with both hands and stretched out over it. "That's *why* we entered into the partnership with the Drumdat Energy Corporation. They spend the money, *they* get the Helium 3, and *we* get Moon Base Alpha. Now, let's have no more questions of budget cuts. Today is a happy occasion."

The interviews switched to the astronauts, and Robert did not disappoint them. He answered his questions with the charm that wooed Brooke from the beginning. His tall good looks, disarming smile and clear blue eyes were enough to sway some of the men, let alone the women in the audience. Being the first human to visit the moon twice made him a special novelty for the reporters. They clamored to get his picture and comments time and again. *Though I'm jealous, I still love the guy.*

When the session wrapped up and Brooke headed for the exit.

Before she could get there, she felt a tap on her arm. Turning, she saw one of the admin clerks standing there. "Administrator Higginbottom would like to see you in his office."

"Right now?"

"He says it's important."

She followed the clerk into the office area where the administrator was getting into his chair behind his desk. "Close the door behind you, Brooke, and take a seat."

When she sank into in the large wing-back chair close to his desk, he almost disappeared from her sight. Between his small stature and the mountain of paperwork on the desk, she found it advantageous to sit on the edge of the chair and lean forward to maintain eye contact. "You wanted to see me, Bart?"

The administrator hunched over in his chair, looking as unlike an astronaut like Robert as possible—short, balding, with a paunch at his waistline and thick glasses perched on the bridge of his nose. He entered something into his comp pad and leaned back to look at her.

The administrator folded his hands behind his head. "So what did you think of the press conference?"

Is that all he wants? What a piss off. He knows how much I've been pushing for my turn in space. "It seemed pretty standard. The usual photo shoot, lots of personal questions for the astronauts. I've been to a few before, nothing out of the ordinary."

"Insidious, isn't it. One can hardly notice the distinct flavor of things."

She gave her head a short quick shake. "I'm sorry. I'm not following you."

He reached for a manila envelope and held it out for her to take. "The budget constraints. Too many questions focused not on what

13

we're doing but on whether we should be doing it at all."

She accepted it. *What the hell is this?* She turned it in her hand. Sealed. "You seem to have handled it pretty well."

The administrator bounced out of his seat and came around the desk. "Unlike my predecessors, I didn't rise through the ranks of astronauts to this position. I toiled my way through the financial department and earned this post because the people in Washington believed I could work wonders with the numbers. It was all about reining in costs." He took the other guest chair.

"I thought the president favored maintaining the existing programs?"

"The president is the exact reason you have that envelope in your hand. He wants the space program to provide him something to crow about. But the Senate is killing him when it comes to spending. It's the reason we're using the Russian rockets for the moon missions. It's why the astronauts are all from different countries. For the past couple of years, we've been robbing Peter to pay Paul."

She looked once more at the packet. "So what's in it?"

The administrator smiled and leaned back. "Go ahead. Open it."

Brooke undid the string and broke through the tape. Inside A congratulatory letter on her mission posting, signed by the president of the United States greeted her. She looked up to see Bart still smiling. "Is this for real?"

"Absolutely. We're going to send the habitat module sitting on the launch pad there, instead of the moon. Likewise, the return rocket is scheduled to lift off in two months giving you just over two years to get yourself up to speed before you go."

She shuffled through the balance of the contents. Her posting orders and all other documents required were there. Everything seemed in order. "I'm surprised. Why me?"

"Plain and simple. You're the perfect fit. We made a mistake with the first mission to the moon being all men. The women's rights activists had a field day. That's a beating I don't dare take again. But likewise, you're single, older, and an unknown. Should something terrible happen, the public won't crucify us. I hate to be so blunt, but your death would be considered an acceptable loss."

"It's nice to know I'll be missed."

The administrator chuckled. "That's the spirit, Brooke. You've got toughness in you."

She put everything back into the envelope and folded her arms over it in her lap. "Just one thing. I studied the proposed program on this before. If things go well, the dollars to keep it running will be more than what the moon base is costing. How are you going to justify the expense?"

Bart reached out and patted her hands. "You just leave that to me. Remember, I'm the number cruncher. I'll make it work. I envy you. On the outside, I have every appearance of the mild-mannered pencil pusher people expect of me, but deep inside, I long to be like you, to explore outer space. I'll have to settle for you as my surrogate. Be happy; you're on your way to Mars!"

CHAPTER 4

Nate Drummond stormed into the office of Drumdat CEO Alban Moceri. "What the hell is going on, Al?"

"Sorry, Nate, what *is* going on?"

Alban's expression told Nate everything he needed to know. *He hasn't heard.* Nate sighed. "Come with me. The president is making the announcement shortly."

The CEO rose and followed him to the executive boardroom. Nate hit the switch turning on the full wall screen, grabbed the remote, and switched to one of the news stations. Plopping down into his usual chair reserved for him as President of the Drumdat Energy Corporation, he waved at Alban to sit. "Make yourself comfortable; you're in for a shock."

Alban approached a wall cabinet and withdrew a bottle of scotch and two glasses. "If I'm in for a shock, it might be best to brace for it. Single? Or a double?"

"Double, no ice."

"You sure? You know what your doctor said."

"Screw the doctor. Pour the drink."

Alban made the cocktails and handed one to Nate. He settled back into the soft leather seat and focused on the screen.

The White House press room showed on the television, with the press secretary trying to hush the room. "Ladies and gentlemen, the president of the United States."

"Hail to the Chief" began, and President Samuel Davidson made his way to the podium. "Good afternoon, everyone. I trust you've all received your briefing notes. This is a historic moment for America.

We are sending a manned mission to Mars. Not since the heady days of the Apollo missions and the Space Race, has such an event defined our nation. We are a nation of explorers, of pathfinders, of leaders into new worlds. We discovered our country. We conquered the moon. And now we dare to go to another planet."

The reporters began to clamor for attention. The president held up his hands for calm and then pointed to a woman in the front row, probably one of his favorites. "Yes, Susan."

"Mr. President, Congress has…"

"Call me Sammy. You know how I prefer to be called Sammy. Although I'm the president, I still like to think of myself as one of you. I don't want any title making you forget that."

Always with Sammy. What a smug bastard he is. No respect for the office.

"Uh, oh, yes…Sammy. As I was saying, Congress has already severely cut your funding on a number of your initiatives, including NASA's. How do you intend to fund such a program? How did the mission get approved in the first place?"

The president sported one of his toothy grins then chuckled for a moment. "Notwithstanding the financial concerns of Congress, NASA has always operated with some leeway. As long as there is no budget shortfall, amendments to its programs have been commonplace."

A different reporter jumped up. "But Mr. Pres…I mean, Sammy. My sources tell me it would run many billions of dollars to mount such an ambitious program. Surely, there isn't enough cost cutting going on at NASA to make this happen?"

"I have the assurances of the NASA Administrator Bartholomew Higginbottom that he fully intends to operate within the budget set for him.

17

"But Sammy—"

The president held up his hand. "Ladies and gentlemen, please. This is not a debate, but an announcement. All of your questions will be answered in due time. For now, allow me to introduce the team of astronauts who will be the first to set foot on another planet."

Three men and a woman dressed in silver and blue NASA uniforms entered the room. The president introduced each by name but by then, Nate wasn't really listening anymore. As numerous cameras flashed and the reporters crowded in, he hit the mute button and turned to Alban. "So what do you think?"

Al took a moment as if collecting his thoughts. "If he can pull it off, it'll get him a second term."

"Oh, he'll pull it off, alright, but at our expense. I wondered why the second habitat platform had not been deployed to the moon yet. Our investment return in nuclear fusion energy is going to be set way back. We've been funding the development of Moon Base Alpha on the condition of earning the mining rights for the Helium 3. Hell, those platforms were bought and paid for with our dollars! He can't do this! Get our legal department on the matter right away. Those are our platforms."

"Not right now, they aren't. I remember the contract, Nate. We agreed NASA would have exclusive use of the platforms for ten years. Ownership will only revert to us after that time."

"Yeah, but that was on the moon, not Mars. How the hell are we going to use it on Mars to get Helium 3 from the moon? We already have three new reactors under construction across America. One habitat on the moon won't provide the housing we need to get production of Helium 3 up to the capacity necessary to feed the reactors. We're going to lose billions…billions!"

Alban got up and put away the scotch. "I'll get to work on it right away. But something tells me we're going to lose this one. In the meantime, I'd halt production of those reactors until we get some answers. I suggest you pay the president a personal visit. Your campaign contributions alone should entitle you to a few moments of his time. And calm down; the doctor gave you explicit orders about that. I'm a lawyer, not a medic. I don't know CPR if you go into cardiac arrest."

"Okay, I'll calm down, but I'll be damned if I'm going to let the president get away with this. I'll go see him. You get to work on the legal end. We'll squeeze the bastard from both sides."

As Alban left the room, Nate hit the mute button once again and returned the sound to normal. The president posed between the four astronauts, with that same big toothy grin on his face. "I only wish I could be going with them. What a sight to see. And with the lower gravity, I bet I'd be able to beat my old time in the forty yard dash."

A chorus of laughter filled the room, then the president shook hands with the astronauts and left. Nate watched for a few minutes more as the reporter summed up the events. "A startling announcement here today. With Congress breathing down his back on fiscal issues, one can only wonder how the president intends to pull this one off."

He turned the program off. "Yeah, I wonder."

CHAPTER 5

Akihiko Fujiyoshi looked at the online memo with some trepidation. A summons to his NASA boss's office. Cuts were happening everywhere. Would he would be next?

No sense in keeping the old man waiting.

He picked up his com-pad and made his way into the private office of the program director. "You wanted to see me, Bruce?"

Bruce looked up from behind his desk and motioned toward the one free chair not covered in files. "Sit down, Aki. We need to talk."

He went over to the chair and discovered it was occupied by a number of files. "Where did you want me to put these?"

Aki watched with amusement as Bruce looked round the room several times. Every counter and inch of desk space was covered with files. Bruce finally waved toward the floor. "Sorry about that. Bart has me doing everything in hard copy. Something about keeping a proper set of books. Just put them anywhere."

Aki picked up the pile and dropped it on the carpet next to him. "Seriously, you need to eliminate some of this stuff. Can't you save it all in the system?"

"Everything is. I guess Bart's old school, likes to have hard copies around. But enough of that. We're not here to talk about the state of my office. Obviously, you've heard about the cuts. You're smart, Aki, real smart. I would hate to lose a good man like you. Your knowledge of spatial and quantum mechanics, I suspect, is second to none, including my own. So I've come up with a solution."

"A solution?"

"Yes. Plain and simple, I'm going to lend you out. Of course, you

20

still belong to us, but you'll be working for them."

"Them, as in who, sir?"

Bruce chuckled and leaned back in his chair. "CERN, of course. Those knuckleheads in the European Organization for Nuclear Research have been messing around with that big hunk of junk for twenty-five years now. The stupid thing's broken down more times than I can count."

Aki blinked and gave his head a quick little shake. "The Large Hadron Collider? I thought I read somewhere they were shelving the project."

"You did, and they aren't. It's just what they're telling the European Union to get them off their backs. The thing's a money pit. So they're going back to basics—redefining what the universe is made up of, coming up with a new equation for everything, and then starting the project again when they're ready."

"So how do I fit in?"

"Bottom line, they're paying NASA a pretty penny for your services. They want every top quantum mechanics guy in the field. As a NASA employee, you will still have complete access to our database. Help them solve the ultimate equation. Who knows? Maybe you'll come up with the answer, get published, be famous."

Bruce handed Aki a folder. "Here's the documentation on your transfer. We've made hotel arrangements for you until you can get settled. Provided you're willing to go. You can turn this down, but I can't make any promises that you'll stay here."

Aki opened the folder and scanned through the few pages inside. "It doesn't sound like I have a lot of choices. My old professor always told me I could come to work for him, but as an assistant the pay would be a step backward. I suppose I could scour the job market first, but you probably want an answer sooner than that."

"It's not me who wants the answer, Aki. It's those guys over there. They're under pressure. Personally, I don't think dark energy exists. Otherwise, they would have found it by now."

"I guess I'll take the transfer. It says here I'm on loan for five years. Hopefully, I'll make some progress where they couldn't. I have my own hypothesis."

They both rose and Bruce took his hand to shake it. "Don't worry. You're the smartest guy I ever met. You'll figure it out. And don't let all those highbrows over there give you a hard time about being so young. You don't need a big mass of grey curly hair on the top of your head to be considered knowledgeable in quantum mechanics. I wish you the best of luck, Aki. God knows, you'll need it."

He started to leave then stopped at the door to look back once more. "That's exactly who they're trying to find."

CHAPTER 6

Brooke sat in front of the television, watching the Rus rocket lift off from Russia. "Have fun, Robert."

Her own plans were on hold. The Drumdat Energy Corporation had managed to convince the courts to put an injunction on NASA preventing the launch of the habitat rocket to Mars. She had read through the documentation several times and nothing gave her the impression it would be going away anytime soon.

As she curled her knees up to her chin, the tears came. *It just isn't fair!* If they did not launch in the next two weeks, the aligning of the planets would put the whole project back two years. With the talk in the news analyzing everything, they probably wouldn't be going at all.

She pressed at her eyes with her palms, then threw her hands down in fists of frustration, pounding the sofa. "This is stupid. Crying isn't going to do anything about it. I'll go make myself some tea to calm down."

She shuffled into the kitchen and put on the kettle. Sorting through the different teas in her cupboard, she settled on rose hip, thinking the sweet flavor was what she needed. Wrapping her robe a little tighter, she suddenly felt a chill pass through her, followed by a sensation of loneliness. *Jeez! Robert's only been gone a week and already I miss him.*

Steaming cup in hand, Brooke settled on the sofa once more. Grabbing the remote, she scanned through the channel menu. Maybe she could find a good movie to watch. After rejecting a number of choices, she settled on a nice romance on the Hallmark channel. Ever since she was a little girl, she knew she could rely on a wholesome family movie from them.

At a commercial break, she started to rise to refresh her tea when a news flash came on.

This just in. The drone space habitat held up from going to Mars by court injunction has lifted off from the Kennedy Space Center. Rumors abound as to how this could happen. Full coverage at eleven.

Spilling her tea, Brooke pawed for the remote and spun through the channels to find the all-day news. Her first stop at CNN provided full coverage. On screen, the giant Ares V cargo launch rocket still sat on the launch pad. Though activity around it gave the impression a launch was a go, it had not moved. The image didn't jive with what she had heard on the other station.

"What the—"

A reporter. *This footage shot was shot just before the rocket subject to the court injunction lifted off.*

The engines roared to life, and oh so slowly, the big ship started upwards. As it climbed, the acceleration was clearly visible as it picked up speed. It went through a rotation then discarded the attached boosters. Though the camera still followed it, it appeared as nothing more than a bright dot in the night sky, on its way toward Mars.

"My god, they really have launched!"

The image of the reporter filled the screen. *We take you now to the briefing room at NASA where Administrator of Operations Bartholomew Higginbottom, is expected to provide an explanation.*

Brooke ignored the spilled tea and perched on the edge of her seat, waiting for whatever would come on next. An empty podium showed on the screen. She recalled her last time in that room, when Robert's return trip to the moon was announced. After a brief moment,

Bartholomew made his way to the dais. After swiveling the microphones to his short stature, he adjusted his glasses and lifted a script. She knew Bart too well to think he winged it. He probably wrote the script over five times.

Ladies and gentlemen of the press, I want to thank you for coming. At 4:33 p.m., by presidential executive order, the launching of the Ares V was ordered. At exactly 8:42:15 p.m., our mission to send a space habitat to Mars was launched. All reports are in and the launch has been a complete success. We expect it to rendezvous with the Red Planet in three months, at which time, barring any incidents, it will land at the targeted location and begin the process of preparing the habitat for human occupation two years from now. I will now take questions.

The room exploded into an uproar as reporters fired questions. Bartholomew smiled and motioned for quiet.

Allow me to circumvent a lot of these questions by stating whatever interpretation you want to put on events, despite all other bodies supervising our jurisdictions, in the end, it is the president who calls the shots, and his words to me were quite clear. "Get that damned rocket into space!"

Before any more could be said, her telephone rang. Identi-call showed it was one of the other astronauts scheduled for Mars. "Hi Jesse."

"Can you believe it?"

"It's mind boggling. Who would have thought it?"

"Certainly not me. I figured, with the lawsuit, we were headed for a two-year delay. But for the president to do what he did is suicide. They'll have his nuts in a wringer by tomorrow. My guess is they'll impeach him. Now we'll never get to go."

Brooke allowed a slight giggle to escape her lips. "No, Jesse, don't you see? They'll have no choice. Firing that rocket and habitat off sent billions of dollars moving away from Earth at twenty-five thousand miles an hour. They've got to send us. We're going to Mars!"

CHAPTER 7

"You were lucky to survive this, Sammy."

He waved his hand nonchalantly at Janice. "Pfft! Luck had nothing to do with it, Jay baby. Those bozos in the Senate knew better. Who would want to be the guy to pull the plug on the first manned mission past the moon? Not one of them. It was a sure thing."

Janice sat down and consulted her comp pad. "I don't consider winning a non-confidence vote by two an easy victory. Even some of your staunchest supporters voted against you."

Sammy chuckled. "Yeah, and just like me, each and every one of them getting huge campaign contributions from Drumdat. Their votes were bought, plain and simple."

"Speaking of bought, not only have they cut you off from donations, but their lawsuits are eating away your reserves. You won't be able to run for a second term."

He frowned for a moment. *Damn it! I hate when she's right. I need to think on this.* Rising, he retrieved a cigar from a humidor. "I'm going outside to get some air. Besides, you know how the staff hates it when I smoke indoors."

"That's because you always choose the Blue Room to do it. Tours go through there, Sammy. You can't go stinking it up with cheap cigar smoke."

"Cheap? Who said anything about cheap! These Cohibas are damned expensive. I'm just glad my predecessor finally opened up trade with Cuba. Without these…. You'd know what a cheap cigar is if I had to smoke American ones."

Janice peered at her pad. "Sammy, hang on a sec. You won't

believe this. Nate Drummond is holding online to talk to you."

"Put it through." The screen on his desk changed to the image of the owner of Drumdat Corp. "Good afternoon, Nate. How can I help you?"

"Sammy, you got through this one by the skin of your teeth. But, god damn it, I'll see you sunk before this is over."

"Nate, Nate, Nate. Don't take it so personally. Why don't we sit down and talk. Work this out. I'm sure we can figure out something. When can we get together and smooth things over?"

"I'm in town. I can be there in fifteen minutes."

"Fifteen? Great. I'll be out on the South Lawn." He terminated the call and reached for the humidor once more. "He can't resist one of these. He's a scotch man, too. Have the staff bring out a tray with some of the good stuff. I'm going to work."

Janice smiled and headed for the door. "Don't sell the farm."

"It's the pound of flesh I'm worried about. It would put one hell of a crimp in my manly figure."

***

As his car rolled through security, Nate sat in the back looking out the window toward the South Lawn. *There's the bastard now.* "Driver, pull over up ahead. I'll walk around."

"Yes sir, Mr. Drummond."

The limousine pulled to a stop and he climbed out. Rushing to greet him was Sammy's chief of staff, Janice Roberts. He couldn't resist looking her up and down, from head to toe. *I can see why he keeps her around. She is one fine looking lady.*

"Good day, Mr. Drummond. The president is expecting you. If

28

you would be kind enough to follow me."

"I know my way, girlie. You best stay here. I wouldn't want to hurt your sensitive ears with what I've got to say."

She hooked an arm into his. "Believe me, Nate. Hanging around Sammy, I've heard it all before. At times, he could make a sailor blush."

He gave her a sideways glance. Despite his mood, her spunk made him smile. "If ever you get tired propping up this bum, come see me about a job."

"You never know. Come three years from now, I might be taking you up on that."

They found the president in the process of lighting a cigar as they neared. "Hello...*puff*...Nate...*puff*...I brought one...*puff*...out for you."

Apparently satisfied he had enough of a light going, Sammy put the lighter down and extended a Cohiba. Nate shook his head, and then looked to Janice as he accepted the cigar. "You got anything to drink with this?"

"Scotch, Mr. Drummond? I have a selection here. Anything you prefer?"

He glanced over the four bottles, all single malts from Scotland. Recognizing one, he indicated it while trying to light his own Cohiba. By the time Janice handed him his drink, he had seen the red circle of his cigar being fully lit, had given one final inhale and allowed the smoke to seep from his mouth. *If my doctor could see me, he'd scream.* "Okay Sammy, the only thing missing is the barbecued ribs. But I didn't come out here for a soiree. We've got business to discuss, serious business."

"I appreciate that. And while out here getting some fresh air, I've

29

come up with a fresh idea. What do you say toward about being partners on Mars?"

"Partners? What the hell are you getting at, Sammy? There ain't nothing on Mars I'd want. It's too damned far for any commercial venture."

"I know. No, I was thinking more along the lines of property domain. Obviously, my people will get the notoriety and acclaim for being on the Red Planet first, but any and all items and or science resulting will belong to Drumdat. Who knows what might be discovered. It's an open-ended opportunity."

"Bah! They won't find anything of any size worth keeping."

"Are you so sure? Those methane plumes aren't just Mars rocks having a bad case of gas. Think smaller, Nate. If microorganisms are discovered, it could have immense possibilities."

He's talking potential bio-lab developments. "I'm listening."

"You'll have the inside line, first crack at the stuff for a year. I'll guarantee it."

He took another drag on his cigar, then a sip of his scotch. "I don't know, still sounds pretty risky."

Sammy came over and wrapped a big arm over his shoulders. "Nate, what's risky is you continuing on with your lawsuits. What have you got to show for it so far? Nothing. And cry foul all you like, there's no way the habitat is coming back home. It's pulling into Mars orbit next week. NASA has a go to commence landing procedures as soon as it does. Now tell me, don't you think it would be better to be onboard?"

The bastard has me over a barrel. Alban says the lawsuits are fifty-fifty at best. As bad as this deal sounds, something is better than nothing. "Alright, Sammy. Here's my counter offer. I get the complete package. Everything that comes off *that* planet is mine, no one year

30

limit. I'll even provide the crew vessel. But I still retain ownership of both it and the habitat, in case there's ever a need for them again. Deal?"

Sammy pulled at his chin. Nate waited. Finally, Sammy held out his hand. "Deal, but you gotta go public about supporting me and all."

He grabbed Sammy's hand. "Deal. I'll have Alban send over the paperwork." He dropped his cigar in the ashtray and placed his drink down. "I've got to get going. It's been a pleasure doing business with you, Mr. President."

Janice escorted him back to his limo. As he climbed in, he gave her a quick wink. "See you in three years."

Once the door was closed, he told the driver to head for the hotel. *Either I just made a whopper of a mistake, or the deal of the century!*

CHAPTER 8

Bartholomew stared at the large screen showing the rocket standing on the pad. Nearly two years had passed since they'd launched the habitat to Mars. He turned to his mission administrator, Bruce. "I never thought I'd see this day. You've done a complete recheck on the habitat and the return vessel?"

Bruce handed him his comp pad. "Everything is ahead of target. The unit has converted more than enough of Mars' atmosphere to fill the air tanks to capacity, and the water tanks are already three-quarters full. The hydrogen fuel for the return mission is just over fifty percent and once the water reservoir is full, a greater percentage of the air can be dedicated toward fuel. None of the equipment is showing any signs of breakdown. I'm thinking we will have capped off all tanks before a decision is required to land on the planet. I still wish we had waited until the return rocket was in place on Mars. If we abort before landing, it's a long time getting back home. I'm not sure the crew's bodies can survive the trip without organ failure."

"This isn't a joyride. They all know the risks associated with this flight. I doubt a single one of them would opt out, even if your numbers weren't up to snuff."

"If my numbers weren't, as you say, up to snuff, I'd abort right now."

"That wouldn't be your decision, just a recommendation. You know how the president wants to see this mission through."

Bruce shook his head. "Thank god it doesn't have to come to that. I'd never forgive myself if we sent these people to their deaths."

"You and me both." Activity on the screen brought

Bartholomew's attention back to it. "Look, the astronauts are boarding. There's no turning back now."

***

Brooke walked with Jesse, Mark, and Brian, holding her helmet under her arm. She felt so nervous that, with every step, she imagined tripping and falling, injuring herself and having to stay home. Even the brave words from Robert, returned from the moon, gave her little comfort.

The technician accompanying her stepped into the elevator as well. "Everything's going smoothly, Lieutenant Jones. You must be excited. I mean...Mars, this is the ultimate trip!"

She laughed. "Are you kidding? This is nerve wracking as hell. If I hadn't already gone, I'd piss myself right now."

He smiled and pressed the button to start the lift. "You'll have plenty of time to get rid of those jitters on the way. It's a long trip."

From the open car, she watched as the supporting structure beams were passed, and through them, the shell of the Ares rocket. In reverse order, the letters passed for both NASA and the USA and as she reached the actual capsule, EROS I was blazoned across the hull. "What better name than the first son of Ares. He was, after all, besides his recognition as the god of love and beauty, known as the firstborn light coming into being and ordering all things in the cosmos. And it's into the cosmos we go."

As the technician helped her into the capsule, he appeared sullen. She paused. "Is something wrong?"

"Nothing, Lieutenant. I apologize. I was merely dwelling on my own knowledge of Greek mythology. I could not but help but think of

33

you, being the only woman onboard, in place of Psyche, the daughter of Eros. Hers was not a happy tale, filled with many hardships."

She smiled and tapped a gloved hand to the man's face. "Don't worry. I, too, know the tale. In the end, she was happy. What more trial could I face than the one I am about to take? In the end, I, too, will be satisfied, no matter what."

His face brightened. "Then, fair Psyche, may the gods be with you."

She settled into the seat and waited as the technician installed the harness around her. When he was finished, she blew him a kiss. "About to be launched toward Mars, I am already blessed with good fortune. Tyche, the daughter of Zeus, as mistress of fortune must be favoring me."

He lowered the helmet over her head and made sure the seal was tight then exited the capsule. Beside her, Jesse was settling into his own chair. "All set, Brooke? This is going to be one hell of a ride."

Mark sat behind Jesse. "Yeah, as long as we can avoid the Mars Curse and aren't consumed by the Great Galactic Ghoul!"

She gave Jesse the thumbs up then listened to the pre-launch chatter from Ground Control. *It won't be long now.*

***

Aki watched the cafeteria television. Over two years since he had been loaned by NASA, he felt a small pang of disappointment. History in the making; he should have been there.

His team supervisor, Dietmar, sat down next to him. "How long until the launch?"

"Seventeen minutes."

"Ah, the Americans. They always have to be first at everything. First on the moon, and now, first on Mars. They are never willing to share the glory. I understand they turned down a sizable contribution from the European Space Agency rather than accept one astronaut not born in the United States."

Aki fought an urge to chastise the man. *Doesn't he realize I am American? Perhaps due to my Japanese descent, the guy has forgotten.* "I heard the Russians wanted to go as well. No space race this time. Going to Mars is just too damned expensive."

"Ach! For what? Another box full of rocks? There's nothing there worth going for. It's a big waste of money to benefit American propaganda."

"Oh, I don't know. Those methane plumes indicate something's alive there. Who knows what kind of microbiological life exists? Bringing some back, we might find some amazing cures. You have to figure anything able to survive there has to be made of pretty hardy stuff, what with no shielding from the sun's radiation and all."

Dietmar nodded a few times. "Yes, I suppose. It's possible." He turned to face Aki. "In the meantime, I understand you have some questions about our decision to give up on dark energy."

Aki grabbed his comp pad and brought up his report. "I've been working on my own theory on the Standard Model and why we have been unable to create the stuff. *I think* dark energy is made up strictly of Higgs bosons. I think, after the Big Bang, all the Higgs particles merged to create the first black holes in the universe. My theory would explain how the different galaxies gained formation and provide a basis for the creation of super massive black holes at their cores."

He handed the pad over to Dietmar, who browsed through it for a few moments. "Forward this to me, Aki. I'm going to need some time to review it. Is it complete?"

"No. Right now it's a work in progress. It's going to take some time for me to sort out the entire math—months, maybe."

Dietmar smiled and offered the tablet back. "Well, when you do, then I'll listen. For now, we'll keep on the path we're on. Work on it. Prove you're right. You know how scientists are. They won't believe a thing you say without quantitative statistical verification."

"Okay, I'll send you what I've got for now." Aki took the pad and forwarded his computations to Dietmar's account. When he looked up, the countdown had reached one minute. "Sixty seconds. Let's hope there's no problem. I'm nervous just sitting here."

Dietmar chuckled. The two of them listened to the announcer count down. *Ten, nine, eight, seven. Starter ignition. Fuel ignition. Four, three, two, one. Booster ignition and liftoff of the Ares rocket carrying the Eros 1 spaceship and four astronauts on their way to Mars*!

It heartened him when, throughout the room, a small cheer went up. Aki smiled and felt a certain sense of satisfaction. He was still proud to be an American.

CHAPTER 9

The long months in space started out as ecstatically hopeful for Brooke. The majority of the time was filled with the mundane necessary exercise routine that pent up her anxiety, until as they neared Mars orbit, it became unbridled anticipation.

Brooke stared out the viewport at the Red Planet in all its glory. When they passed within the orbital path of the moon Diemos, Mars had looked no more than a dusty orange ball, but as they entered the space between the moon Phobos and their destination, the details became clearer. Olympus Mons was visible. "Do you think we'll find any gods there?"

Jesse looked up from where he sat on the exercise machine. "What?"

She turned to look at him. "Olympus Mons. Mount Olympus. Don't you know your Greek mythology?"

He rose from the bike and moved over to look out the viewport. "A little. Home of the gods, right? Jupiter and Mars and all those others."

"No, that's Roman. Mount Olympus is Greek. It would be Zeus and Ares, not Jupiter and Mars."

Jesse scratched at his head. His facial features contorted to scrunch toward the side he scratched, giving him a comical look. "So why did they give it a Greek name when the planet's is Roman? Seems silly to me."

"That's why they call it Olympus Mons, not Mount Olympus. Olympus Mons is the Latin name for Mount Olympus. Latin is the language of ancient Rome. Don't you know anything?"

"Well, then it *is* Roman, and I was right all along."

"No, Roman mythology did not have the gods living on Mount Olympus because that would mean the gods live in Greece, not Rome. The Romans believed their gods lived wherever they were, in their homes."

Their debate abruptly ended when a communiqué came in from Flight Control. "Eros I, countdown to insertion into the Martian atmosphere and landing has commenced. In one hour you will be setting down on the planet. Please begin landing procedures. Pressurized suits will go through a complete systems check in thirty minutes, so get them on."

Jesse pressed the button to respond. "Copy that, Command." He turned to face the rest of the crew. "Well, ladies and gents, you heard the man. Let's get our gear on."

Mark jostled Brooke with his elbow. "And make sure your tray tables and chairs are in the upright position."

Along with Brian, she laughed, and began the process of putting on her suit. Although cumbersome, in no way did it compare to the one Robert wore on the moon. Mars had a lot more gravity and somewhat of an atmosphere, so the suits were leaner and offered greater flexibility. Still, struggling into them was really a chore in zero G. The point six gees they had maintained during the long trip by spinning until insertion would have really helped. But they had to stop their spin before entering orbit.

Satisfied that all the connections were sound, Brooke began to strap herself in. She was startled by the sound of a bell combined with the warning red light flashing on the console. Jesse read the screen and then cursed. "Brooke, you have a leak somewhere. My indicators show it's at the helmet. Try taking it off and putting it back on."

The monitor on her wrist flashed the warning as well. A moment of panic subsided to tenseness in her shoulders and hands as she worked to lift the helmet over her head. All eyes watched her go through the process. *Please, not now. This isn't fair. Not now!*

She reattached the helmet and checked the connections once more. Jesse studied the screen on the console. Several moments passed and she grew impatient. He held up a hand and kept his eyes on the screen. Finally, after what seemed like forever, the green light blinked on. Once her suit had fully pressurized again, she exhaled the breath she'd held and gasped for more air. Everything was fine.

They waited until Control came back on. *We're reading a failure in the suit of Lieutenant Jones. Please advise, Eros I.*

Jesse shot her a quick look and she gave him the thumbs up. His features relaxed behind his face shield. "Everything's fine, Command. During the time lapse between communiqués, we fixed it. We're ready for final descent."

Her body slumped within the suit. She finished strapping herself in and settled back. More time passed before Flight Control came on once more. "Confirmed, Eros I. Insertion is a go. Good Luck!"

Mark gave a loud guffaw. "And now the fun part, seven minutes of hell."

Seven minutes of hell. She knew of it well. Seven minutes of the ship screaming down through the Martian atmosphere. The years of preparation prior to lift off, the long months in space before arriving in Mars orbit, all boiled down to seven minutes of pure pandemonium when the craft would bear the full brunt of flaming its way down to the surface. Either the heat shields would hold, or they wouldn't. The habitat had landed safely, as had the return rocket, but the percentages were stacking up; only one in five launches made it to Mars safely. Her hands clenched involuntarily onto the arms of her chair. She could sense her weight returning which could only mean they were within the gravitational pull of the planet and the outer reaches of the atmosphere.

It began with a mild shaking. Soon Brooke could hear a rumbling, growing in intensity. She glanced at the viewport. Flames flowed from where the heat shield would be. The vibrations continued to increase, but no worse than they were at lift off. "How many minutes left in this ride?"

Mark glanced at the readout. "Three and a half! Halfway there!"

The vibrations waned and the amount of flame shooting by the viewport decreased. Then, abruptly, they stopped. In the next moment, a popping sound was followed by the tug upward as the parachutes opened.

Brooke checked her screen. "Radar has kicked in. Ground telemetry is coming in. Landing rockets should fire when we reach an elevation of fifty meters above ground."

Jesse took hold of the controls, preparing to land manually should it be necessary. "We've leveled off. I'm green lighting the computers to take us the rest of the way down."

She could feel a new boost against their fall as the rockets kicked in. "There they go! Forty meters until touchdown…Thirty… Twenty… Ten…"

A jarring feeling passed through the ship as they hit the ground. Mark hit the release on his safety straps first and scrambled out of his seat. "And bingo! We're on the ground! Hallelujah!"

The others chuckled and began to follow suit. Jesse hit the com. "Hello, Control. The Eros I has safely landed. We're on the planet Mars. Open the champagne."

They spent the next fifteen minutes checking all the sensors and systems on the ship. It had landed without problem and was almost perfectly perpendicular to the ground. They noted the external readings and temperature and atmospheric levels.

Brian pointed to his screen. "Hey, everyone. Good news. We're only two hundred and thirty-two meters from the habitat. I'd say that was pretty pinpoint accuracy by the boys back home."

Jesse stretched. "Then the first thing to do is go check it out. Who's up for a walk?"

Brooke and the others chorused. "I am!" Another round of chuckles followed.

Mark kicked at the hatch. "Well, open the damned door already!"

Jesse held up a hand. "Just a minute. I'm waiting for Control to respond."

As if on cue, the com came on. "Eros I, congratulations. You are a go to proceed to the habitat."

Jesse hit a button, and the air began to cycle out of the ship. When the readings reached a comparative air pressure to what was outside, he hit the hatch release. A small hiss let Brooke know the seal was broken and Mark spun the locking mechanism and swung the door out. The red glow of the Martian sky flooded through the opening. He turned to Jesse and bowed. "After you, mon capitaine!"

Jesse paused in the doorway and looked back at them. "I've been thinking all the way here on what to say. When Neil Armstrong was the first to step on the moon, his words, 'That's one small step for man, one giant leap for mankind' were forever immortalized. It would be blasphemy to compare myself to Neil, but something needs to be said for this moment to be best remembered."

He turned and faced the Martian landscape. "It is the nature of humanity to look out, to wonder, to question, to explore, to brave the unknown."

Jesse stepped out, and Brooke followed right behind. NASA had given explicit instruction as to the order in which they were to step onto the surface. Poor Mark, for all his urgency, was to be last. Immediately outside the door, a camera would record and beam back the images as they planted their feet in the dusty red soil.

When she got outside, the first thing Brooke did was complete a three-hundred-and-sixty degree spin to scan the horizon in all directions. The landscape varied little, with what looked like rocky sand dunes everywhere. In the distance, she could see some hills, but not very high. The only break in the dusty red appearance was the discarded parachute some one hundred yards off to her left and the white gleam from the habitat to her right.

Once Mark had secured the hatch, Jesse pointed toward the habitat. "Okay, everyone, let's go. We can do some sightseeing once we've checked into our new home."

She fell into step beside him, with Brian and Mark bringing up the rear. "This is unbelievable! I'm actually walking on the surface of Mars!"

CHAPTER 10

Bart's vid lit up with the face of his secretary. "He's arriving, Mr. Higginbottom. He'll be here any moment."

"I'm on my way."

Bart closed the link and, with some effort, got up from his desk. The doctor had told him to stay home for a while, insisting he needed a break from the stress of work, but he had ignored the suggestion. He sighed as he pulled on his suit jacket from where it hung by the door. "No rest for the wicked."

He made it to the helipad as the copter set down. Making a feeble attempt to brush away a few wrinkles in his clothing, he put on a brave face and stepped forward to greet his honored guest. "Good afternoon, Mr. President. Thank you for coming to visit with us."

President Samuel Davidson shook his hand, the man's grip totally enveloping his own. "Glad to be here. That's what I like about you, Higgie. Always ready to accommodate me. Once I heard the news, I knew I had to stop in and pay you a visit."

Bartholomew cringed at the moniker the president had given him. "Yes, it's been quite a success. The landing was textbook."

Samuel put his arm over Bartholomew's shoulder. "That's not what I was talking about, but yes, the successful landing couldn't have been better. And no more of this Mr. President stuff, Higgie. I told you before, call me Sammy. All my friends call me Sammy."

"Yes, Sammy. Shall we go inside?"

The president waved his hand in a grand fashion toward the building and bowed slightly. "Show me the sights."

He guided the president through the various departments. To him, the man seemed almost oblivious to what was actually going, staring off into space when things were being explained, but he never missed a hand to shake. After walking through Mission Control, he suggested they retire somewhere for a private chat. Bartholomew took him to the small conference room and dropped into the nearest seat. *Thank god. I don't think I could have walked another step.*

The president had ordered his security team to remain outside the room and strolled casually around; poking into everything he came upon. "So tell all the good news. I understand you found some fossils? What do they look like? Were they like dinosaur bones? Tell me."

Bartholomew chuckled. "Nothing like that, I'm afraid. Microscopic stuff. Our microbiologist, astronaut Brooke Jones, identified the life forms in some slate pieces they extracted from one of the craters. They're only visible through a microscope, but definitely there. Here, let me bring them up on the big screen beside you." He sent the images from his own pad to the viewer.

Sammy squared himself before the screen and whistled. "Well, this is fantastic news though, isn't it? I mean, life on Mars! I need to go public with this."

"If you don't mind, we'd rather keep that quiet for now. Until we get the sample for further study. We don't want another ALH 84001. Bill Clinton had plenty of egg on his face when he announced life on Mars back in '96. It wouldn't look too good for your re-election campaign. By the way, how's it going?"

"It's in the bag. Being the president who put the first humans— Americans, mind you—on the planet Mars, has led to a huge windfall of public support, as I expected."

"Then with four more years in power, maybe we can see some budget restoration?"

44

The president came and stood near him, slapping a hand onto Bartholomew's shoulder. "That's what I like about you, Higgie, always ready with the quip. Yeah, we'll get you a few more bucks, but don't get your hopes up too high. I still have a few other budgets to fund."

A staffer brought refreshments and, once he left, the president turned to face him, a serious expression on his face. "Listen Higgie, we have a small problem."

What's he talking about? I've done everything he's asked up to now. My job is done. This better not be some ruse to get me to do something I don't want to. He gave his head a quick shake to clear it. "What problem, Sammy?"

"The reports from Eros I. You haven't been forwarding them to Drumdat."

"That's because we're not finished with them yet."

"That's beside the point. Look, we made a deal with Drumdat. They have exclusive rights to anything Eros I brings back from this mission."

So this is what he's after. I'll be damned if I'm going to give away everything I've fought so hard for. In his years climbing the corporate ladder, he had dealt with all kinds of bullies. The president was no different. Bartholomew took off his glasses, produced his cleaning cloth, and wiped them thoroughly. Replacing them, he looked up at the big man standing before him. "*You* made a deal, Sammy, not NASA. Besides, the way I look at it, Eros I is yet to return, so technically, they haven't brought anything *back* yet. But have no fear, when the ship lands safely, I will be more than pleased to give Drumdat whatever we have."

"But...but...that will be several months from now!"

"More like seven. The one month left on the planet, then the six

45

month journey home. That should give us plenty of time to review everything."

Feeling somewhat revived, he stood up, causing the president to step back a bit out of his way. "Now, if you don't mind, Mr. President. I have many duties to attend to. I want to thank you for your visit. Rest assured, your private little deal will be honored. I never could have got my people there in the first place without it. They were my first priority, and for that, I thank you. We have a big day tomorrow, and I still have a number of things to look into."

The president stood still for a moment, looking dumbfounded, and then he broke into a loud guffaw. "Ha! That's what I like about you, Higgie, you're a tough little cookie. Okay, I'll get out of your hair. And I'll tell Drumdat they can damn well wait for their data."

After escorting the president to the waiting helicopter, Bart returned inside to find Bruce waiting.

"Did everything go well?"

"With all the times the president said he liked me for one stupid reason or another and called me Higgie, I'm really starting to detest that man. But I got what I wanted. We don't need to turn over the data at this time, and he even promised a budget boost in the new year."

His body ached from the walking once more. But as he dragged himself toward his office, he still found the strength to smile. He'd managed to hold onto the reports from Mars until his crew got back. *Played him like a fiddle.*

CHAPTER 11

Brooke settled into her seat in the rover. The cave was over forty miles away, and the contraption they had for wheels had a top speed of twenty. What with dodging rocks and avoiding deep sands, Jesse rarely drove above ten. "Let's put a little pedal to the metal today, Jesse. I want to get there before it's time to come home."

Mark stowed the gear and jumped in the back. "I'm with Brooke. This is the only cave anywhere close, and I want to get some spelunking in. Time to get down. Ha!"

Brian filed into the last seat. "For once, I'm with these two. Even at top speed, if we spill, it won't damage our suits, especially at less than point four gees."

Jesse stepped down on the accelerator. "Okay, okay. I get the message. Just so you know, if we tip, *you* guys are doing the lifting to straighten it out. I'll be watching."

He kept the speed up, and the vehicle bumped and bounced on its way. They almost tipped over twice, but both times Jesse managed to maintain control.

Adrenalin rushed when she spotted the hole in the ground. "Look, there it is!"

Mark broke into song. "Spelunking we will go. Spelunking we will go. Hi ho the derry-o, spelunking we will go."

Everyone chuckled as Jesse pulled the vehicle to a stop some fifty yards from the hole. Brooke could hardly contain her excitement. She faced her last chance to find life before the return mission to Earth. So far, the fossilized remains discovered in the shale were the closest she had gotten. *There must be life down there. I know it.*

Brian handed out the climbing gear. "Now remember our training. As it is, those few exercises Earthside probably didn't prepare you well enough for the climb down in this low gee."

Brooke clipped the team line to her belt. "I'm trusting in you, Brian. After all, you are the resident expert. Just tell me what to do."

She'd envisioned an open entry into a dark corridor like a mine in an old Western, but the cave was more like a large hole in the ground. Satellite readings indicated it ran for a long distance below the surface, perhaps an old lava tube or former river course. As they neared the lip of the cave, Brian tapped at the ground with a long metal rod he was carrying. "Just stay behind me until we get to the opening. Who knows how much this expands below?"

They reached the edge and looked down and in. To Brooke, it looked deep. "I can't see the bottom!"

She and the others followed Brian around the roughly circular opening. It couldn't be more than eighty feet across. When he was about a third of the way, he stopped and pointed in. "There's the bottom. I'd say about forty yards down. This looks like our best point of entry. The sun is in the right spot to light the way, and I see a number of ledges and grades to make the climb down easier."

Producing a hammer from his kit, Brian pounded the metal rod deep into the ground near him. Attaching a line to it, he threw the balance of the rope over the edge. "Okay, I'll go down first. Along the way, I'll plant a number of anchors and feed the rope through it to establish the path I want you to follow. Coming down is the easy part, but you'll need those when we go back up."

Mark gave him a playful shove. "You're the man. Lead the way."

Brian lowered himself over the edge and rappelled down the wall of the cave. Because he kept stopping to hammer in the anchors, it took him half an hour to reach the bottom. His helmet light faded off into the distance in two directions when he turned around.

"This thing is huge! I can't see either end of it. Okay, everyone, come on down. The line is secure."

Jesse attached his belt to the line. "My turn, folks." It took him only five minutes to be at Brian's side.

Brooke hooked onto the line. "Well, here I come." She half-rappelled, half-scrambled and, for a couple of yards, half-fell into the hole. Once at the bottom, she looked back up at Mark's descending form. "That wasn't as bad as I thought it would be."

Mark landed with a thump next to her. "Time's a-wasting. Let's check it out. Which way, Brian?"

Brian pointed downhill. "That way. My guess is at one point there was an underground stream that ran through here. The opening above our heads is merely the result of a cave in. This could go for miles. Who knows, maybe tens, or even hundreds of miles. But one thing for sure, water runs downhill. So that's the way we go."

Brooke and the others picked their way through the rock debris when the roof caved in, but after several hundred yards, the way cleared and widened slightly, and making travel easier. Brian pointed out what once must have been the underground river bed. Much of the course was filled with sand and ice. She would stoop now and then and scoop up a rock that seemed interesting. But relying only on her helmet light and those of the others, it was too difficult for her to really study them. Those most promising she dropped into a large pocket by her hip.

After almost two hours, Jesse pulled everyone to a stop. "It's time we head back. Our oxygen will be nearing the halfway point soon, and I want to have enough to spare. Besides, by the time we get home, it will be night. Suits or no suits, I'm not taking any chances."

Mark leaned against a wall. "Aw, Jesse. You spoil all the fun."

As much as she wanted to press on, Brooke was weary and figured Jesse was probably right. She was about to comment about it when Mark tumbled to his knees. "Mark, you okay?"

He bounced up. "I'm fine. My hand slipped when I was leaning on the wall is all. Don't I look the fool."

An alarm went off in her head. *Could it be?* Brooke walked over to the wall Mark had leaned against. "Slipped? Let me take a look. Shine your light on the spot where your hand was."

Mark turned and pointed. "Right there. That's the spot. You just can't trust a rock wall nowadays."

Brooke pulled a knife and scraped at the spot, her excitement building. "Jesse, what's the temperature?"

Jesse held up the box he carried that indicated all of the environmental readings. "I'll be damned! It's only four below zero Celsius! That's pretty warm."

She packaged the scrapings and looked farther down the cave. "Jesse, a little farther please. Can we go just a little farther?"

Jesse checked his apparatus. "Okay, fifteen more minutes. Then we're out of here."

Brooke paced to the lead, an awkward jogging due to the confines of her suit. She could hear Mark calling to her to wait up. She glanced back to see everyone scrambling to catch her. Turning forward again, she pressed on.

Jesse continued to examine his readings. "Minus two! Now, minus one!"

The distinctive sound of splashing brought Brooke to a halt. She looked down. She was standing in about an inch of liquid.

Mark came up beside her. "Can it be? Is it really water?"

50

She started forward again. "Let's find out."

She charged through a few more puddles, each larger than the previous, then the view before her became reflective and she came to a stop. Before her, as far as the light would allow, lay an underground lake. The walls, too, glinted in the light. Retrieving her knife once more, she scraped a sample and watched as it pared from the wall like thick jelly. "Living organisms! There's life on Mars!"

Jesse came to stand beside her. "What is it, Brooke? Moss?"

"Nothing so complicated. My guess is some kind of single-celled organism that has multiplied to such extremity it has the appearance of a thick gel."

Mark was standing at the lake's edge. "Whatever it is, it's in the water, too. It's purple! I sure wouldn't want to have to drink that."

She finished packing up the sample from the wall. "I'm out of containers. Get me a sample of what's in that lake, will you, Mark?"

"Ugh! Okay, will do. I bet this stuff would make one hell of a purple Jesus!"

Jesse tapped at the panel on his arm. "Time's up, people. We have to head back now."

She sighed and looked around the cavern. "We need to come back."

Mark handed her the sample. "Yeah, and bring my swim trunks!"

CHAPTER 12

When Brooke peered up at the opening, the sky was on the dark side. "Jesse, we got back late. It must be night."

Jesse looked at his wrist panel. "No, there should still be daylight." He stared up. "I think it's a sand storm up there."

Brooke held her hand up in the light from her helmet and noticed a dusty mist drifting around it. "You're right. I can see it now. Boy, this stuff is fine."

Mark tried to scoop some up in his hand. "If we can grab enough of it, maybe we can make a beach to lie on down by the lake."

She giggled. "You never stop, do you, Mark?"

"Not if I can help it."

Jesse moved toward the dangling ropes. "Enough already. This stuff can gum up the rover, and I don't want to walk back to the base, so let's get going. Brian, get up there."

Brian saluted. "Aye, aye. I'm on it." He took hold of one of the lines and planted his feet on the wall.

Brooke watched him scamper up the rock face. "The guy's a human mountain goat."

When Brian reached the top, he waved down. "Okay, Brooke, you first."

She took the rope and hooked it to the harness on her outfit. Grasping the climb line, she began her slow ascent. She could feel Brian's tug from above as she grabbed onto the pitons he had placed. *This is easier than I thought it would be.*

She stepped onto each spike like a staircase, keeping her eye on the opening above her head. About two thirds of the way, her foot slipped from one of the spikes. Clinging to the rope, she twirled in midair then banged hard against the rock face. Jesse's voice rang in her com system. "Hang on, Brooke. Brian's got you."

She looked at the wall and realized she wasn't falling, only dangling. Reaching around with her foot, she found one of the pitons to secure her footing. "I'm okay, just got bumped a bit."

Grabbing another spike, she once again began her journey up. When she got to the top, a wave of relief flooded through her as Brian grabbed hold and pulled her to safety.

"You okay?"

She detached the line from her suit and handed it to him. "Yeah, I think so. Just a little rattled."

"Well, stand back so you don't trip over the ropes while I help the other two up." Brian lowered the line, and Brooke walked over to the rover.

As she stepped around the many stones strewn on the ground, something caught her attention up and to her left. She paused to watch a large bubble floating down through the storm. Sand swirled all around it, but none entered. *Isn't that weird?*

After a moment, the oddity headed straight her way so she stepped backward to avoid its path. Doing so, she tripped over one of the stones and landed heavily on the ground. A warning siren blared from her intercom. She glanced at her wrist panel to discover the flashing red light indicating the seal of her suit was compromised.

Jesse's voice came over the com. "Brooke, what happened? What's going on?"

"I...I fell. I'm leaking air! I think it's my helmet again."

"I'm on my way up. Listen! You'll only have one chance to do this right. Your suit will decompress quickly so you're going to have to do what you did before and get the seal to take. That means taking off your helmet and re-seating it. You'll have only about twelve seconds to do it before you black out. Fifteen, tops. Take several deep breaths then completely exhale before you do it. Otherwise, the bends will get you, and we're too far away from the base to pressurize you to get rid of the nitrogen in your blood."

She brought her hands to her helmet but couldn't bring herself to do it. "Jesse, I'm scared."

"You can do it, Brooke. You have to. Take off your helmet and re-seat it. Do it now!"

"Okay, okay. I'm doing it."

She grabbed hold of her helmet with both hands and gave it a twist to free it from the attachment ring. Just as she completed freeing it, to her amazement, the bubble descended and enveloped her. *What the hell?*

She could feel a dizzy spell coming on and tried to focus on the task. Something black flew into her right eye, and she winced them both shut. Forcing the helmet back into place, she twisted again and the siren's wail stopped. Colors flashed before her, and a terrible sense of vertigo caused her to collapse. Alternate flashes of black and white exploded in her vision then darkness took over.

***

"Brooke, can you hear me?" Nothing. No reaction. Jesse lifted her into a sitting position and leaned her against a rock. "Brooke...Brooke?" He placed the glass of his helmet next to hers to see as close as possible. She was breathing. Her eyes were closed. He raised her arm to examine her vitals on her wrist panel. The sand

54

continued to whirl about him but not enough to obscure the readings. Everything was green. "Thank god."

Mark knelt down on the other side of her. "How is she?"

"Her suit is functioning fine. The containment is complete, so she must have been able to re-seat her helmet, but she's out cold. Her vitals are fluctuating a bit. I can't really interpret it like this. My guess is she's suffering from the bends. It's probably why she blacked out. We need to get her back to base, pronto."

"Hey, you're the doctor here. Let's get going then. I'll give you a hand to lift her."

Together, the three of them hoisted Brooke off the ground and carried her to the rover. Once they had her strapped in, Jesse jumped into the driver's seat. "Let's hope I don't spill this thing, but I'm going to open it up as much as I can. If she's got the bends bad, time is of the essence."

Mark grabbed hold of the roll bar overhead. "Let 'er rip!"

CHAPTER 13

Robert stepped off the scale and took a deep breath. He didn't need the doctor's quiet clucking to tell him what he had seen with his own eyes. His weight was still down by seventeen pounds. "So what's the verdict, Doc?"

The doctor glanced up from his comp pad. "Are you still taking those pills I prescribed?"

"Every day, morning, noon, and night, just like you told me."

The doctor tossed his pad onto the nearby table. "For whatever reason, your bone mass doesn't want to rebuild. Without the bone strength, your body doesn't want to add any more muscle because it knows your skeleton won't handle it."

His hands bunched into fists as he struggled with what was being told to him. "So what do you think I should do?"

"I think we're going to have to try something different, perhaps a marrow transplant. I don't know."

"Don't you think that's a bit extreme?"

"Perhaps, perhaps not. You're healthy, Robert, healthy enough to live a normal life, for now. But if I don't do something, you won't see seventy. Once old age gets hold of you, what little bone you have left will fail quickly."

I'm never going to get better. Robert let his fists drop and his shoulders slump. "So what now?"

The doctor smiled and clapped a hand onto his shoulder. "Keep up the physiotherapy. Every little bit helps. And who knows, perhaps some gene will trigger and start building bone again because of the demand. The human body still has a lot of mysteries we haven't solved.

And every now and then I get amazed by some act of recovery no science can explain."

He started to get dressed again. "Well, I guess I better get back to the grind. Thanks again, doc. Same time next week?"

"See you then."

As he strolled out of the medical facility, he retrieved his phone from his jacket pocket. Three missed calls and two messages. One from Administration. He hit send. "Hi, it's Robert Tangler. Someone looking for me?"

"Hello, Captain Tangler. Yes, Administrator Higginbottom would like to have a word with you. Please hold."

The administrator? What does Bart want?

"Hello, Robert. I'd like to see you right away. Come by my office, will you?"

"What's this all about?"

"It's about Brooke. There's been an incident. I figured you better hear it from the horse's mouth."

"Sure thing. On my way."

He pocketed his phone and made straight away for the Kennedy Space Center where the administrator's office was. *What could have happened? Was she killed? It must be bad if they won't tell me over the phone.*

Upon arrival, Robert was ushered into the private office right away. "Hello, Bart."

The administrator shook his hand. "Thanks for coming, Robert. Sit down. Sit down. Let me brief you on what's going on."

Bart sat behind his desk.

"There's some big news, Robert. Big news. Your friend has discovered microbial life on Mars."

57

Robert let out a sigh. He hadn't realized until then that he had been holding his breath. "That's good news, isn't it? I mean, real good news."

"Yes, well, not all the news is good. Brooke's suit lost containment while retrieving the samples. She suffered a real bad case of the bends. Jesse is a first class doctor. It's why we put him in charge of this mission. He tells us they got her back to the base and have her in the airlock trying to pressurize the nitrogen out of her system. She's unconscious. We don't know yet the severity of her injuries."

The tension that had left him began to rebuild. "Why didn't you tell me this first?"

"Because I wanted to make sure you were in a state of mind that could handle it. Listen, Jesse thinks he got her into the chamber in time. He thinks she's going to come out of it okay. He's not finding any visible signs of internal bleeding, meaning her organs are still sound. It's just her neurological issues he's concerned with. She should have regained consciousness by now."

"You mean…she could have brain damage?"

Bart waved a hand in dismissal. "Nothing so severe. No, it's more like confusion, memory loss, and visual abnormalities. And she may be subject to mood or behavioral changes. These are things you can help with when she gets back."

The administrator got up from his chair and came back around the desk, a signal it was time to go, and Robert rose as well. "Thanks for letting me know first. You'll keep me informed. Right?"

Bart clapped him on the back and guided him out the door. "Yes, yes. It's all arranged. Now go home and take care of yourself. We'll notify you as soon as she's awake."

Robert's muscles ached. His bones ached. His head ached. In fact, everything ached. But he wasn't going to let it stop him. He had only half a mile to finish his nightly jog. Of course, carrying the twenty pounds of weights on his back didn't help. But if he gave up now, he might be packing in the rest of his life.

Besides, it helped him keep his mind off Brooke.

When he got home and finished a hot shower, he called Mission Control.

"I'm sorry, Captain Tangler. The last report says she's still unconscious. It's a seventeen minute communication delay at the moment. We're in contact as much as the speed of light allows."

"Okay. I'm going to bed, but call me when she wakes, no matter what the time—even if it's four in the morning."

"Will do, Captain Tangler."

In the kitchen, he poured a large glass of cranberry cocktail. He figured, what the hell, and decided to spice it up with some gin. He was tired and sore, and the bed called his name. After downing the drink, he clambered under the blankets, but not before making sure his phone within easy reach.

Some sleep is what I need.

Robert, help me!
Brooke?
Help me, Robert.
How? How can I help you?

I think I'm dying.

They said you're fine. They said they got you back in time.

I'm dying.

You're not dying. You're just unconscious. All you have to do is wake up.

Wake up?

Yes, wake up, Brooke. Wake up. Wake up!

Robert shot upright in bed. Sweat drenched him, and the sheets wrapped in a tangled mass around his body. All was quiet and dark in his room. A shiver ran through him.

The clock by his bed said 3:21 a.m. He reached for the phone and called Mission Control. "Have you heard anything?"

"Nothing, Captain Tangler."

"You're sure?

"I would have called, sir. We've heard nothing."

"She's awake. I know it. I'm coming down there."

He hung up, struggled free from the bed linens, and jumped into some clothes. Halfway to the space center, his cell rang. "Good news, Captain. She's awake. We just received the communiqué from Mars."

"Thanks, that's great. I'll be there soon."

He checked his watch. 3:38 a.m. *How freaky is that? I have a dream, and she wakes up within seventeen minutes.*

CHAPTER 14

"You've been out for a long time, Brooke."

She contemplated the statement. Despite being awake for some half an hour now she felt like she hadn't slept more than a few minutes. "How long?"

"Two days. I was really starting to worry."

"It was that long? It was really strange. It seemed like I was in a whirlpool, and in the center it was all black and drawing me in. I thought I was dying as I spun toward the middle. When I got there, I woke up."

"Hmm, I guess some kind of variation of the falling dream people have. So how do you feel now?"

She sat up and swung her legs over the edge of the bed to put her feet on the floor. "I think I want to try and get up. If what you're telling me is true, I've had enough beauty sleep. Besides, I want to take a look at those samples we brought back."

Jesse grabbed her arm and helped her to rise. She felt a brief dizziness, but it passed quickly and she walked into the main room. "I think I'm fine. Perhaps a little groggy. Is there any coffee?"

Mark hopped over to the small kitchenette set in one wall and poured a cup of the steamy liquid. "Here ya go, kiddo. It's a couple hours old. That ought to perk you up."

She sat at the small table and took a sip. "Yeech! You're right about that. Get me some cream and sugar, will you please?"

Mark handed her a packet of each, along with a spoon. "Warned ya. Are you up for something to eat?"

"Maybe in a minute. First, where did you put the samples? I want

61

to take a look at them."

Brian waved her over to one of the science stations. "I started some preliminary work on them. Best I can tell, they're some kind of methanogen, but the cellular structure is different. You're the expert. Come take a look."

She felt a moment of panic. Her chest constricted as she feared what mistakes might have happened. "Did you quarantine the samples first?"

"Absolutely. Even better than that, I mixed a batch of my blood with one to see if there was any reaction. So far, results are negative."

She sat in front of the microscope and placed her eyes to the device. Brian was right. The physical configuration was unlike anything she had ever seen before. "What about the kill box? Did you take it out of the freezer?"

"No, not yet. I figured I'd better wait for you on that one."

The kill box. She understood the hesitancy of her crewmates to handle it. "There's no time like the present."

She crossed into the storage section and punched in the code to unlock the special freezer compartment where the kill box was kept. She slipped into a protective suit and opened the box to retrieve one of the plates inside. Each glass plate contained numerous miniature cells. Although many were filled with harmless microbiological life, many more were filled with either harmful bacteria or viruses. She slid the glass plate into the containment unit. Made sure the seal was complete, returned the kill box to its freezer unit, and then doffed the outfit.

Returning to the seat before the microscope, she typed in the instructions for the first quarantined sample, the lake water, to be injected into each cell in the plate. "Now we watch and see what happens."

Mark grinned and shivered. "Brr! It's always bothered me having those things onboard. What if one of them plate cells should rupture? Or all of them? How many different ways would we die?"

Brooke laughed. "Don't worry. The fail-safes are plentiful. First of all, the unit is sealed tight. If something should happen, and one was to break open, a laser flash is programmed to incinerate the cell immediately. In fact, I can't even take the plate out of the containment unit without all cells being torched first. Just in case."

"But why are we doing that here? Shouldn't they be doing this in some high tech lab when we get the stuff back to Earth?"

She returned to the microscope to examine the cells. "You're right, that makes the most sense. The problem is, when we get back home, we have to surrender the samples to the Drumdat Corporation."

"Figures. Big money wins all."

She tried to adjust the magnification, but a wave of nausea overtook her and a sudden throbbing at her temples. "Oww, my head." She looked to Jesse. "I keep getting dizzy. How long will I have these spells?"

Jesse produced a retinoscope and held it before her eyes. She blinked as the bright light shone in.

"Hmm. I don't see any problems here. My guess is its temporary, a holdover from your bout with the bends. You should be right as rain in no time."

She rubbed at her right eye. "You know, just as my helmet came loose, I got something into my right eye. I wonder if that's the problem."

Jesse looked again with the retinoscope. "I can't see anything there. It was probably a piece of sand. There *was* a sandstorm blowing at the time if you remember."

"That's just it. Right at the moment I disconnected my helmet, I was enveloped in an air bubble. There was no sand in there. You saw it, didn't you Brian?"

Brian waved a hand in denial. "Not me. I was busy helping Jesse with the climb."

A chime rang, interrupting the discussion. Jesse glanced at the screen and then moved out of the way. "Brooke, it's Control for you."

"For me?" She took his place and tapped a key to display the message. Robert Tangler's image popped up on the screen.

Hi honey,

I got word of your recovery, and they let me be the first to say hello and pass on the congratulations on your discovery. Life on Mars!

It's still a long time until you get home, but I'll be waiting, counting the minutes.

All my love.

She smiled and recalled their last night together, a warmth filling her.

Over her shoulder, she could hear Mark's voice. "Aww! Ain't that sweet. Where's the kisses?

She spun quickly, put a hand on his face, and shoved him away. "Mark, you're such an ass!"

He laughed and danced off. She turned back to the screen and began to record her response.

CHAPTER 15

The weather wasn't cooperating. As he stood out in the open on the deck, Sammy tried his best not to get sick. Twenty-five foot swells bashed the sides of the vessel, and a light rain whipped across the deck. Even though the aircraft carrier was very stable in the water, the sense of movement had his stomach roiling. "Ugh! Somebody better get me a Pepto. I think I'm going to lose my load any moment now."

Janice handed him some pills and a glass of water. "Didn't you take your sea sickness pills like I warned you? Honestly, Sammy, sometimes you take this macho thing too far."

He popped the medication in his mouth and drained the glass. "Thanks, kiddo. I don't know what I'd do without ya."

"Pff! Probably be in jail by now...or dead."

He smiled at her quip then settled back into the scowl befitting his demeanor. *It's that damned Higgy getting even with me when I cut his funding again. Stalling the reentry so's I can get sick out here.* "Any word on how long?"

An ensign standing near pulled up his comp pad and showed it to Sammy. "Telemetry has them on target to splash down off our port side in seven minutes, sir."

"Huh, I guess I can last that long. Where's Rear Admiral Jenkins at? See if he can keep this tub steady until then."

"He's up in the bridge, sir. Did you wish me to radio him with that request?"

Sammy chuckled. The young ensign wore such a sincere expression, he didn't know if the fellow was serious or not. "Naw, I'll manage. How long did you say it will take to retrieve the capsule?"

"Thirty to forty-five minutes. It all depends how far away it lands."

"Hmm." Sammy looked at the empty glass in his hand. "Jay girl, see what you can do about getting something a little bit more potent to celebrate with when they get onboard, will you?"

Janice pulled the glass away. "You can't drink after taking those pills. It will only make you sicker."

"Now ya tell me! I knew I shoulda toughed it out."

The ensign handed him the pad again. "We have visual, sir. It's right on target. The chutes should be deploying any second. Rear Admiral Jenkins has already started to move toward the splashdown point."

He hoisted the pad and watched as the parachutes opened, slowing the descent of the capsule. The ensign nudged him and pointed. "Look up there, sir. You can see it coming down from here."

Sammy moved forward a couple of steps, shielded his eyes with his left hand, and looked where the ensign was pointing. Plummeting down, right toward them, was the EROS I, the three large chutes splayed above it like giant mushrooms. "Ain't that a sight!"

To his left, two large helicopters lifted off the deck and began to move out. It surprised him how fast the capsule was falling. Perhaps fifty feet from hitting the water, the parachutes cut free and flew away. The EROS I plummeted the final few feet. He had always thought it would float down, like a feather on the wind.

When it hit the water, the sound of the splash was louder than the noise from the helicopters as a large spray erupted from the impact point. The capsule bobbed up and the helicopters reached it in moments. A cable lowered from one, while men were jumping into the water from the other. They scrambled up onto the capsule, grabbed hold of the lowered cable and attached it to the top. The helicopter hoisted the EROS I up and returned to the deck of the carrier.

Upset stomach forgotten, Sammy stepped quickly to where the capsule was lowered onto the deck. The ensign put a staying arm in front of him. "Please, sir. No closer. Not until the cable is detached."

He felt like a kid waiting for a ride on the roller coaster. Many of the other dignitaries onboard huddled near. His excitement had him fidgeting. "Jay, you got the stuff?"

"Right here, Mr. President." She produced a case and opened it, exposing four medals on ribbons.

The moment he had been waiting for had finally come. The capsule was being opened. Four wheelchairs were lined up, and two men climbed in the ship. After perhaps two minutes, they emerged with Captain Jesse Cain between them. Sammy joined in a cheer and a round of applause erupting from everyone gathered. Jesse waved a hand as they sat him in the farthest chair.

It took less time for the team to retrieve the next astronaut, Brooke Jones. She stood and waved before being seated. The other two followed suit and once all four were on deck, Sammy stepped forward, Janice right behind him. "It is with great honor that I am here to greet the four of you today. Never has mankind traveled so far, or withstood such dangers in the name of science. It is my esteemed privilege to decorate each and every one of you with our highest honor, the Presidential Medal of Freedom."

He reached into the case and retrieved the first one which he placed over Captain Cain's head. Taking the man's hand, he shook vigorously at first but quickly softened his grip. *Damn, the man's as weak as a kitten! Janice warned me that might be the case.*

"Congratulations, Captain. Your leadership in this endeavor will forever be enshrined in the halls of Washington."

Jesse winced for a moment, but then the smile returned to his face. "Thank you, Mr. President, but the pleasure was all mine. The chance to be the first to step on the Red Planet was beyond my wildest dreams."

"I envy you. I truly do."

When he moved to astronaut Jones, she surprised him by rising and taking his hand firmly. "Mr. President, it's an honor."

He chuckled. "No, you got that wrong, the honor is all mine. Being the scientist who discovered the first alien life is something no one can take away from you. What an accomplishment indeed." *So how come she's not weak?*

He completed the ritual with the other two astronauts, both of them frail like Jesse, then turned and faced the crowd and the cameras. "All the people of America, correct that, all the people of the planet Earth are in your debt for the service you have done for us. Never again will the question be raised, are we alone? Never again will the ingenuity and determination of humanity be questioned as we reach out, first for the planets, then the stars. I salute you."

He raised his left hand in salute, and everyone else followed suit. When he finally brought his arm down, the thunderous applause and cheering drowned out the thanks from the astronauts.

He stepped away from the crew and let the media swarm in. When he managed to reach his own personal helicopter, he paused to look back one last time at the intrepid crew of the EROS I and smiled.

Damn. I wished it could have been me.

68

CHAPTER 16

"Once again, Brooke. I want to get another reading."

Brooke took a deep breath then mounted the treadmill again. "I don't understand, doc. I thought all these electrodes you have hooked up to me took all my vitals already."

"Just do it once more, then I'll let you go."

"Ugh. Okay, one last time." She began jogging with the machine at a pace she had always been comfortable with. As she pounded out the steps, the doctor reached over and spun up the speed. "Hey!"

"I don't think you're pushing yourself hard enough. It's only a mile. Let's see if you can make it."

"Okay, but if I fly off this thing, you're going to owe me *big* time."

She had already found the faster pace a challenge to keep up. She glanced at the setting and recognized it was higher than she had ever run before. *I can't do this. No way.* "I'm going to fall."

The doctor never took his eyes from the machine readings. "Keep trying. Concentrate on each step. See how far you go."

She turned her attention to her feet, pounding away. Watching the moving track below her for an instant affected her balance, and she wobbled but managed to straighten out in time. *Concentrate, I have to concentrate.*

Her mind turned to the mechanics of what she was doing. The lifting and stretching forward of each leg. The planting and pressing off of each foot. She imagined them like the pistons of an engine, pumping up and down. They just needed more gas or in her case, more blood feeding the necessary oxygen and nutrients to the cells in her muscles.

As she imagined this process, her steps steadied and her stride lengthened. When the bell sounded the mile mark had passed, she found herself in full flight on the machine. Grasping the handles, she slowed down with the belt below her then stepped off. Her breathing, though heavy, didn't hurt in her lungs. "How'd I do?"

The doctor paused to mark down a few notations on his comp pad and then looked up at her, smiling. "A personal best. You shaved almost twenty seconds off your best time."

"Twenty seconds. Really? That's amazing. Are you sure?"

"Sure as I'm standing here. I don't know why, but your state of health is unlike anything I've ever seen before with returning astronauts. Your bone mass is normal, your conditioning stronger than ever. Jesse and the others suffered massive bone and muscle loss. It will take all of them years to rebuild it. You've even put on fifteen pounds, though it doesn't show. In fact, you're the first astronaut to ever return from an extended mission having gained weight. What's your secret?"

She chuckled. "Come on, doc. It's simple. I'm a woman. We are the stronger sex, you know."

"Hmm. Well, laugh all you want. I'm going to need to get to the bottom of this, and I'm afraid that means more testing. Now I promised you could go, but I'm going to expect you back. I'll send you a schedule once I've decided how we're going to proceed."

The elation of beating her time faded quickly at the thought of more testing. *Is there something wrong with me?* "Okay, doc. I want to get back to researching the stuff we brought from Mars."

After cleaning up, she made for her office in the lab. When she walked in, she was surprised to find a man sitting at her desk, accessing her computer. "Who the hell are you?"

The fellow spun in the chair to face her. "Good day, Lieutenant Jones. My apologies, I waited as long as I could before starting. It's just you took so long in returning, I couldn't wait anymore. My name's Terry Bradford. I'm with the Drumdat Corporation. I've been assigned to download any and all files regarding the life forms returned from Mars. Once I've wiped your computer clean, you can have it back."

"What? Wiped it clean? Are you nuts?"

Before she could say another word, Frank, her team leader, arrived and pulled her out of the office. "Brooke, come with me please. Let the man do his job."

She yanked her arm free from his grasp. "Are you crazy? The guy says he's going to wipe the memory from my computer. You can't allow them to do that."

"I can, and I will. I've got a court order sitting on my desk that says *all* things recovered from Mars and *all* data relating to it are rightfully owned by Drumdat. There's nothing we can do about it."

"We can fight it. Appeal to the Supreme Court. This is important to the country. They can't do this."

"The order *is* from the Supreme Court. Brooke, you knew when you went that Drumdat had funded the Mars trip and that they were entitled to what we brought back."

She knew it. But it still pissed her off. Aiming a well-placed kick at the nearest garbage can, she gave it a boot halfway across the room. "Fine. They can have it. It's just that I want to be part of the team that unlocks their genetic code. See if they can help mankind in any way. If Drumdat does that, they'll make billions in profits selling it to us."

Her boss righted the garbage can. "Relax. They're nothing but methanogens anyways. It will take years to unlock that weird genetic code of theirs, if not decades. The only thing we proved so far is they

71

weren't harmful to human life, or any Earth life, for that matter. Their biological makeup is so different; I doubt they could interact within anything on this planet. Let Drumdat spend the time and money trying to figure them out. The good news is, when it comes to alien life forms, it appears they cannot contaminate us, nor we them. The unlimited combinations on the configuration of life make such a possibility a distinct reality. Let's hope that's a constant across the universe. It means we can go anywhere without fear of dying from some alien disease."

She allowed a smile to cross her lips as she calmed. "Yeah, I guess you're right. And who knows. If Drumdat can develop something worthwhile, then it won't have all been for nothing."

"With Drumdat involved, nothing is for nothing. You can be sure of that."

CHAPTER 17

As he walked down the hall, Aki thought about Dietmar's email. A request to attend the supervisor's office at 2:00 p.m. carried serious overtones. *He didn't agree with my theorem. I know it. I know the math is sound. What could be the problem?*

He arrived promptly at Dietmar's door. Unlike his and so many others, it was closed in true German fashion. He knocked and waited. From behind it, he heard the scrape of a chair pushed back, steps approaching, and then the handle turning. Dietmar waved him in. "Thanks for coming, Aki."

Aki waited for the supervisor to sit, and then found a chair for himself. "So what did you think?"

Dietmar rubbed at his face, sighed, and then turned his monitor so Aki could see the report on the screen. "I studied your theorem in detail. Do you really expect me to accept this, Aki?"

Aki shuffled his chair closer to better overlook the open file on the screen. "There can be no other explanation as to why we can't actually see the Higgs boson." He reached over and tapped the screen. "See? By amending the Standard Model, here…and here…and again over here, we achieve the same results."

Dietmar settled back in his chair and sighed once more. "So you want me to believe that we'll never actually view the Higgs boson in action."

He's not buying it. "'Fraid not. Not unless we can visit a black hole."

Dietmar chuckled. "That's not hard. We just visit my wife's bank account. No matter how much I deposit, it disappears. Now *there's* a black hole."

Dietmar leaned forward again to study the screen. "Still, your hypothesis that the Higgs bosons imparted mass to everything back at the time of the Big Bang and have since gone to form the super-massive black holes at the center of every galaxy lacks balance. There is far too much matter in the universe to be offset by the amount contained in those black holes."

Aki nodded. "Hence my supposition as to the existence of what constitutes the dark matter roaming the cosmos."

"Then why haven't we seen any around here? It's believed dark matter is everywhere."

"That's the one thing that's puzzled me. My only conjecture would be solar wind."

Dietmar tapped at his keyboard. "I want to show you something. Remember when you first broached this idea with me? What did I say? I said for your hypothesis to be accepted, it was going to need to pass the test. Prior to inviting you here today, I forwarded this to five other noted physicists here at Cern. Can you guess at their analysis?"

Aki pressed his lips tight. *I don't like where this is going.* "No, but I suspect you're about to tell me."

Dietmar hit one more key and his email box opened with the top message from one of the other scientists.

Without going into too many details, this analysis is hogwash.

Dietmar went to the next message.

Aki is a bright kid; he shouldn't be wasting his time on such useless conjectures.

The following three were no better.

"Understand, Aki, I think deep down you might be right. But who am I to argue this? These people have spent a significant portion of their lives trying to find the Higgs boson and you want to dash their careers away with one single swoop. No, without support from the scientific community, there's no way I can consider your analysis, despite my inner reservations." Dietmar rose from his seat.

Aki took the clue and rose as well. *That's it then.* "Just so you know. I've submitted my paper for review elsewhere. Someone somewhere will endorse it. Then what?"

Dietmar clapped him on the shoulder and laughed. "Then? Then I get to go and relax as a professor in my home town of Dusseldorf."

Aki left and made his way to his own office. Along the way he passed one of the people who had scorned his report. The first temptation was to avoid eye contact and step wide, but he resisted it. Instead, he did his best to hide his feelings and gave a polite hello without stopping to talk. *I'll prove them all wrong.*

Slumping into the chair at his desk, he opened his email. He decided to send one to his old supervisor back at NASA.

Hey Bruce,

I hope you've had a chance to complete your review of my theorem on the Higgs. Your last email said it looked promising but you needed more time. Everyone here thinks I'm nuts.

Aki

He had spent the next hour reviewing the daily reports when the ping of a new email caught his attention.

Hi Aki,

In fact, I did finish and I concur your analysis is possible. I'm just waiting for one of my colleagues here to agree. Sounds like it's time for you to come home. I have an opening. Interested?

Bruce

Aki allowed himself a smile. He typed a quick message and hit send.

You bet!

CHAPTER 18

Robert was feeling romantic. He was nearly ready. The wine was chilling and dinner in the oven. He went round the table placing the last of the silverware and stuck a match to light the tapered candles set in the middle. It had been a long time since he had prepared a fancy dinner on his own. He knew it was one of Brooke's favorites.

When he heard the door open and Brooke call out she was home, he felt a high level of pride in getting things done right and right on time. He met her in the foyer. "Hi hon, you're punctual tonight. No fashionably late as usual?"

She gave him a kiss as she entered. "When I heard what you were cooking, it took all of my willpower not to be early." She handed him a box filled with fancy Italian pastries. "Figured I'd bring dessert."

Taking the box into the kitchen, he returned with the bottle and two glasses. "Some wine?"

She accepted a glass and waved it at him. "Silly question."

He gave her a liberal amount then poured one for himself. "I'm thinking maybe a toast in is order. This is our first chance to have a night together without either one of us having to be at work early tomorrow."

Brooke sidled up and gave him another kiss and a one-armed hug. "You have something in mind?"

The strength of her momentary hug caused him to lose his train of thought for a moment. *How is it she's so healthy?* He looked into her eyes and smiled. She was beautiful—more beautiful than he remembered. She almost glowed. And the laugh lines around her eyes seemed more muted.

She tilted her head and narrowed her eyes, studying him. "Well?"

"Oh…uh…I was just lost for a moment there. Of course I've got something planned. What red-blooded American male wouldn't be thinking what I'm thinking with a gorgeous creature such as you in his arms?"

She pushed him away and laughed. "You beast! I should have figured."

As if she wasn't thinking the same thing only a moment ago.

"Maybe I *was* thinking the same thing, but it could wait until after dinner. It smells divine. When can we eat?"

He laughed. "It's ready. Sit. I'll go get it."

He walked into the kitchen and pulled the stuffed lake trout baked in a tomato and white wine sauce from the oven. He prepped two plates with sides of spiced wild rice and zucchini and marched out to the dining room, a napkin draped over his arm. *I hope she's impressed.*

Seated, Brooke looked up as he entered. "Wow, just like a professional waiter. Must be looking for a big tip?"

He placed a plate before her then one across the table and sat down behind it. "Wait until you taste it. I followed my usual recipe, but one never knows."

She laughed. "It'll be fine."

He raised his wine glass. "To us and a romantic evening. It's been a while."

She clinked glasses. "To us."

They dug in and he paused to watch her from over his hovering fork. She mumbled through a mouthful of food. "Divine!"

Satisfied, he paid more attention to consuming his own dinner. Every now and then he'd stop long enough to ask Brooke a question about the mission to Mars. She would take the time and detail to share as much as she could of every facet of the trip. Finally, he felt ready to let loose the question he'd been hesitant to ask. There were some odd things in the written report from Jesse. "What actually happened when you were forced to take off your helmet? Why were you unconscious for so long?"

She paused to wipe her mouth and put her utensils down. "I had lost a foothold when climbing out of the cave and banged into the wall. I guess it must have jarred my helmet some, and when I finally reached the top, I tripped and it unsealed. Brian was busy helping Jesse, and I was some distance away toward the rover. Jesse knew the problem and was yelling for me to reseat my helmet. Understand that during all of this, a sandstorm was blowing. Just as I went to do what Jesse wanted, the sand around me cleared, and I found myself in this air bubble with the sand swirling all around the outside of it. It looked like a perfect circle. It was the weirdest thing. Anyway, I knew I didn't have much time so I took off my helmet, and then reseated it. Then I passed out. I woke up in my bed two days later."

"Yeah, you know, I read Jesse's report. His version is a little different than yours. He figured you were in the middle of a dust devil, and that your bends-induced vertigo caused you to recall things differently."

"I know. I read his report as well but I refused to change mine. I know what I saw. It was the shape of a globe, I'm certain of it."

Robert looked down at his three-quarters finished plate and decided he was full and pushed it away. *I used to always finish this.* "You know, of course, there's no such thing as a spherical dust devil. It's scientifically impossible."

Brooke scraped the last morsel on her plate onto her fork. "That's what everybody keeps telling me. But I don't care. I'm sticking to my story." She gestured toward his plate. "You not going to finish that?"

"You can have it, if you want it."

She grabbed the plate and slid the remnants onto her own. "Thanks. I'm still a bit hungry."

Funny. It was always the other way around. I would eat fastest then finish hers.

She scooped another mouthful in. "It's funny, isn't it? You used to always finish mine before. But ever since I got back, I've had a bigger appetite. I guess years of space food can do that to you."

An alarm triggered in Robert's head. "You know, I think that's like the third or fourth time tonight you've said what I was thinking."

Brooke paused, fork halfway up in the air. "Really? I guess we must be like an old couple then, knowing each other's thoughts."

"Pff! I've been feeling like an old man ever since I got back from the moon. But you seem the picture of health. Frankly, I'm a little bit jealous—and worried. You're not going to want to stick with an old fuddy-duddy like me."

Brooke finished everything on her plate, got up from her seat, and came over to sit on his lap. She wrapped her arms around his neck and gave him a big kiss. "Come on. I think I know what you need to be young again."

CHAPTER 19

Sammy pounded back the last of the scotch in his glass, smacked his lips, and then let out a loud sigh. He saluted Nate Drummond with the empty. "Ya owe me, Nate. Big time!"

"Sammy, you owe your political existence to me. You managed to serve two terms when you probably didn't deserve one. I'm not going to appoint you president of the board of Drumdat, and that's final. And asking for a salary of fifty million? That's outrageous."

"Fifty mill is peanuts to ya." Sammy poured himself a liberal dose of scotch from Nate's private bar.

"Help yourself. It's only $200.00 an ounce."

He broke into one of his wide, toothy grins. "Nate, baby, you're too tense. Look, my term of office is just about up. I need something to do, and after all the things I got passed your way, the least you could do...."

"Is what? Give you a job for which you have no qualifications? The shareholders would eat me alive."

Sammy closed the gap and draped an arm over Nate's shoulder. "Naw, they'd accept me. I'm a president, remember? I'm used to being in charge. I ran the country. I can run Drumdat. No prob."

Nate purpled for a moment. "You're insufferable!" He moved out from under Sammy's arm and pressed a button on the intercom. "Send Alban in here, will you?"

"Right away, Mr. Drummond."

Nate turned on the large wall monitor.

Alban strolled in. "You looking for me, Nate? If you're wondering about the report from that Barnaby fellow, I got it."

"Yes, I am, Al. But not on that issue. Who do you have working on the Mars biology program? I want you to bring President Davidson here up to date."

Alban had a comp pad in his hand and after hitting a few keys managed to bring the view screen to life and post a report on it. "Here's the latest. Our lab boys say the methanogens are practically useless. The difference in the DNA structure is so variant as to be incompatible with life on Earth. Their only hope is they show a strong propensity to populate in our warmer climate. Who knows, in a number of years they might actually generate enough methane to be commercially viable. As a heating fuel, and with absorption, a number of commercial applications, there are some significant long-term prospects."

Nate waved at the screen without taking his eyes off Sammy. "At what point would you expect the payback to occur for the over ten billion dollars spent on the Mars mission?

Alban chuckled. "I don't think you'll live long enough to see it."

Nate walked over, hit a button, turned off the screen, then folded his arms, and grimaced. "So, you see, Sammy, that little stunt you pulled to get re-elected has got a long way to go to recompense me. And *you* want a board position to retire with."

He pursed his lips and made a snicking sound out of one side of his mouth. *Time to play hardball.* "Listen Nate, Don't start pulling that crap with me. Who set ya up with the exclusive deal for the Helium 3? Me. Who signed off on all those expropriations so ya could build your reactors where ya wanted? Me. Ya been making a lot of hay as a result, and I think I'm entitled to a piece."

"Entitled…entitled? The only reason you're in office is because I bought every delegate on the floor. Did you really think you got the party nomination on your own? Ha! You're a jock. That's all. In my mind, at best, we're even."

His mouth open to retort, Sammy stopped and smiled again. *Play it cool, Sammy. Play it cool.* "Hey Nate, how's about ya have a drink with me? Ya need to relax, unwind. You're letting this whole thing stress ya out. I've got a couple of Cubans in my pocket, want one?" He pulled cigars from inside his jacket as he tried to determine from Nate's body posture whether the old guy would calm down.

Nate shook his head. "Sammy, one of these days you're going to push me too far. I'm working. I don't have time for a drink and a cigar. Besides, my doctor says I've got to quit. They're not good for my health. Now, if we're finished here, then perhaps it's time you get going."

He replaced the cigars. "Okay, Nate. I get the message. I'm outta here. But before I go, I just want to make sure we have an understanding."

"Huh? What understanding?"

He held out his hand. "That we're even. So if I bring you one more sweetheart of a deal, the position's mine."

Nate hesitated then shook. "It better be one hell of a deal. Don't try and fool me with some low-end thing."

Sammy chuckled. "Would I try and con you? Nate, you're the man. I would never try to pull the wool over them eyes." He headed for the door. "Okay, I'm gone." Opening it, he found Janice standing nearby, talking with Alban. "You been listening at the keyhole all this time, kiddo?"

Janice smiled and matched his stride as he continued down the hall. "Of course. If I didn't try and stay ahead of your antics, I wouldn't be doing my job."

Sammy pulled her into a quick hug. "That's my gal, always

looking out for me. Come on, the limo's waiting." They made their wait out to the waiting car, the security guys falling in behind.

Once they climbed in and the car began to move, Janice kicked him in the shin. "Are you nuts? You can't go promising Nate anything else. You're already under investigation over the land deals, and half of Congress is upset with the way you handled the Mars mission."

He chuckled. "Hey, but it got me re-elected, didn't it? I mean, the people still love me, and that's what counts."

"Obviously you haven't been looking at your approval ratings lately. You're dropping like a stone. As more and more of this stuff leaks out, people are starting to question your motives."

He let loose a short raspberry. "Huh, ain't no matter. I can't get elected for a third term anyways. My time's almost up, Jay baby. I gotta prepare for my future."

"Not if that future's in jail. No more deals with Drumdat. That's final."

"Okay, okay, I'll think of something else."

He sat in silence the rest of the way and stared out the window. *There's gotta be another angle for me. I just know it.*

CHAPTER 20

Brooke settled down onto the bed of the MRI machine. "Is this really necessary, doc? I feel great."

The doctor placed a staying hand on her shoulder. "Relax, Brooke. This will only take thirty minutes. And yes, this *is* really necessary. Your peak physical conditioning is an enigma. I need to understand it. The implications of why you are so robust can have a major impact on future space missions. This neuroimaging may help me understand what's going on inside you. So far, the only thing I've discovered is a high level of hemoglobin in your blood. Your body has a very intense regeneration going on. I need to know why. So far, the only thing I can think of is your metabolism has sped up from your long duration in space and hasn't returned to normal yet."

"Okay, just don't scramble my brains with this thing."

"You'll be fine. Even though it's clamped down, try not to move your head. The test will be over before you know it."

The platform she lay on slid into the machine. Despite knowing there would be no problems, she still couldn't resist holding her breath every now and then during the process. But as the doctor promised, the scan was over in half an hour. She got up and went into the washroom to put her clothes back on. When she emerged, she waved to the doctor. "Okay, I'm off."

"Don't you want to see what your brain looks like?"

"I've got a lunch date. I'm sure if there's any bad news, you'll track me down. In the meantime, I gotta go."

She dashed out the door and jumped into her car for the ten minute ride to the bistro where she was to meet up with Robert. He was sitting at one of the outdoor patio tables and got up to greet her when she arrived.

Robert gave her a quick kiss. "I thought you were going to stand me up."

"Don't be silly. You know I was at the doc's." She took the seat opposite his. "What looks good on the menu?"

Robert sat down as well. "I don't know. Nobody writes them in English anymore. You picked this place, not me. I figured you would know what's what. I can't seem to find a cheeseburger on the list anywhere."

She laughed. "*Really*, Robert. You need to widen your taste experiences." She scanned quickly through the choices. "I think you want that fourth one down."

Robert lifted the menu close. "Bu-lette-au-gra-tin-crois-sant? Are you kidding me?" He dropped the menu and lifted his hands in surrender. "Fine. I'll have that. Next time, *I* pick the place."

She patted his hand. "Whatever you say. Here comes the waiter. I'm starved."

They placed their orders and she relaxed back into the chair and glanced around at the pleasant day. The sun was shining, people smiled as they enjoyed their meals; all was right with the world. Still, she frowned as she thought about the unviewed brain scans back at the doctor's office. She should have taken the time to go over them with the physician.

"Penny for your thoughts."

She snapped out of her reverie to look at Robert. "What?"

"You looked lost in thought there. I was wondering what's bothering you."

She gave him a weak smile. "Oh, it's just all these tests. The doctor won't let me be. He has me visiting him practically daily trying to figure out why I'm so healthy. You'd think he'd be glad. Instead of wasting his time studying me, he should be working to help you." Robert's jaw dropped; she had gone too far. "I'm sorry. I didn't mean it that way."

He pressed his lips tight together then let out a sigh. "It's okay. I know what you meant. He's doing all he can. He says I've had a very small amount of bone re-growth. It's a good sign. I'm hoping I'll be back to normal soon."

The waiter returned with their meals, and she was thankful for the break in conversation. "Ooh! It looks good. Time to dig in."

Robert held up his plate. On it was an open faced croissant bun with a slice of meatloaf garnished with cheese and shredded lettuce. "This is a cheeseburger?"

"Oh, shush. Try it, you might like it."

"Whatever." Robert took a bite and gave an approving nod. "Good."

"See? I told you." She grabbed her fork and knife and dove into her own meal. *Hmm, could use some salt and pepper.* She absently reached for the salt shaker and sprinkled some on.

"How'd you do that?"

Brooke stopped shaking, and took the moment to glance at Robert. "Do what?"

"You…the salt shaker jumped into your hand."

She turned the shaker to look at it, and then returned her stare to Robert. "What are you talking about?"

"I watched it happen. You reached for it, and it seemed to move the inch or two to meet your grasp."

A moment of panic ran through Brooke. *Could Robert be telling the truth?* She returned the shaker to the table and extended an open hand toward it. "Nothing. Are you sure?"

Robert stroked his forehead. "I think I'm sure. It was so quick. Now, I'm not certain."

He dropped his fist down on the table hard. The table wobbled and the shaker fell into Brooke's hand. "Oh, see? It was just a wobble that caused it. You must have bumped it then and it just looked like the salt jumped into my hand."

"Yeah...yeah, maybe that's what happened." He broke into a grin. "Sorry about that. It must have sounded real stupid."

"Don't sweat it. I've had plenty of stupid moments in my life. I won't tell if you don't."

"Deal." Robert looked at the unfinished sandwich on his plate. "And I'll not tell anybody that this is supposed to be a cheeseburger."

She laughed. "I thought you said it was good?"

"I lied."

"Well, when you pick, make sure it's not some dirty, greasy hole in the wall just because you say they've got good burgers. I like a little ambiance with my food."

"I promise. They'll even serve you wine with your lunch. As long as you don't mind drinking it out of a coffee cup."

"You're incorrigible."

They finished eating and she kissed him good-bye before she headed for her car. She hadn't said anything, but she suspected the lie about the sandwich was not a lie at all, but a subterfuge to hide the fact he couldn't finish it. He never finished his meals anymore. As she climbed in her car, she stopped to wipe her eyes as the tears came. *There's got to be something that can help—anything.*

88

CHAPTER 21

Bart tapped his pencil on the desk. "So, Doctor, let me get this straight. What you're telling me is that you don't know."

"Now that's not exactly what I said. What I said was, I can't explain it."

"Explain, know, what's the diff?"

"The difference is that I know what's going on, I just can't explain why it's happening."

Bart sighed, dropped his pencil on the desk, and leaned back in his chair, folding his hands behind his head. "Alright, tell me again. But simple English please. All those big terms you used before fly over my head. I'm only an accountant, not a medical scientist."

He watched and read the man's anger as the doctor paused to glare at him. *Fine. Let him be pissed off. I don't care.* "Well?"

"It's like I said before. For some reason, when I took my readings with the electroencephalograph, the rapid fluctuations of voltage, between parts of the cerebral cortex, that are detectable, are at an accelerated rate. In short, her brain waves are greatly enhanced. Her mind is operating at an incredible speed. This has resulted in other aspects of her physique also benefitting from an enhanced pace. Like her health. Those parts of her body designed to correct deficiencies in her system are operating at such a level, she is the picture of perfect health. The only quirk is she's put on better than twenty pounds since her pre-flight weigh in, but damned if I can see where."

"So, what…she's some kind of super woman?"

"In a manner of speaking, yes."

He returned to a normal sitting position and picked up the doctor's file. "Okay, leave this with me. Have you told her yet?"

"I was going to do that next."

"I'd prefer if you didn't at this time—at least for a couple of days. Give me a chance to investigate this from my end. Will that make a difference to her?"

The doctor pulled at his chin, obviously in thought. "No, I don't think so. If anything, she should only get better. But at some point, I need to tell her. I have a duty."

"Fine. It's our little secret for now. Two days is all I ask. Then you can tell her and all the world to your heart's content."

The doctor exited Bart's office and he reached for the phone. "Yeah, Frank? Can you come see me in my office? Just come see me."

He picked up his pencil and began the drumming once more as he waited for Frank. It was only a matter of moments before the research head came into his office. He rose, switched the pencil into his left hand, and offered a handshake. "Sit down, sit down. We need to talk."

After Frank gave him a weak handshake, he sat in the empty chair across from Bart's desk, but avoided eye contact. *Did he know about Brooke's condition already? No. The doctor said I was the only one who knew. So what's bugging him?* "How are things going, Frank? I haven't had a chance to go over your reports lately."

Frank hesitated before answering. "I'm sorry, Bart. My apologies for not coming to you sooner."

Now his curiosity was really piqued. The pencil back in his right hand, he had been drumming again but he stopped. "Sooner? What am I missing here?"

Frank wrung his hands. "It's Brooke. I should have told you. But I was afraid those guys from Drumdat would show up again."

"Why? What did Brooke do? Did she hide something from

them?"

"No. Nothing of the sort. It's just…well…she's completely rebuilt the file—from scratch."

"From scratch? What do you mean from scratch?"

"Just that. She's managed to recall every aspect of the methanogens from Mars. Right down to the smallest detail. I didn't think it was humanly possible. No one can recall that much. I don't know if it's all accurate, but the rest of the staff combined couldn't refute any of it. They think she's bang on. So we've been running hypothetical analyses on them ever since."

He placed his finger on his lips in contemplation and started drumming again. He sighed. "Okay, Frank. It's okay. After what the doctor told me about her freakish physical health, I'm not surprised. You keep working with that data. I don't think Drumdat's boys have a claim to it. But let's keep this under wraps for a couple of days. And your staff as well."

"Will do. Mum's the word."

Frank got up and excused himself. As the door closed, Bart threw his pencil in the air. As it hit and clattered across his desk, he rose and left his office. He waved to his secretary. "I'm going down to the cafeteria for a coffee."

He trudged in, grabbed a coffee, and while he was at it, a jelly doughnut. *These will be the death of me.* Looking for somewhere to sit, he spotted Jesse Cain and Robert Tangler at a table not too far off. He moved near. "Mind if I join you gentlemen?"

Jesse pulled one of the chairs out. "Sure thing, Bart. How're things at the upper end? You still fighting for pennies with Congress?"

"If they made them anymore, I'd take them, what with the price of copper these days."

Robert laughed then pointed at his doughnut. "You know, those things are going to be the death of you. You need to eat smart."

Bart took a bite. "Mmm, they still taste good. You know, that's exactly what I was just thinking. You must be a mind reader."

Robert held up his hands in a defensive posture. "You're looking at the wrong person. You should try Brooke for that skill."

His hand halfway back toward his mouth for another bite of his doughnut, Bart froze it where it was. Could it be true? "Reading a man's mind is a simple thing. The female sex has been doing it since Adam and Eve. They call it woman's intuition. My wife knows the second I've done something wrong."

"Hmm...I don't think so. We were having dinner and it seemed every time I thought of something, she said it."

"And she does this all the time?"

"No, just the one night. It was kind of spooky, really. I'm thinking it was a freak thing."

Jesse leaned in. "What's freaky is how quickly she recovered from the trip. I'm only now getting my legs back, and it's been months. She was out dancing her first night home."

Robert gave his elbow a nudge. "That's not true. She didn't leave the base for a week. She had to go through the same recovery program you did."

"Yeah, but that's just it. She's out in a week. Maybe less. It takes time, and you know it."

Robert slumped in his chair and took a sip of coffee.

Jesse sighed. "I'm sorry, Rob. I didn't mean it that way."

The report on Tangler's condition popped into Bartholomew's head. "It's been two years now, Robert. How is the recovery coming?"

"Doc says I've gained point oh four percent bone mass over the

92

last six months. So I suppose that's something." Robert reached to put his coffee cup back on the table, fumbled it, and it spilled. He tossed the empty on the table. "Oh hell, you know my stats. There's no sense bullshitting anybody. I'm not getting better. Okay?"

Jesse rose, placed his hands on the Robert's shoulders and started to rub. "Easy, Rob. I shouldn't have blurted out like that. We all know what you're going through."

Bartholomew patted Robert's forearm. "Have faith. You know we'll move mountains to help you."

Robert pulled away. "Yeah, well you better get Brooke to help you there, too."

Bart sat back and sighed. "I can understand you being a little jealous, but be happy she is healthy. After what she went through, it could have been a lot worse. She almost died out there."

"No, you don't understand. Listen, Brooke would have my nuts if I told you this, but the other day, I could have sworn I saw her move the salt shaker without touching it. Promise me you won't say anything."

Now how did Frank put it? "Mum's the word, Robert. Mum's the word." He rose. "Well, gentlemen, my doughnut's done and I need to get back on the job. Take care of yourselves. America needs its heroes alive and well."

He turned and headed back toward his office. *And the hits just keep on coming. So what next, she can fly?*

CHAPTER 22

Agnes got home from work to find the kitchen a mess. Three teenagers and not one could put a single thing in the dishwasher. She cursed their laziness then set about cleaning up and making dinner.

After about an hour, her husband, Hank, came home, the screen door banging behind him. "Hey, hon, how's dinner coming?"

"Hank, you've got to talk to those children of ours. I got home to disaster zone. As a result, dinner won't be ready for at least half an hour."

"Okay, okay, I'll talk to them. They're just kids."

"They're not just kids anymore. Bobby's going to be eighteen soon. It's high time they took on some responsibilities around here."

He paused from hanging his coat to give her a quick kiss on the cheek. "Alright, I said I'd talk to them. But later, okay? I've got bowling tonight. In the meantime, anything I can do to help?"

She let out a huff of air. "No, I'll manage. Just stay out of my way."

"Suit yourself." He sat down at the dinette table and picked up the paper. He rustled through the pages.

The noise irritated her. "Do you have to do that now?"

"Do what?"

"Crumple the pages like that."

He put the paper down. "What's the matter, hon? Bad day at work?"

"No, not really. Nothing I want to talk about."

Hank got up and stopped her from dicing the salad vegetables by putting his hand on top of her forearm. "Hey, we had a deal. No secrets.

I can't help if you don't tell me."

She pulled away and resumed chopping the celery. "No, it's nothing like that. I'm under orders, that's all. I'm not supposed to talk about it to anyone."

"And anyone includes me? What do they think down there at NASA, that you're married to some international spy? Come on, spill it."

She scraped the chopped veggies into the salad bowl, wiped her hands, and sat down. "You know that astronaut, Brooke Jones? The one who went to Mars?"

Hank returned to his seat at the table. "Yeah, what about her?"

"Well, she works in our department and she's charted out the genome of those methanogens that were brought back from Mars."

"So? That's good, isn't it? Doesn't that make your job a lot easier? So what are you telling me, you're jealous?" He picked up the paper once more.

"Hank, don't you remember? Drumdat Corporation took *all* the methanogens and *all* the data files some months ago. She did it from memory. We're talking thousands of variables. It's inconceivable."

He dropped the paper. "You're kidding."

"I am not kidding. And what's more, it's all hush hush. I'm feeling like an idiot working beside her."

Hank reached out and took her hands in his. "Listen, it's probably all some hoax, just to make her look good. You know, news propaganda. Girl goes to Mars *and* is top bio scientist. Don't let it get to you. The truth will come out sooner or later. They're feeding her the data. There can't be any other explanation. You'll see."

Hank gave her another kiss on the cheek, and then got up. "Listen, I'll grab a dog at the lanes. You feed the kids. I'll talk to them when I get back. Everything will be fine. I'll see you later."

"Have fun."

As the screen door banged again, she got up and set the table. A small doubt nagged at her. *I hope Hank's smart enough not to talk to the guys about it.*

***

Suzie ran across the playground to where Timmy played with the other boys. The news she was about to tell him gave her a sense of pending satisfaction. "Hey Timmy, I talked to my mom last night and you're wrong."

He came over, the other boys falling in behind. "Wrong about what?"

"You're wrong about Superman."

"What are you talking about?"

"My mom says that there is no Superman. He's only make-believe."

"Shucks. I knew that."

"Yeah, well, that makes Wonder Woman the best superhero of them all."

"Aw, you're just a dumb girl. Wonder Woman is make-believe, too."

"No she isn't. I know because my mom knows her."

"Your mom knows Wonder Woman? I think you got rocks in your head."

She stomped her foot. "It's true! My mom says she's one of those astronauts. She knows because she works in the hospital at the base. She says this lady is super. She has like super powers or something,

96

like Wonder Woman."

"Sheesh, Suzie, you're nuts. Wait until I talk to my dad. He's an in-ves-ti-ga-tive reporter. He knows everything. He'll find out the truth. He's a lot smarter than your stupid mom."

"My mom is not stupid. And you're just jealous because Wonder Woman is a girl and you can't stand it that a girl is the best."

"You just wait until tomorrow, Suzie. I'm going to prove you wrong."

She stuck her tongue out at him then turned away to go back to the girl side of the playground. *Just wait until his dad finds out my mom is right.*

***

Mark plopped down in his seat. "It's your shot, Jesse."

Jesse hefted his cue stick, and took aim at the cue ball. "Seven ball in the corner." He took the shot and the seven rattled in and out of the pocket. "Damn!"

Mark got up to take his turn. "You're not on your game tonight. Something bothering you?"

"Nah, I just suck, that's all."

He went to the table where their drinks were and signaled the waitress for another beer. From the pool table, the sound of balls clashing and the distinctive noise made when one entered a pocket had him turning his head to look. "What've you got left?"

"Only the eight."

He watched as Mark lined up his shot and sank the ball.

Mark reached for the ball rack. "That's game. Play another?"

"Nah, come sit down. I ordered us another round."

"Sounds fine, you lost so you're buying." Mark plopped down in the chair opposite and took a swig of the beer in front of him. "Just in time, too. Looks like this one is about done."

Ever since he had lunch with Robert the other day, things had been gnawing at Jesse. "How are you feeling, Mark? A hundred percent yet?"

"Yeah, right as rain. I'll feel a whole lot better after you buy a few more rounds. Why do you ask? You still not there yet? After that last pool game, I was starting to wonder."

"No, I'm fine. I was only curious." He took the last sip of the beer in front of him, scanned about for the waitress, and then returned his focus to Mark. "I'm wondering whether you had any side effects like…Brooke."

Mark laughed. "I wish! She was up and about in days. I wonder what her secret is. If it's a girl thing, then I might just think about a sex change if it means getting well so fast."

"So you haven't heard then."

"Heard? Heard what? Oh no, let me guess. She's pregnant? Whatever anyone says, it wasn't me, man."

The waitress finally arrived with their beers and placed them on the table. "I wonder if you can be serious for more than five minutes. I'm talking about her extra…. Oh, what's the word I'm looking for? Powers, special skills, mystic talents… Oh, whatever, she can do things. Stuff like you only see in the movies."

The waitress had removed the empties but still stood there. "You mean psychic abilities."

He turned to look up at the girl. "Pardon?"

"Psychic abilities. I'm leaning all about them in class. I only work here to get through school. I'm taking psychology as a major. There are

98

all kinds of psychic abilities, but the ones most people know about are ESP, telepathy, psycho kinesis...."

"Psycho what?"

"Psycho kinesis. Mind over matter. You know...levitation and stuff like that. Magicians claim to have that ability all the time."

Mark, after having a drink from his new beer, shuffled his chair in closer. "Are you saying Brooke has these skills now?"

Jesse held a hand in front of Mark's face. "Shh! I'm not saying anything."

The waitress looked from Jesse to Mark and then back again. "Well, I've got other tables to tend to. I wouldn't worry about it. In almost every case, they're proved to be frauds."

Jesse waited until she left. Once he was sure she was out of earshot, he turned back to Mark. "Blast it, you've got to watch what you say around people. They might get the wrong impression."

Mark scratched at his chin. "What do you think they might think—witchcraft? Hey, with a figure like hers, I'm sure she puts a lot of spells on guys."

"Pff! Don't be silly. But apparently she can do those things the waitress mentioned. Robert swears he saw her levitate a salt shaker. And he thinks she can read his mind."

Mark laughed. "No shit. If she can do that, he'll never get away with fooling around on her."

"Oh, never mind. Let's drink up and go. I want to get out of here."

"Okay with me, but you still owe me two rounds from pool."

Jesse signaled to the waitress to bring the bill. "We'll get them at the next bar. I just don't want to stay at this one anymore."

They finished their beers, Jesse paid the tab, and they headed for the door. As he left, he could see from the corner of his eye the waitress watching them all the way out.

CHAPTER 23

Brooke sat at her console, examining the results of the latest hypothetical run regarding the methanogens from Mars. *Damn! If only we still had a sample. There's only so much you can do this way.*

She got up and headed for Frank's office. She stepped past his secretary and went straight to his open door. Peeking in, she saw him at his desk. "Frank, can I have a minute?"

He bolted upright in his seat. "Uh, oh hi, Brooke. Sure, come on in. What's on your mind?"

I must have startled him. But he seems real nervous. I wonder what the matter is. "Listen, I've been thinking about those Martian methanogens Drumdat took. I'd like you to have a sit down with them and see if you can iron out some kind of joint venture to work on the stuff. My research has me thinking there might actually be a big use for the things. How about it?"

Frank folded his arms across his chest. "That's beyond my scope. I'll have to talk to Bart. See whether he can finagle it, but aren't you busy enough?"

"Busy enough? Are you kidding? That's exactly why I need those microbes. I'm at the limit of what I can work with." *I'm sensing something here. Something's bothering him.*

Frank turned to his computer. "Yes, busy. You're logging twelve hours a day in the lab. Sometimes more. If not for your visits to the doctor's office, I'd bet you'd be here twenty-four, seven. Go home. Get some rest and get healthy."

"What's Doc been telling you? I'm fine. I don't get tired. If anything, I find it hard to sleep, so I'd rather be working than lying around doing squat."

"Doc? Oh...nothing. He's told me nothing. I just assumed there might be a problem, considering how often you go."

"*Frank*, you're hiding something from me. Now what is it?" She stared at him and concentrated. In her mind, she heard his thoughts. *The doc says you're a freak.* A freak? She stepped back, the surprise of what had just happened hitting her.

"Listen Brooke, maybe you better go talk to Bart. I'm...I'm not the guy you need. Go see him now. I'll call and tell him you're on the way."

"Yeah, yeah, maybe I'd better." She left Frank's office, dazed. *I read his mind. His mind! I could see what he was thinking. And more. He's afraid of me. What the hell is going on?*

When she entered the senior administrator's outer office, she found him waiting for her.

"Brooke, come on in. Frank called and told me to expect you."

"Thanks Bart, if it's not too much of an inconvenience."

He led the way into his personal office. "No problem at all. Clear off a chair. Sit. Tell me what's on your mind."

She moved the files off the chair closest to the desk then sat and stared at him for a moment.

Bart sat down, picked up a pencil, and began to tap it. "I got an idea from Frank what you want, but why don't you tell me in your own words."

She hesitated and concentrated. Nothing.

He tilted his head. "Brooke? Speak up. Tell me your plan."

Nothing still. Maybe it was my imagination. "Sorry. I was just concentrating on how best to put it. But now that I'm here, I'll lay it on the line. You've got to get those samples back. Or at least get me

102

working on them at Drumdat. I'm on the verge of a breakthrough."

"A breakthrough, you say? Seriously? Tell me about it."

"I think I can unlock how these microbes defend against cosmic radiation. Think. Mankind could travel the stars without fear. For Drumdat, it means their workers on the moon would be free to spend limitless hours scouring for Helium 3. And not just cosmic rays. Deadly exposure to uranium and the like would be a thing of the past. But I need live Martian methanogens to test with. Not computer simulations."

"Yes, I've heard of your successes in the lab from Frank. Quite astounding, I must say."

She bit her lower lip, contemplating. "You know, that's another thing I wanted to talk to you about. I get the impression Frank knows more about my visits with the doctor than he's supposed to."

Bart dropped the pencil on the desk. "I'm afraid that's my fault. I owe you an apology. I might have spilt the beans to Frank after I met with Doc."

Whatever happened to doctor-patient privilege? "So you know, too?"

My dear, there is nothing that goes on at this base that I don't know about. Or at the very least, find out about. And your unusual good health is an important concern. Very important."

"But it's my"

"It's what? It's something private between you and the doctor? Surely you must understand that whatever the secret is to your amazing recovery, it could help future astronauts, or even past ones—if you catch my drift."

She did. And after her moment of defiance, she shrank down in the chair. *He's talking about Robert. If there is anything I can do, I need to do it.* "I'm sorry. I guess I got a little offended. I should have known better."

The administrator picked up his pencil and started his incessant tapping again. "That's better. Nothing like a little humility now and then to make you a better person. Now let's see what we can do to get you teamed up with Drumdat."

She perked up. "Really? You think you can do it?"

"Ha! They didn't call me the Maneuver Master for nothing."

"They did?"

"No. I just made that up now. But have no fear, I'll get it done."

She got up and grabbed his hand with both of hers, causing him to drop his pencil. "Thank you, Bart. You won't be sorry. I know I can do it."

"I have no doubt you can."

CHAPTER 24

"How's it coming, Aki?"

He looked up to see his supervisor peering in. "Hi, Bruce. I'm still going through some old data from Voyager 1. It operated for almost fifteen years once it got out of the solar system. I figured it was the best place to start."

Bruce came over and sat next to him. "What are you looking for?"

"Anomalies. It's my hope I can find some collaborating evidence in the galaxial solar wind."

"Still no support in getting your theory accepted? I've never been a big quantum mechanics guy. I understand it, but have never approved of it. Every decade, someone comes up with some newfangled theory on how the universe works at the microscopic level, and every decade those theories get disproven. Look at your recent stint in Geneva. All these years and billions upon billions of dollars later, and still no final proof their theories are correct."

"My approach is different. Unlike Higgs, whose boson, in his formula, is needed to create mass, I approach it from a belief that instead, it imparts energy and mass is a byproduct of the effect."

"Yes, I read your theorem on it. But then you go on to explain that these particles don't become one of the building blocks of matter, but instead clump together and form black holes. It's this aspect of your analysis that is challenged."

"Look." He brought onto his monitor the images of other galaxies that had been taken over the years, from Hubble forward. "It is now standard theory that there is a black hole at the center of each galaxy. Some..." he pointed to a couple of the images, "show jets of energy spewing from the poles light years into space. While others..." Aki pointed out different ones, "have none. The prevailing theory is that black holes are made of incredibly dense mass compressed into a singularity where not even light can escape. Yet these jets of energy do. Physicists go on to theorize that the black holes can only eat so much matter at a time and must reject the rest. They also formulize that those super-massive black holes without jets are in a dormant stage."

Aki faced Bruce. "Now just imagine, instead of super-massive black holes being formed as the result of an immense gravity well, they're the result of my particles clumping together., Yes, they would still have a large gravity, but not the singularity as espoused. No, whatever it draws in, it spits out, energized. It would explain why some black holes emit such massive jets, and why others appear dormant."

"Okay, so how does looking for anomalies outside of our solar system help? It's fifty thousand light years to the nearest super-massive black hole in the center of our galaxy. You're not going to find one floating just outside our heliosheath. Heck, not even a regular black hole could exist that close without our knowing about it."

"No, but that's not what I'm looking for. I'm looking for micro black holes."

Bruce bounced against the back of his chair. "Micro black holes? Seems to me I recall them being theoretical at best. And why do you need to go outside the solar system to find those? Wouldn't they, if they exist, be everywhere?"

"It goes back to the formation of the solar system. When our star was born, the initial solar wind from that birth cleared the area of them. Any that remained probably fell into the sun as there were no planets with the gravitational well to pull them in."

"So how would Voyager have recognized one?"

106

Aki smiled, triumphant at having the answers to justify his theory. "I'm hoping they picked up the variances in speed of nearby photons within the Schwarzchild radius."

"If you find one and can verify it with some statistics, it will validate your theory?"

"That just about sums it up."

Bruce slapped his hands onto his knees and rose. "Well, sounds like you've got it all figured out. I appreciate you have a burning desire to prove your quantum theories, but don't forget, there's still work to do."

"Okay, I get the message. I promise to make up the time."

Bruce stopped in the doorway. "Out of curiosity, should someone else in our department, or anyone else at NASA for that matter, come across one of these micro black holes, what exactly would they find? How big are these things?"

"They're really small, as small as twenty-two micrograms in size or one planck. They would be imparting energy to anything near them so imagine a sphere of influence around them."

"Twenty-two micrograms, eh? Sounds pretty small. What would that work out to?"

"About the size of a flea's egg."

"Well, if I hear of anything that small, I'll be sure to let you know."

Bruce left and Aki switched to the assignment he was supposed to be working on. Then it hit him. He jumped up and dashed out the door. Bruce was just down the hall. "There's something else I forgot to tell you."

Bruce turned to face him. "What was that?"

"Good luck spotting one. They're black."

Bruce laughed. "Silly me. And I was hoping for pink with green polka dots on them."

CHAPTER 25

Nate Drummond perused the reports from the company divisions. Two of his reactors were yet to be operational because of a lack of Helium 3. His contracts with several states to provide fusion power involved gave him leeway until moon operations were in full swing, but it irked him still.

It had been a smart thing to invest in power grids all those years ago. If there was one constant that Americans would always need, it was electricity. Rates climbed every year without fail, and until his decision to invest in nuclear fusion, profits had always been tidy. Traditional power sources were running out, either of supply or favor. The solar and wind fads were still out there, but they just couldn't produce the wattage necessary to feed big cities. Coal burning was history, nuclear fission unpopular, and hydro-electric too damn expensive. *Dam expensive. Now that's funny. I must remember to tell Alban that one.*

Which is why he had gambled on nuclear fusion. Rates had grown to such a high level; he constantly had to fight to keep states from legislating how much he could charge.

It had taken tremendous resources to get the project to where it was now. Losses in the past few years had been in the tens of billions. The shareholders were screaming and the creditors had a few things to say as well. But there was plenty of good news as well. Reports indicated returns in triple figures from the operational reactors. It boded very well once all of the reactors were in full production.

That whole Mars expedition had turned out to be a big bust. Billions spent and nothing to show for it except a few measly microbes.

Come to think of it, where is that report?

Clicking through to Research and Development, he scanned the relevant report. It spoke of a promising breakthrough with the Martian methanogens. *Well, this is good news.* Also that the work was about to be shared with NASA. *What the hell?* He speed dialed his CEO. "Al? What's the story on NASA worming its way back into the research on the methanogens? I thought we went to a lot of trouble to purge their files of this stuff."

"We did. But they managed a breakthrough regardless. It could save R&D years. And we have a newly-negotiated one-year lead on any new findings."

"One year. Is that enough?"

"Enough to prevent anyone else from catching us. And there's one more thing."

"What's that?"

"The lead scientist on this is that astronaut Brooke Jones, the one who went to Mars."

"I know who she is. What of it?"

"Did you know she returned in better condition than when she left? She's agreed to a whole battery of tests. Think back on that lawsuit we dealt with from the two Helium 3 miners. If we can make our people safe from cosmic radiation *and* provide them a method of quick bone recovery, we could save millions."

"Okay, you sold me. Keep me in the loop."

I think I'll cover a few extra bases, just to be sure. Next, Nate called the security chief.

"Security. Smithson here."

"David, come see me in my office, will you?"

"On my way, Mr. Drummond."

Nate buzzed his receptionist to send David straight in, then rose from his chair and went to his private bar to get a drink. It was located behind a bookcase that swung out into the room when he pressed a button. Normally, he liked to keep its identity private, but when he needed to remove tension with a simple libation, it served its purposes well.

The security chief entered. "Hi, Mr. Drummond. You wanted to see me?"

"Yes, David, I did. You remember that Upshaw case? The one where that employee was suing us on false pretenses? That investigator we used before, the one you recommended. What's his story again?"

"You mean Barnaby? We worked together when I was still with the agency and we were investigating the rumor of CEO Alban Moceri's ties to organized crime. After we were fired and while you took me on, Barnaby opened up his own private investigation firm. The case was closed after that."

He chuckled and handed David a drink. The man's penchant for alcohol was what got him fired from the FBI in the first place. "Yes, Barnaby. That was the name. Did I ever tell you he reminded me of an old television character named Barnaby Jones? I used to watch it as a kid."

"Yes, sir. A couple of times."

"I did? Well, never mind that. I want you to get that fellow doing a special background check on Miss Brooke Jones, the astronaut from NASA."

David had been sipping at his beverage and choked for a moment. Obviously the poor fellow had been surprised. "Miss Jones, sir? We already have a complete dossier on her. Can I tell him why?"

"Yes, you can. Apparently now, she will be working at our

research lab. I was just apprised of it. You know how I like additional background checks that don't use the regular channels on certain people. Get Barnaby to do this one. Keep it on the hush-hush. Bring the report to me when it's finished."

"Will do, Mr. Drummond, sir. I can tell him the usual rate applies?"

"Yes, yes. Now be off and get him started. Time's a wasting."

David looked at the glass in his hand, took a quick gulp, and then put it on the counter. "On my way."

After he left the room, Nate picked up the man's glass, drained of all but the ice. He dumped it in the sink. *What a waste of good scotch.*

CHAPTER 26

Robert jogged around the corner. *Just a few more blocks until I get home. My legs are killing me.*

He had adjusted his program from carrying twenty pounds on his back to ten pound ankle weights on each leg. Although the total weight was the same, the distribution was different. According to the doctor, the bones in his legs had stopped recovering. They were going to stay thin. *Not if I have anything to say about it.*

He crossed a street and almost tripped going up the curb. A sharp pang coursed through his left leg. He slowed until the twinge eased then accelerated again. Home was only another two blocks.

As Robert stepped down off the next curb, pain flared through his leg at a much higher intensity. He crumpled to the ground. "Augh! What the hell?"

He tried to get to a sitting position and winced at the deep throb in his shin. Looking down, he spotted a bulge halfway up. "Well, that's done it. It's broken."

He glanced around. *Of course, no one in sight. Maybe I'd better try calling out.* "Help! Is anyone around?"

A dog barked in the distance but he heard no other sounds. *I can't lie here forever. Time to get up and get off the street. And stupid me without my cell phone.*

He managed to balance on his right foot and both hands. Slowly, he inched his palms backward until he could stand. "Alright, I guess I'm hopping the rest of the way."

No sooner had he started when from down the street, the headlights of a car caught him in motion. *That damned idiot is coming fast.* He put as much as he could into his hopping and cleared the lane just as the vehicle roared past behind him, the driver leaning on his horn. As he tried to hop up the curb, he tripped and fell into a large bush. The aching throb in his left leg was joined by a searing lance in his right. Using the lower branches, he dragged himself into a sitting position. The ugly angle of his right foot told him all he needed to know. *I can't believe this. I've broken them both.*

He felt dizzy. "Help! Help?" He slid back down to lie on the ground. "Some...one...help...me? An...y...one?" His mind fogged. *Someone help me...please?*

***

Brooke pulled into the driveway next to Robert's car. *He's home. I've tried to call him for an hour. Why hasn't he answered? I've got a lot to tell him.*

She headed for the door and then paused. Something itched at her mind. Instead, she walked to the end of the drive and looked down the road. The streetlights stretching off in the distance offered an alternating mix of illumination and shadow. She couldn't see anything of note, but something nagged her to go.

She began to walk, but then felt the urge to speed up, to hurry. In half a block she dropped her purse and was at a full tilt run. She didn't know why but she felt the need to cry out. "I'm coming!"

She bolted across the intersection, dodging two cars in the process. Racing the whole next block, she spotted him lying under a bush. He looked passed out. She dropped to her knees beside him. "Robert, what happened? Are you okay?"

He opened his eyes. "Brooke, is that you? How'd you find me?"

"I-I don't know. I just did. Something told me I'd find you down here. Come on. Let's get you up."

He groaned and pushed at her when she tried to hoist him to his feet. "No, don't. I think I've broken both my legs. Call an ambulance."

She cringed. One leg was turned sideways with a nasty lump above the ankle. The other looked like he had a second knee in the middle of his shin. *Oh my god.* "I don't have my phone. I dropped my purse. I can't leave you here. Let's get you home and get that ambulance."

"I'm too heavy. Just go get help."

"No way. I'm not leaving you here." She scooped him up with both arms, rose to her feet, and ran back toward home.

Robert stared into her face. "How are you doing this?"

"Don't talk. Save your strength. We'll be there soon." She hardly slowed down when she scooped up her purse. "My key is in there, if you need it."

Robert fumbled through his pockets. "No, I have mine." He inserted it in the lock and opened the door. Brooke dashed in and placed him on the sofa. Grabbing the phone, she dialed 9-1-1.

With an ambulance on the way, she returned to sit on the edge of the sofa next to Robert. "How are you doing?"

"Some pain killers would be nice." *What she did was incredible. In fact, impossible.*

She patted his cheek. "No it wasn't. It's amazing what you can do when necessity demands it."

She's reading my mind again.

"No, I'm not! I'm just…I'm just, oh my god. Robert, I'm sorry. I just…just, oh, I don't know what I'm doing." A huge pang of despair wracked her, and the tears came in a flood. "What's…what's wrong

115

with me?"

He took her hand. "Nothing. In fact, right now you're as perfect as can be. Whatever happened to you back on Mars made you all the better. You're different, that's all. So listen, you're going to have to control it, keep it quiet. People don't like different, even if it *is* better."

Screeching sirens approached their house. "I'm going out of town to work on the Martian methanogens. Drumdat Corp. has given NASA permission. I wanted you to know. But I don't know what to do. You're going to need me now."

Vehicle doors slammed in the driveway. Robert glanced toward the open door then smiled at her. "Don't worry. I'll be fine. I'll get to watch a lot of TV and eat junk food. Go. Make the next big scientific discovery. Heaven knows you deserve it. It should have been your baby in the first place. I'll see you when you get back."

The front door swung wider as the ambulance workers rushed in with a gurney. "Stand back, miss, so we can get to him."

They checked Robert's legs and he told them what had happened. After checking his vitals, they loaded Robert up and wheeled him out the door. Brooke followed and watched as they loaded him in. He reached for her and she bent close to hear. "I love you."

She kissed him. "I love you too." The tears started again.

Once the driver gave her their destination, he closed the door and the vehicle sped off, siren blaring. She watched it go until it was out of sight then jumped in her car and drove to the hospital as quickly as possible.

CHAPTER 27

Nate grasped the data stick. "Thank you, David. I'll look this over in a moment. You've kept this hush-hush as I requested?"

"Absolutely, Mr. Drummond. No one knows about it except you, me, and Barnaby."

"Good. Did you have a chance to review the report?"

David glanced at the bar before replying. "Yes sir. Quite interesting. It seems she is subject to some weird rumors."

Best to appease the big oaf. "Would you like a drink?"

"Oh, why, yes, sir. Thank you, sir."

He poured David a healthy scotch. "So, weird rumors, you say. How so?"

"Well, it seems she has some special skills. Psychic stuff. Like tele— something or other."

"Telepathy?"

David paused to take a healthy sip from his glass. "No, I don't think that's the one. Teleporting things, like in Star Trek."

"You mean moving things? Telekinesis, possibly?"

"Yeah! That's it. Telekinesis. And that's not all. It gets even weirder. They say she has super powers, like…like Superman!"

What's he talking about? Nate gave the man a close look. "David, I know you have a penchant to drink now and then. You sure you haven't been imbibing before getting here today?"

"No, sir, never. You gave me a chance to restart my career, even after I had worked on that case investigating Alban. I would never betray your trust. As to Miss Jones, it's all in the report. You'll see. Apparently she can outrun, outjump, and out-lift just about anybody, including men. And out-think them too. Supposedly she's got like a photographic memory. The rumor is she got infected with something back on Mars that's made her better than everybody else. But they don't know what it is. It ain't natural, I tell you."

He always reminds me of that investigation. They closed the file but did they discover anything? "If that's true, our doctors are going to find that out soon enough. She's scheduled for a full battery of tests."

"Aw, I don't believe it anyways. So far it's only rumors. I don't think she could beat a professional fighter, such as myself."

He chuckled. "I learned a long time ago never to underestimate anybody. One never knows."

David reddened. "What? You think she could beat me? I'll have you know when I was in the service; I was the toughest guy in my division. That's how I landed that job with the FBI. They were looking for someone with my set of skills."

Nate held his hands up in defense. "No, I'm not saying that. I'm merely pointing out that one should never automatically eliminate possibilities. Every rumor has a grain of truth to it."

David sighed and his shoulders slumped. "Yeah, I suppose you're right, sir. It says in there that she takes classes in self-defense. I guess for the average guy, if she's really fit, she'd be more than a match."

I tweaked a nerve suggesting the woman could beat him. There's a lot of pride in David. I guess that's what makes him good at his job, despite his drinking problem. "See? There's always something. You're a smart guy, David. I know that. Otherwise you wouldn't have this job. Your physical attributes are strictly a side benefit. The experience you gained working for the government has been a boon. But never take anything for granted."

David finished his drink and assumed an at-attention posture.

"Right-o, Mr. Drummond. I guess I'm a little defensive about what I can do."

"Only natural. But getting back to the telekinesis, that's something truly remarkable."

"Huh. That ain't nothing. I see magicians do that stuff all the time. Lots of people must have that talent. In fact, I've got a cousin down in Texas who claims something of the sort."

Nate walked over to his desk and placed the memory stick into a drawer. "You're wrong there. They're charlatans, every one of them. I don't think telekinesis has ever been scientifically proven. Magicians and others trick you into believing they have the gift. I assure you, no one can really do it."

"I suppose so, sir."

His patience had run out. "Alright then, David. I'll go over the file when I find the time. In the meantime, you get back to your duties."

David glanced into the empty glass then deposited it on the bar and left. When the door closed Nate quickly retrieved the data stick and inserted it. He scanned through all the information as quickly as he could. It was all there, just as his security officer had said.

Confidential interviews with her fellow employees, NASA medical staff, and even the statement of a cocktail waitress claiming to have overheard a conversation with two other astronauts from the Mars mission.

This investigator Barnaby was detailed. He had worked in the FBI, just as David had. But unlike his security officer, whose alcoholism had led to his dismissal, Barnaby had left because he had gone over the confidentiality line into private business. Some of the reports in the file indicated the man still had ties back at the agency. Handy to know.

Nate was intrigued by this woman. Emailing R&D, he inquired where he could meet her. When he learned she was delayed for a day because her fiancé had been injured, he cut the link. *Women. Always allowing emotions to interfere in their judgment. It's no wonder I never married.*

CHAPTER 28

Better late than never. The fence surrounding the Drumdat Energy Corporation's R&D facility stood at least fifteen feet tall. Brooke lifted her sunglasses to get a better look at the sign hanging on it.

Caution—Electrified Fence

She gave a short burst of laughter. "I wonder whether it's to keep people out or in?"

She pulled up to the gate and rolled down her window. One security guard remained in the booth while the second circled her car. *Boy, these guys take their job seriously.* "Hello, my name is Brooke Jones. Where am I supposed to go?"

The fellow in the booth smiled at her. "Miss Jones, we were expecting you a couple of days ago."

"Yes, I know. A close friend of mine had an accident, and I wanted to make sure he was all right before I came. I did call."

"Yes, they informed me to watch out for you today." He handed her a large, rigid card, with A12 on it. "I want you to put this on your dash. Just follow the drive until you come to Lot A. You can't miss it. Parking spot 12. Then go on inside. Someone will be there to greet you."

"Thank you." After the gate lifted, she drove slowly past the booth. As she neared the building, the lots moved down the alphabet from F, through E, D, C, and B. Lot A was right by the front doors. "Ooh, executive parking. I like that."

She moved down the front row. "Seven...eight...nine...ten...eleven...twelve! Here's my spot." She was surprised to see her name emblazoned on the parking curb. Wow. They're really rolling out the red carpet.

She parked then headed for the front door. An elderly man and a young woman met her right inside. The man extended his hand in greeting. "Doctor Jones, It's a pleasure to meet you. My name is Francis Weatherby. I'm the team leader on the methanogens project. This is Sarah Cooper. She's the coordinator for Drumdat's security here at R & D."

The girl also extended a hand. "Pleased to meet you as well, Doctor Jones." The woman produced a plastic card on a neck chain. "This will grant you access to the building, all of the common facilities, and those departments you are sanctioned for. It works just like a hotel card. Should you lose it, let us know as soon as possible, and we'll deactivate it and get you a new one."

She slipped the neck chain over her head. "Thank you. I'm looking forward to getting started. Where do we begin?"

Francis swept a hand to his left. "How about the grand tour? Allow me to be your guide. Perhaps we could start in the cafeteria and get you a coffee or something?"

"That sounds like a wonderful idea. Lead the way."

Sarah once again shook Brooke's hand. "You won't be needing me for that. I'll return to my duties. You're in good hands. Good-bye."

Brooke noticed an abruptness in both her tone and grip. "Did I say something wrong?"

Francis chuckled. "Pay Sarah no mind. She's *always* like that. She's also head of security around here, so it doesn't take much to put her nose out of joint."

"That little girl?"

"They say she has a black belt, but around here the only thing she's ever had to do was rip up someone's security card when they got the axe."

"Nice. So, about that coffee?"

Francis strode down the hallway. "Right this way."

She hurried to keep step. "They keep a pretty tight lid on things around here, I see."

They entered the cafeteria and got in a short line. "Yeah, I guess industrial espionage is pretty big stuff. Take a look at our fusion reactor design. They built the first one right here. Sure, it was a small version but it powers this entire place and feeds the grid for the towns around here."

They each got a coffee and sat down at the nearest table. "That's mechanical engineering. The methanogens are biological. You do both?"

"What, me? Ha. No, I didn't work on that project. But methane gas and its application as an energy source *are* my specialties. I can't tell you how excited I was to get those methanogens from Mars. There's another team working with them for medicinal potential. You'll get to meet them later. By the way, I wanted to tell you how impressed I was on your work to date. Your breakdown of the organism seems quite exact. I can't wait to run it through my own battery of tests. Did you really mock them up from memory?"

"That's what I'm here for, to conduct my computer generated tests with real methanogens, and yes, I did."

Francis slumped back into his seat. "That's amazing."

What Robert told her about keeping her new skills secret popped into her mind. "But I had plenty of help from the staff at NASA. Let's say, it was a concerted effort."

"Even still, very impressive." Francis rose. "Come on. It's time

123

for the rest of the tour."

They walked through the main building which was mostly clerical and management. They passed by Sarah's office, who gave them a perfunctory nod.

Francis headed toward another exit "All of the out buildings are where all the labs are."

She followed him to a structure with no windows. The building, made of concrete, was three stories high and just about as wide.

"This is where the fusion reactor is housed. You can see it, but we have to take precautions in case of radiation leakage."

"I thought one of the best things about fusion was there wasn't any harmful radiation?"

"Not quite true. It still gives off a small amount. In all honesty, the shielding around it prevents most of it from getting out, but they like to err on the side of caution. They have detectors all over the place should any kind of a leak occur. This is much smaller than most of our reactors."

Francis took two wristbands from a box by the door, unwrapped them, and slipped one on her. "Here, you need to wear this. It's mandatory. Just in case you pick up any radiation, it will warn you."

"What will it do?"

"It will change color. Right now it's white. It goes yellow, then orange, and finally red. If it gets to red, you're dead."

She held her wrist up to the light. "It looks kind of yellow right now."

Francis chuckled. "Yeah, mine too. We've been meaning to get a new shipment of those in. Don't worry. Yellow is only mild caution. The damned things pick up that much radiation just from regular sunlight. Let's go take a peek."

He showed her through the facility. She was amazed at how small the reactor was. *If this is all it takes to generate that much power nowadays, Drumdat must be making a killing!*

They left the building and entered another about the same size but a more office type looking structure with windows. "Here's home most of the time. Let me introduce you to the gang."

They entered a large lab and Brooke shook hands and exchanged hellos with half a dozen people. Francis led her to a number of offices along one wall. "We've opened up this one for you. I hope it meets your expectations."

She glanced inside. It was your standard fare office with a desk and two computer stations. "I figure I'll be out in the lab most of the time with the rest of you, but thank you. It will do just fine."

He led her around, pointing out the various work stations and equipment, ending up in a kitchenette in a back corner of the building where a number of the employees were seated at a couple of tables. On the counter was a coffee machine with a full pot on the burner. "Oh, is that fresh? I could use another cup."

One of the guys there volunteered he had just put it on.

"Great. Can we take a break here?"

They took their coffees to a small table. As he sat down, Francis pulled his wristband off. "We don't need these anymore. You can take it off now."

She tugged her band free and handed it to him. "What do you do with them?"

"Garbage. As long as there's no high levels on them." He paused to look them over. "Huh. Now isn't *that* interesting."

Brooke paused her coffee drinking with cup poised before her. "What?"

"Your band is completely white. Wasn't it tinged yellow at the start like mine?"

She reclaimed it then held it up to the light once more. "It was. Is that bad?"

Francis laughed. "Bad? Are you kidding? You have to be the first person to ever have had her band lose radiation. It must have been defective. No other explanation makes sense."

"Alright, as long as I don't have anything to worry about."

"Not a thing."

She returned to drinking her coffee but noticed Francis throw his band away and put hers in his pocket.

CHAPTER 29

Aki sat at his desk staring at the monitor. His head felt fuzzy. *Ugh. I just can't think today.* His stomach churned, and he rubbed at it in hopes of allaying the cramps.

He got up and headed out, waving to Bruce as he passed him. "I don't feel good. I'm going to the doctor's office and find out if he'll see me. Maybe he can give me something to pick me up."

"I'll let him know you're on the way."

"Thanks. See you in a bit."

The walk to the medical facility across the complex helped relieve the cramps. When he arrived, the receptionist ushered him in. "You're lucky. The doctor wasn't taking patients, but when I told him you were coming by, he decided to take a break from his project to see you."

"That's great because I feel lousy."

She brought him to an examination room. "The doctor will be with you in a moment."

"Sure thing." He hopped onto the table to wait.

In a matter of seconds, the doctor entered. "Hi, Aki. I hear you're not feeling so good. You want to tell me about it?"

"I've got a bad case of cramps, and my head's all fuzzy."

"Hmm. Let's have a look. Open wide."

The doctor peered down his throat. I'm glad you came by. I've been staring at a computer screen all day. My eyes aren't what they used to be. It's been giving me a headache."

"Doesn't your staff do all the clerical work?"

The doctor poked an instrument into his ears. "No, this isn't that. I'm going through some brain scans. My counterpart over at the

Drumdat Corp. wants me to verify something."

"Drumdat? What's that got to do with NASA?"

The doctor lifted one eyelid than the other, examining his eyes. "Astronaut Brooke Jones. They're doing the same tests on her there that we did here. They want to know if my data will corroborate theirs."

"What is it they want you to find?"

The doctor pressed two fingers to Aki's wrist and looked at his watch. "I don't think I should be telling you."

"Listen, doc, *everybody* knows about Doctor Jones's amazing condition. It's no secret. There's nothing to spill."

The doctor put away his medical tools. "Just a case of the flu. I'll get you some medication to ease the cramps. You'll need plenty of rest and lots of fluids. As to Brooke's status, I suspected as much. But don't fret over it. I checked the images over and over again, and what they're claiming isn't there. When I ran the scan, I saw something *like* what they were looking for, but it was in a different location. At the time, I thought it was a glitch in the machine. It couldn't be a blood clot or cancer cells in either case, because on my next reading it had moved, and apparently, according to them, moved again. That would be physically impossible. Besides, I know what those look like. This didn't look anything like them."

"Don't ask me. You're the doctor. What was it, anyways?"

"Like I said, a glitch. Nothing medically explainable. A tiny black dot. It's probably a lost pixel."

A coldness crept over Aki. *Could it be?* "Doc, did you say a tiny black dot?"

The doctor began writing out a prescription. "Yes, just that. A tiny black dot."

"How big is this dot?"

"Oh, the business end of a pin, I'd say."

Aki jumped up off the table and headed for the door. "I gotta go."

"Wait. Don't you want the prescription?"

He grabbed the paper out of the doctor's hand. "You're right. I've got no time to be sick."

He hurried back toward his building. *Am I dreaming? Is it possible?* He had heard a number of rumors but never really took a lot of stock in them. But he did remember when Brooke had fallen sick during the Mars mission. Something nagged at him that he needed to verify.

He marched into his department head's office and plunked down in front of him. "Bruce, you're not going to believe what I have to tell you. But first I need you to do something for me."

"What's that?"

"Pull up the records from the Mars mission. Specifically, what happened when astronaut Brooke Jones fell ill."

Bruce started typing. "Give me a moment."

After a dozen seconds he smiled. "Now ain't that a hoot. It's a good thing you came to me. The file requires a senior administrator to access it. I'll just type in my au-thor-i-za-tion…and voila! So what is it you wanted to know?"

"What's the official version of what happened?"

"Simple. She lost containment and suffered a severe case of the bends. That's it. Even I knew that."

Aki circled Bruce's desk to get a better look at the screen. "No, I got that wrong. Not the official one…her version."

It took Bruce a bit of searching but he finally pulled up the file. "Okay, says here she bumped against the cavern wall on the way up, and she thinks that's why her helmet loosened. When she got to the top she was walking through a sandstorm toward the transport when the seal failed. As she tried to reseat it, she was enveloped in a sphere empty of sand."

"And then what?"

"And then, just as she was reattaching her helmet, something black flew in her eye. The next moment, she passed out."

Aki returned to his chair and stared at nothing in particular as he contemplated what Bruce had just said.

"Aki? Aki, what is it?"

He shook himself from his reverie. "Bruce, we found it. Brooke brought it back with her."

"Found what? What the hell are you talking about?"

"The micro black hole. It's in her head!"

CHAPTER 30

Brooke felt uncomfortable seated alone in the middle of the room. She was circled by a number of assorted gadgets and whatnots of which she had little or no real idea of what they did. "Are you sure this is absolutely safe?"

Francis peered around one of the devices and gave her a smile. "Fear not, little lady, I will ensure no harm comes to you or my name isn't Sir Galahad."

She couldn't resist smiling. In her few months in the lab, Francis always found ways of doing that to her. She had found in his passion for science a kindred friend. "Last I checked, you aren't Sir Galahad."

"No? Then maybe it was Sir Lancelot."

She shook her head. "Nope."

"Oh, then maybe it was Sir Gawain."

"Not even close."

"Sir Percivale?"

She sighed. "It is your intention to go through all of the Knights of the Round Table?"

"Naw. Those are the only ones I could remember. My next was going to be Sir John Cleese."

"I can't seem to recall him being one of King Arthur's knights."

"He wasn't. He was part of the cast of that comedy group, Monty Python. Don't tell me you've never seen Monty Python and the Holy Grail? It's one of the funniest movies of all time!"

"Never seen it."

"Too bad. You've lived a sheltered life." Francis rose from where he had been crouched. "There, that does it. We're ready to go. Now don't move, Brooke. We need you to be absolutely steady for this to work right."

"I'll try."

Francis signaled to a technician on the far side of the room. "Okay, let's turn it on."

The equipment hummed, unnerving her slightly. She gripped the armrests in anticipation of some kind of pain but there was nothing. After a few moments, Francis signaled to shut the system down.

"There, that didn't hurt, did it?"

She let go and flexed her cramped fingers. "I didn't feel a thing."

"Go relax, have a coffee. I'll call you when we've had a chance to examine the results."

"Screw the coffee. I need a glass of wine."

Francis helped her up. "You're in luck. I always keep a bottle in the mini-bar in my office. Let's go have a glass, shall we?"

"Yes, let's." She headed for the exit.

Francis paused beside her. Yeesh! Look at that! How hard were you gripping that thing?"

Brooke turned to look back at the chair. The aluminum armrests were crushed. She could even make out finger grooves. "Damn! I did that? My adrenalin must have been running a little high. Never mind. Where's that wine?" *Just how strong am I going to get? Is there no end to whatever is happening to me?*

She followed Francis to his office where he produced the promised bottle and two glasses. "I've been saving this for a discovery with the methanogens, but if what is expected with you is true, then this occasion will do."

She settled into a chair and accepted the filled glass. "I have to admit, when I heard the news at first I thought, oh my god, I'm going to

132

die! But then I realized, if that was the case, I'd be dead by now. Besides, if anything, I've never felt better. And the doc says I'm as healthy as anyone could possibly be. So whatever it is inside my head, I'm kinda glad it's there."

"Once you think about it, it all makes sense—the reports of your extreme good health, your perfect memory, and your ability to go with almost no rest. According to the theory hypothesized by your fellow NASA scientist, Akihiko Fujiyoshi, the micro black hole has accelerated the neurons in your mind. It's led to a host of good things— vastly increased hemoglobin, endorphins, adrenalin, and whatever else the body needs. It's possible you will never age."

"Not grow old? I'm not so sure I want that." *That answers a lot of questions though.*

"I said possible, not for sure. At the very least, you should live to a hundred and twenty or more. The maximum life expectancy in humans."

"So I'm going to be an old spinster for a very long time. Somehow, Francis, I don't think you're helping."

Francis laughed. "You're missing my point. Even at a hundred and twenty, you'll be the picture of perfect health. No worse than you are today."

She finished her wine. "How long do you think until they know for sure?"

"Hmm. You know how we scientists are. They'll want to check and recheck their answers before they tell anyone—maybe even get an outside opinion to be sure. I doubt we'll know today."

"Then I'm going to call it early. Waiting around until I hear will drive me crazy." She rose to leave. "Thanks for the wine. I'll see you in the morning."

She headed out to her car. When she got into her hotel room, she opened the mini-bar and found a bottle of wine. *One negative about this thing, I can't seem to get a buzz.*

Wondering how Robert fared, she gave him a call. After five rings it went to voice mail. "Hi Robert, how are you doing? I suppose you heard about me by now. Freaky, huh? I miss you. Call me. Love ya. Bye."

After Brooke poured the wine into her glass, her phone rang. She read the caller ID. "Hi Jesse, what's up? I suppose you heard as well?"

"Hi, Brooke. Yes, I heard, but that's not why I'm calling. Robert's taken a turn for the worse."

She took a sharp intake of breath. *Something wrong with Robert?* "What? What happened?"

"His legs aren't healing. The doc's worried. They've got him on IV antibiotics, but he thinks Robert might lose them."

"Oh no."

"He has a high level of infection. They're worried he might develop gangrene. It's real serious. He's asking for you."

"Shit. When did this happen? Why didn't anyone call me before?"

"He asked me not to. He didn't want to interrupt your work, but that was before they shipped him to the hospital."

"I'm on my way."

CHAPTER 31

Nate bit back a flurry of expletives he wanted to unload. "You're telling me she up and left?"

On his screen, his security officer Sarah blanched. "Yes sir. She called in to say her friend was real sick, and she was going to go see him at the hospital back home."

"I'm finding this hard to believe. No sooner do we discover an incredible find, in her brain, no less, than she hightails it back to NASA. I won't stand for it. My contract says I'm to get everything that comes back from Mars, and as far as I'm concerned, that includes that thing in her head."

"I don't see how, sir. Although Francis thinks he can capture it, he said the physical removal of the micro black hole was impossible without killing Doctor Jones. It's all detailed in that report."

"Everything is possible. He just hasn't figured it out yet. Tell him to get to work on finding a solution."

He disconnected without giving Sarah a chance to say good-bye. He still seethed over the recent turn of events. He returned to the report he had reviewed only moments before. Yes, it was indeed believed to be a micro black hole residing within astronaut Jones. Yes, it was having an amazing effect on her neural network, accelerating her neurons to such an extent that all of her physical aspects were enhanced to an absolute maximum. And yes, it was expected to extend her life for a very long time, if not indefinitely. *I must have that thing.*

He got up and paced, thinking of all the possibilities should he obtain the micro black hole. *What am I to do? There must be an answer.* His pacing brought him to the bar. Staring at the scotch, an idea hit him. He went back to his desk and made a call.

"Security here."

"Smithson, get up to my office."

"On my way, sir."

Was the big oaf up to the job? He doubted it. No, a more subtle approach was needed. When the security man entered, Nate smiled and rose to greet the fellow. "David, I need you to contact that friend of yours, Barnaby. I have a special job for him."

"What's the job, Mr. Drummond?"

"I'd rather not involve you. Your ties to this organization would be very detrimental if anything should go wrong."

"You can trust me, sir. I owe this organization everything. As I told you before, I even managed to delete my old FBI files."

Always the old hint. He admired the loyalty, however misplaced. No, best keep it arm's length. "Just have Barnaby give me a way to contact him without anyone knowing. The sooner the better."

"Will do, Mr. Drummond. Consider it done."

The rest of the day passed with the reading of other reports and his usual afternoon meeting with Alban. Tired, he headed out the door.

As he approached his waiting limousine, a man standing off to one side approached him. "Good afternoon, Mr. Drummond. I'm Barnaby. You asked to speak with me. I wonder if it wouldn't be too much to ask if I can get a ride with you."

A moment of being startled passed, and he eyed the lanky fellow. "How did you manage to be waiting here?"

"I walked in. It's amazing how easy it is to bypass your security when one doesn't drive up."

"Still, I asked for a means to contact you, not the other way around."

"Please excuse my abruptness, but I prefer to remain off the radar as much as possible, including contact information."

Is this the real McCoy? Do I chance it? Hell, who else could do it? "Hmm. I shall have to have a talk with David. Never mind that for now. Get in."

The chauffeur opened the door and both he and Barnaby climbed in. As the car pulled out of the complex, he returned his attention to his surprise guest. "So where did you want me to take you?"

"I'll get off anywhere once we have concluded our business. So tell me, Mr. Drummond, what is it that you so urgently needed to speak to me about?"

"I'm going out on a limb telling you this, but I think you're the kind of man who can understand that whatever the cost of something I need, I can afford it. I'm looking for someone to complete a very special job, someone with the kind of skills to put together a team that can do it. Understand, you're going to have to break quite a few laws. Are you up to the task?"

"I'm intrigued, and I understand the ramifications. What is this *special* job?"

He sighed. "I'm an old man, Barnaby, and I'm getting older by the minute. I don't know how many years I have left. For all I know, I could drop dead tomorrow. When an opportunity such as the one I am about to describe to you presents itself, you need to grasp it with all your might. But what good is it if you end up in jail for the rest of your life. This is something that I cannot be implicated in. You understand that."

"I do, but until you tell me the nature of this thing, I can't tell you whether or not I'll be able to help you."

Nate pulled his comp tablet from his briefcase, pulled up the

137

report he wanted, and passed the device to Barnaby. "Read this, and you'll figure it out."

Barnaby took the tablet and studied it for some time. After a while, he handed it back to Nate. "I think I understand. This is going to require quite a number of skilled people. Doctors, quantum mechanics scientists, the necessary tech people to build whatever is needed to capture this thing, and who knows what else."

Nate took a deep breath. "Are you up to the job?"

"I think it's possible, but the price tag is going to be pretty heavy."

"Name it."

"Fifty million dollars, plus equipment expenses. I have no idea how much that stuff is going to cost."

"Get to work on it but wait until I give you the go ahead. I'm going to give my own people a chance to come up with a solution. I'll forward you ten percent as a startup fee."

"Then I guess this is my stop. Ask your driver to pull over, if you wouldn't mind."

When the car glided to the curb and stopped, Barnaby opened the door and began to stand, but Nate put a hand on his arm. "Understand, Barnaby, I am not a patient man. Not when it comes to something like this. Make sure you're ready."

Barnaby calmly pried Nate's fingers from his arm and stepped out. He then looked back in. "I will be."

He closed the door and walked off.

Nate slumped back into the leather seat. "Let's go home."

CHAPTER 32

Brooke arrived at the hospital to find Jesse waiting for her in the lobby. "They've got him on IV antibiotics, trying to fight the infection. So far, no luck."

"What room is he in? Can I see him?"

"Sure, follow me. I'll take you to him."

As Jesse led her to the elevators, Brooke played through her mind, once more, the terrible possibility of Robert dying. *I can't let that happen. They better be doing all they can, or so help me—*

They exited the elevator, turned right and, three doors down; she followed Jesse into Robert's room. Stretched out on a hospital bed with an IV in his arm and crumpled white sheets covering him, he appeared asleep. She stopped where she was, just inside the door, not wanting to wake him. She sat in the chair next to the bed and looked Robert over. Had he been this gaunt when she left? His cheekbones pressed through and tight lines ran from the corners of his eyes to the edges of his mouth. His tousled hair hung across his brow, dotted with beads of glistening perspiration. The stubble on his unshaven jawline showed a lot of grey, accentuating his already haggard look. She started to cry. *Robert, what have they done to you?*

Jesse squeezed her shoulder. "He'll make it, Brooke. Just wait and see. He's a tough bugger. Five tours in outer space, including two trips to the moon. He's always come back from them. He's a warrior. He'll fight through this."

Brooke wiped away her tears, got up, and started for the door. "Show me where I can get a coffee before he wakes up. But first, I need to freshen up."

Jesse pointed down the hall. "There are washrooms over there, and the only cafeteria is in the lobby area. I'll meet you down there and get the coffees."

"Thank you, Jesse. I won't be long."

Once inside the ladies room, she washed the tear stains from her face then gathered herself and stared into the mirror. "You've got to be strong, girl. Robert's going to need you and going all to pieces isn't helping."

She took a deep breath, and then made her way to the cafeteria. Jesse was already sitting at a table, and she took the empty seat across from him.

Jesse passed her a tray. "I got you a coffee and took the liberty of buying you a biscotti as well."

"Thanks. I haven't eaten much today. It was a long drive to get back here. I blew out the door right after you called and pulled an all-nighter. I haven't told the people at Drumdat when I would return."

Thinking of Drumdat reminded her of the testing they had done the day before. She pulled out her comp pad and opened the report from Francis. He had attached a personal note as well.

Hello, Brooke.

I hope all is well. I heard a close friend of yours is very sick. I wish him a speedy recovery so that you can return and help me with these methanogens.

As to your own status, Mr. Fujiyoshi, I believe, is quite correct. Your body has been invaded by a micro black hole. You are well aware of your own personal physical benefits of as a result of this. I have some suspicions that there is more than even you may know. The bracelet, for example, was cleared of all radiation. This implies the benefits you are enjoying extend past your physical form. Whether the

140

sphere of influence is mere millimeters or farther, I cannot tell.

As to any danger from this occupation of your mind, I also am at a loss to predict, though one would have to wonder whether the maintaining of this predicament you find yourself in would be healthy in the long term. Some of my colleagues, however, have predicted dire consequences. Personally, I find their doom and gloom prognosis poppycock. Unfortunately, I can see no methodology to remove said item without causing you severe injury, most likely death. At this time, my suggestion is to leave it be, kept under constant observation, with an instant reassessment should any new characteristics manifest.

Personally, I am excited for you. This is a phenomenon of the most extraordinary nature, and you are at its epicenter. It must be very exhilarating.

Once again, wishing your friend well,

Francis

She glanced through the report but much of it dealt with quantum mechanics, a field of research she knew little about.

She returned her attention to Jesse. "I bet I could do it."

"Do what?"

"Heal Robert. I just need to get close enough. This thing in my head is the key."

She handed the comp to him. "Read this report. Then you'll see what I mean." She got up.

"Where're you going?"

"Back to Robert's room. I'm going to get in that hospital bed with him. When you're done reading, come see me."

She made her way back to his room, slipped off her shoes then climbed in next to him. Robert stirred but didn't wake. *They must have put a lot of drugs in him. I just hope I'm not too late.*

141

In a few moments Jesse came in waving the comp pad. "You know, I had my suspicions, and the rumors were pretty rampant, but this is beyond what I had imagined."

"Shh. Let's let him sleep. Just make sure no one comes in to disturb us."

Jesse moved a chair in front of the door and sat in it, blocking anyone from entering. "Okay, Brooke. Let's hope this works."

She laid her head against Robert's chest. The steady beat of his heart reassured her that all would soon be well. *I'm here for you, Robert. Get better quick.*

It must have been an hour or so when there was a knock at the door. Jesse got up and peeked out. "Yes?"

A terse female voice met her ears. "I'm here to check on Captain Tangler."

"Not right now, if you don't mind. His fiancé wants to spend some private time with him."

"I'm sorry, sir. But I have to do my job. Please step aside."

Jesse stuck his head back in. "Brooke?"

She shook her head. "Tell them later. Robert's still out."

Jesse disappeared out the door again. "Like I said, not right now. Come back in a while."

"Sir, if you don't let me pass, I'm going to have to call security."

"Fine. Have it your way. Jesse stepped back into the room and shrugged his shoulders, hands up in the air.

The nurse entered and froze. "Miss, what are you doing? You're not supposed to be doing that. Please get out of the bed."

Brooke gave the nurse a defiant stare. "No."

The nurse looked from Jesse to her and back to Jesse again. He gave her a sheepish smile. "She said no."

"We'll see about this."

The nurse dashed out, and Jesse closed the door once more. "She'll be back, and soon."

Brooke ran a hand across Robert's brow. "Robert, come on, honey. I need you to wake up."

Moments later there was a hard knock on the door and the nurse returned, accompanied by a doctor and two security people. The doctor pointed at Brooke. "Ma'am, I'm going to ask you nicely to please vacate the bed. Mr. Tangler is in no condition for your company. I don't want to have to order these men to remove you."

She reached out and grabbed the metal rails on both sides. "I'm not leaving until he's better."

The doctor signaled to the two men. "Remove her."

The security guys tried to pull her arms free, but she continued to hold on. The one closest tried to pry her fingers off one at a time. "Sheesh! She's got a grip like iron!"

The other one pulled out a club. "Enough of this shit."

He swung it at her other hand. She grabbed the club in midair and gave it a hard twist.

The club came free from the man's right hand. He grabbed his wrist with his other. "Yeow!"

She dropped it on the floor and re-fixed her grip on the rail. "I told you. I'm not ready to leave."

She felt movement beside her and turned to see Robert awake.

"Brooke? Is that you? When did you get here?" He looked around the room. "What's going on?"

The doctor moved in. "Out of the way."

Brooke let go of the one bar and moved enough for the doctor to get to Robert. The doctor looked into his eyes, ears, and mouth and

143

checked his pulse and forehead. He stood straight and sighed. "Well, I don't know what happened. But the infection is gone and so is the fever. This woman came in here and was disturbing your rest. I was about to have her removed when you woke up."

Robert put an arm around her. "No, if it's alright with you, she can stay."

"Hmm. This is most out of the ordinary, but I can see no harm now that you're past the worst. But if you feel any of the symptoms again, she's got to go."

"Don't worry, doc. I'll be fine."

"Okay, I'll be back in an hour to check on you. Just to be sure and order some blood tests. Get some rest."

The doctor ushered everyone out of the room. The guard Brooke had disarmed was complaining his wrist was sprained. She gave Robert a kiss and dropped her head on his chest once more. "I'm glad you're better."

Robert nuzzled her hair. "I don't know what happened, but me, too."

She snuggled closer. *Everything is going to be fine.*

CHAPTER 33

After she visited Robert for three days in a row, they released him to go home. The doctors gave him a clean bill of health with the infection gone and the bones finally starting to knit though still very thin.

Robert was resting.

Maybe I'll give Francis a call.

"Hey Brooke, it's good to hear from you. You'll never guess what's happened. I completed that first range of tests you wanted to do, and bingo! We think we can develop a medication against radiation. When are you coming back?"

"That's great news, Francis. I wish I could be there but I think I'm going to be here a while yet. You'll email me the results when you can, won't you?"

"Absolutely. I've had to go out and get another bottle of wine to celebrate. Imagine, two major scientific discoveries in a week. When I report this second one, my fellow scientists will be green with envy."

She thought about the earlier discovery and became a little nervous. "Francis, have you reported the first one? The one about me?"

"Your secret is still safe with me and my staff. I threatened them with life and limb if they talked. Besides, until I can come up with a way to pull that damn thing out of you, without hurting you, there's still a lot of work to do. Mr. Drummond contacted me personally on it just today. He was most disappointed when I told him I didn't have an answer yet."

She wrapped the conversation up then checked on Robert. *Still sleeping. Maybe I'll go stretch my legs.*

As she strolled down the street in the clear night air, she stopped to gaze up at the heavens. She spotted Mars in the sky. *How are you doing up there? Do you miss me?*

At a noise to her left, she turned to investigate. Four men were walking down the sidewalk in her direction. She stepped aside so that they might pass when the one closest looked at her. "Hey, aren't you that astronaut, Brooke Jones?"

"Um, yes."

"Do you think I can get your autograph?" He started checking his pockets. "I've got a pen on me somewhere."

A fan. Bart wants me to make sure I'm always nice to fans. She opened her purse to retrieve a pen and one of the promo cards she always carried. "Never mind, I've got one here. Who do I make it out to?"

While she was retrieving the pen, a cloth was clamped over her mouth and arms clutched at her. From behind her, she could hear the voice of one of the other men. "Nighty-night, sweetie."

She spilled her purse and started to struggle but she was becoming very groggy. The face of the man before her faded out.

***

Brooke woke up from something jabbing into her side. She went to sit up but banged her head. *What's going on?* She reached up and felt what was above her. It didn't take long to recognize the inside of a trunk hood. Her initial disorientation over, she identified the sound of a running engine and the wheels rolling down a street. When the car went over a bump, whatever had jabbed at her did so again. She reached under her hip and pulled it free whatever it was. A little light was sneaking in round the seam of the trunk. Holding the thing up she recognized a plastic oil funnel. *I've been kidnapped!*

From inside the other side of the back seat she could make out the voices of men talking. She calmed herself. *Alright, what do I do now?*

The car stopped then started moving again. *Probably city streets.* She decided she would pop the trunk lid at the next stop and jump out.

Brooke used her hands and searched around the trunk but could find nothing to pry it open. She had no other option than to try and force it. She contorted to give herself the best angle at kicking the lid though the space was so tight she didn't think she could get a lot into it. As the car came to stop once more she kicked as hard as she could. The lid held. She continued kicking.

"You idiot! You didn't gas her enough."

"Bullshit. She should have been out for hours."

"Well it's only been fifteen minutes, genius."

"Quit arguing and pull over somewhere so I can put her back under."

Dammit! They know I'm awake. Brooke continued her kicking while the car moved. Although the lid did not open, it was being bent enough that plenty of light streamed in.

The car swerved around a corner and lurched to a stop. The car doors opened and slammed.

"Man, look what she did to my car! It's a classic."

"Shut up and open the trunk."

She tensed at the distinctive click of the trunk unlocking and the lid moved up an inch or two.

"Okay, let's get her."

The lid swung up and a couple of the men reached in for her. She kicked one and grabbed the arm of the second. Striking down hard with

147

her elbow, she heard a snap and the man howled. As he moved away, she tried to climb out.

"Don't let her get away."

Three of them jumped on her, and she punched wildly. One of them went flying when she landed a hit to his jaw. The other two tried to pin her down and apply the anesthetic cloth to her face. She twisted her head and punched the man in the stomach. He doubled over and moved off. The last man was still on her back trying to get her in a full nelson. She pulled him over her back and tossed him to the ground.

She glanced around to get her bearings but just before she could make a dash for it something hard crashed into the back of her head and she crumpled to the ground.

"What are you doing, man? You could have killed her."

"The bitch deserves it. She broke my god damn arm! Besides, she ain't hurt that bad. She's still not out."

"Quick then, put her back under and let's get the hell out of here."

The cloth came back over her face. Still groggy from the slug to her head, she succumbed to it, and darkness came.

CHAPTER 34

Robert woke from a disturbing dream. Brooke was in trouble. He didn't have the details but he knew it to be true.

He reached for the phone and called her cell. It went to her message service. "Brooke, call me when you can. It's Robert."

He called Jesse.

"Hey, Robert, how are you feeling?"

"I'm okay. But I think something's happened to Brooke. Have you heard from her?"

"I thought she was with you? What makes you think that something's wrong? Have you tried calling her?"

"I tried her cell. All I got was voice mail. I don't know why, but I just know. Can you come over?"

"On my way."

Robert spent the next several minutes maneuvering into his wheelchair. Rolling into the living room, he glanced out the window and saw Brooke's convertible still in the drive. *Then where the hell is she?*

It was another ten or fifteen minutes before a car pulled up to the house. Jesse climbed out and headed for the front door. "Come on in. The door's open."

Jesse entered, glancing back as he did. "That's her car, isn't it?"

"Yeah, and no sign of her."

Jesse sat down. "Maybe she just went for a walk."

"Jesse, you know she's got some special skills, so believe me when I tell you that I think she's telling me she's in trouble. It's some kind of telepathy."

"I've heard. Can you contact her?"

"No. It's one way. For a while now, she's been able to read my mind, and I think she's able to send me stuff. Not words, or anything like that, but emotions—love, fear, anger, the strong stuff. I'm telling you, she's in trouble."

"What do you want to do, call the police?"

He laughed. "I'm not sure. I mean, what would they think? Oh, officer, my girlfriend is sending me mental images she's in trouble. Can you go look for her? They'd probably throw me in the loony bin."

Jesse rubbed at his chin. "I'm thinking we need to go to the top on this one. Let's call Bart. He'll know what to do."

"Higginbottom? The administrator? Do you think we should?"

"Absolutely. At the very least, he can get NASA security to work on it. Who knows? Maybe the FBI."

Robert weighed his options. Should he call Bart? If it turned out to be nothing, he'd never hear the end of it. No. He knew what his dreams were telling him. Brooke was in trouble. "Call him."

Once Jesse managed to reach the administrator, Robert took the phone and ran him through everything up to that point.

On the vid phone, he could barely see the small man behind the mountain of documents on his desk. "This is very serious, Robert. Very serious indeed. I've been fully briefed on what astronaut Jones is capable of and, as a result, I believe you. I'm pulling out all the stops to help. I'm sending our chief of security over right away. Give him every assistance that you can. Let's hope for the best."

In less than an hour the security chief showed up, and he wasn't alone. Four cars filled with NASA personnel accompanied him. Robert's entire house and surrounding grounds were turned into a crime scene. The chief grilled him for a long time in an attempt to

150

extract every single detail of the last twenty-four hours. Others had fanned out into the neighborhood, conducting a search and a door to door canvas for information. Sometime after midnight, one of the teams returned. "Chief, we found something."

"What is it?"

The man held forth a NASA pen and one of Brooke's promo cards. "They were lying on the ground, just off the sidewalk. The area had been recently trampled. I'm going out on a limb here, but I'd say she's been abducted."

Robert maneuvered the wheelchair closer and grabbed at the card, but the officer held it out of reach. "Abducted? Are you certain?"

The chief took the pen and the card and dropped them into a plastic bag. "It makes sense, Captain Tangler. The dropped items, the trampled grass. I'd say she was approached for an autograph then they nabbed her."

The man who found the stuff nodded. "My conclusion exactly. There's no sense in searching around here anymore. In the time that's elapsed, they could be out of the state already. We need to go national."

The chief sighed. "You're right, of course. Call everyone in. I'll bump this up to the Feds."

He placed a hand on Robert's shoulder. "We're not giving up. I'll continue the local search in the morning. For now, get some rest. I'll keep you in the loop as much as I can. We'll find her, Captain. You have my word on it."

Once they had exited, Jesse closed the door and faced him. "Do you want me to stay?"

"No, it's okay. You go on home. I'll be fine. Just keep your cell close by."

"Will do. Goodnight, Robert."

Jesse left leaving Robert alone in his living room. He was too wound to sleep. Instead, he decided to try and focus on Brooke. Maybe, wherever she was, she would hear him and somehow let him know she was okay.

As Robert sat and concentrated, coldness crept through him and he began to fear the worst. *Come on, Brooke. Help me find you.*

CHAPTER 35

Sammy sat in the Oval Office with a comp pad in hand and a ton of stuff to read through. *Jeesh! This shit is getting stale. I can't read all this crap.*

He hit the intercom. "Where's Janice? Tell her to come see me."

"Right away, Mr. President."

He tossed the comp onto his desk and fixed himself a drink.

When he was halfway through his scotch and water, Janice entered. "Sorry to keep you waiting, Sammy. What can I do for you?"

"Where've ya been, Jay girl? I've been trying to muddle my way through this Senate omnibus package and can't make heads or tails of it. Get somebody who understands all this mumbo jumbo to brief me. Let me know what they're hiding in this thing"

"Sorry, I've been busy. We've got bigger problems. I just received a call from the FBI. Seems one of our astronauts has gone missing. They think she's been kidnapped. They're keeping it all hush-hush right now but should it go public there's going to be a hell storm following it."

"Yeah, I can understand the public getting pretty upset about one of their heroes getting nabbed. What are the kidnappers' demands?"

"There are none."

"Then why have they got her? What's the point, if not for ransom?"

"You don't know the half of it. Apparently Lieutenant Jones is carrying something of immense value. Something she brought home from Mars. According to the reports, a micro black hole has taken up residence inside her."

"Say what?"

Janice hit a few keys on her comp and handed it to him. "You heard me—a micro black hole. Nobody knew. It's only been confirmed in the last week. The people at Drumdat discovered it. Everyone there is a suspect, including your friend Nate Drummond."

He paused to read the report on Janice's screen. He scanned through it quickly. With the amazing side benefits that astronaut Jones enjoyed, it was easy to see why anyone who knew would be suspect. As a result, everyone with knowledge was listed by the Bureau as potentials, including a significant number of NASA staff. "This is big shit, Jay. *Big* shit. You better hope the FBI is wrong on this one."

She retrieved her comp pad. "I'm not going to count anyone out, including Lieutenant Jones. She might be on the run."

"Pfft! Now why would she be on the run?"

"Because she knows the truth, and she thinks people want to stop her. Kill her, if they must."

"What truth?"

"I spoke with some science guys who told me the potential danger of a micro black hole worst-case scenario. Sammy, she could destroy the planet!"

He froze for a moment. *Destroy the planet? Is she serious?* "Damn it, Jay. You scared the crap out of me. Now I'm going to have to go and change my shorts. You can't really mean that."

"It's not me saying that; it's the physicists. I don't really believe it either. They said the percentages of that happening were small. But the question is, can we take that chance?"

"You...." He didn't know what to say. Sammy got up and crossed the room to stare out the window. The drink was still in his hand, and he downed it. *Take it easy, Sammy. Don't panic.* He turned back to

Janice. "Call in the team. I want everyone ASAP. We're going to come up with a plan that covers all possibilities. Get going."

"I'll get it done."

Janice stepped out of the room, and Sammy was left with his thoughts. *This is the craziest thing! It's like some cheap science fiction movie.*

He sat down and had his staff get hold of NASA Administrator Higginbottom. "Higgy, are you aware of what's going down with this girl of yours?"

"If you're referring to astronaut Jones, yes, I'm aware of her abduction."

"Not that! That other thing. You know…the micro whatever."

"The micro black hole? Amazing, isn't it. To think that such a thing even exists, let alone that it could be trapped in a human body. And the benefits! Astounding!"

Was the man an idiot? "I'm not talking about the benefits. I'm talking about her blowing us all to kingdom come!"

The administrator cleared his throat, picked up his tablet and after a few taps, read from it. "According to my in-house expert on quantum mechanics, Mr. Akihiko Fujiyoshi, who, by the way, is the one who postulated the theory on micro black holes and, in particular, identified this one, the likelihood of any danger from the micro black hole stands at approximately four hundred and eighty-two million to one. And that was his worst-case scenario. The odds of the best-case scenario involve too many zeroes for me to read them all. Needless to say, I am confident we have nothing to fear."

"Ya see, Higgy, that's the problem. You're applying too much math to it. The bottom line is, there's a chance. And you know what Murphy's law says. If there's a chance it could happen, then it will."

155

"I see your point, Mr. President. But what is it you expect me to do?"

He calmed himself by taking a deep breath and exhaling out loud. "First of all, I want you to get that expert of yours…what's his name?"

"Akihiko Fujiyoshi"

"Yeah, that guy. Get him and whoever else you got hanging around there who understands this shit to come up with some way to defuse this thing. And while you're at it, I want you to come up with a backup plan in case they don't."

"And what would that be?"

"Figure out how to get rid of that thing inside her, or else."

CHAPTER 36

Brooke woke up to find herself sprawled on a cot, hands and feet cuffed. She struggled into a sitting position and took in her surroundings. *Where the hell am I?*

As far as she could tell, it wasn't in a house of any kind. The room was too sterile—plain white walls, ceiling, and tiled floor, and there were no windows. The door was steel. She guessed it to be about fifteen feet square and the ceiling some twelve feet up. It reminded her of the storerooms back at NASA.

Off balance with her hands cuffed behind her back, she decided to make an attempt to bring them in front of her, but no matter how she tried to wriggle them through, she couldn't do it. *Those guys who do it in the movies must be double jointed.*

She paused to catch her breath, and the sound of voices from outside the door caught her attention. Getting to her feet, she shuffled closer in hopes of making out what was being said.

"Stevie, how long do we have to hold on to the bitch? It's not like she's some nobody. They're going to start looking for her sooner or later, and when they do, it'll be big."

"For a few days. Apparently they gotta get equipment of some kind here before they can do whatever it is they wanna do."

"What the heck is it they want with this broad?"

"Shut up for now. We're getting paid big bucks to pull this job. That's all you need to know."

A new voice chimed in. "Steve's right, Nick. That's none of our concern, and I just want to get my cash and blow out of here. The sooner the better."

At least three of them were in the room next door. She remembered four. The creak of a door opening and footsteps answered her question as to the missing fourth. "Hey, guys, I'm back."

"Nice cast, Mikey! How long did the doc say you gotta wear it?"

"Six god damned weeks! Thing itches like hell."

"How'd ya tell him ya broke it?"

"I said I fell down the stairs at home."

"Aw! You should have told him it was at work. That way, you could have applied for comp."

"Nick, you knucklehead. Then they would have called to verify it. At least it gives me a reason to call in sick. How's the girl?"

"I checked on her just a little while ago. Still out like a light. That hit you put on her head was a doozy. It's a good thing you didn't kill her. Then we'd all be in the shitter."

"Like I give a rat's ass. The bitch had it coming. What's to eat around here?"

She shuffled away from the door and back to the cot. *What kind of equipment are they planning on bringing? What is it they want to do to me? It sounds like a have a couple of days before anything happens. Maybe by then I can figure a way out of this.*

She studied the cuffs on her feet. There were a few inches of connecting chain between them. The ones on her wrists must be the same. Maybe she could break them. She tried to pull her arms apart. After several seconds of straining, she gave up and collapsed onto the cot causing it to move and scrap across the floor.

In the next moment, the door opened and one of the men entered. "Well, look who's awake, if it ain't Sleeping Beauty. How's the head, sweetheart?"

She tried to check it, forgetting about the handcuffs, then

glowered at the man. "What do you want with me?"

The fellow laughed. "It ain't me who wants something. I'm just a delivery boy. Now you just sit tight. I'll be rid of ya in a couple of days."

The smell of food wafted through the open door. "Are you going to keep me handcuffed like this the whole time? How am I going to eat anything with my hands behind my back like this?"

"My orders are, not to un-cuff you for any reason. I'll feed you."

"And what about if I have to go to the bathroom? You going to wipe my ass?"

The man backhanded her across the face, sending her reeling backward. "That's enough sass out of you for one day."

Another man rushed into the room. "Nick! What the hell are you doing? You know the deal. She's to remain unharmed."

"Aw, I didn't hurt her none. Just giving her a lesson in manners."

The other man came over to the cot and helped Brooke right herself into a sitting position. "Don't pay Nick no mind. He doesn't have one. My name's Steve, and I'm in charge here. Nick's right though. I can't let you loose from the cuffs, but I can probably come up with some kind of solution."

He turned to Nick. "Come on. Get out of here. Make her something to eat. I'll be back shortly."

It wasn't long before Steve returned with a whole new set of chains. He took the cuffs off and replaced them with something a chain gang would wear in the movies. "This ought to do the trick."

He was smiling, and she didn't feel as threatened by him but she needed to know what their plans were. "What is it you intend to do with me?"

He gave her a warm smile. "Don't worry. My orders are to make sure you don't come to any harm." *She's a good looking babe. Too bad they're going to slice her head open to get at that thing.*

The horrid thoughts chilled her. *I've got to get out of here, and fast.* She returned the smile. "Thank you, Steve. I imagine you'll get quite the ransom for me. Perhaps now I can use the washroom and get a bite to eat?"

Steve's smile faltered for a second, and then he waved toward the open door behind him. "Right this way."

She shuffled slowly through, making sure to take in as much as she could of the layout. The next room appeared similar to the one she was confine to, with the exception of a small kitchenette at one end and another door on the far side. The other three men, sitting at a table, watched her parade past. The next door, unlike hers, though steel, had a large window in it. She entered a hallway with a half dozen different doors running off it. The hall dead-ended to her left and turned a corner to her right. A faint bit of daylight came from that direction. *That must be the way out.*

Steve put a hand on her shoulder and turned her toward the next door on her left. "The bathroom's this way."

A unisex sign hung on the door. She reached up and slid it to expose the woman stick figure and cover the man. "In case someone else is in the building and needs to go."

"Don't worry. We're all alone so forget about screaming. Don't be too long in there. I don't want to have to come in and get you."

"I won't."

She shut herself inside and slipped into the toilet stall. It was big, designed for handicapped users. As she sat down to use the facilities, she dropped her head into her hands. *How am I ever going to get out of here?*

CHAPTER 37

Sammy waited until the standard refrain of "Hail To The Chief" began, then he made his entrance into the White House press room.

"Good evening, everyone. I have a short statement to make then I will open it up for questions.

"As of early this morning I was made aware of the abduction of astronaut Lieutenant Brooke Jones. I have instructed the FBI and the CIA to make every effort to assist all local police throughout this county to recover our prized hero and capture the perpetrators of this injustice.

"As of this moment, no ransom has been requested. Nor have there been any other demands set forth in exchange for her return.

"It is my hope, god willing, that she is found quickly and safely returned to her friends and family and the good people of the United States of America. My thought and prayers are with her.

"Thank you. I will now, as best I can, answer your questions." A number of hands went up and he selected the one closest to him to start.

"Mr. President, when exactly was she kidnapped?"

"I cannot pin down an exact time, but I am told it was somewhere between eight and nine o'clock last evening." He pointed to the next hand.

"Do you think this is terrorist related?"

"There is no reason, at this time, to speculate the involvement of terrorists." He went on to the next hand.

"If not terrorists, and not ransom, then why do you think she was abducted?"

The question he feared had finally arrived. He had mulled over and over again the numerous options available to him. He could say he had no idea, he could reply it was too early to tell, or he could simply fabricate one for the time being. His instincts told him to avoid an answer, but his staff had counseled otherwise. They feared withholding the truth now, if it should come out later, would result in a huge backlash from the public, and the office of the president would be severely damaged. He took a quick breath and let it go. Moments such as this reminded him of his mental preparation before a big play when the ball would end up in his hands. In moments like this, he missed those days. "It's believed that astronaut Jones is carrying within her a micro black hole as a result of her visit to Mars. It's of immense importance for a number of reasons, and ownership of such a thing is a value beyond measure."

The room broke out into a furor with reporters shouting questions and rising from their chairs. He held his hands up to calm them. "Ladies and gentlemen. Please. We will get to all of your questions. At this time, I'm going to surrender the microphone to the director of the FBI for more details, and he has with him Doctor Akihiko Fujiyoshi from NASA who is best suited to provide the technical answers you deserve."

He took a seat to the side and listened as the reporters peppered the two men with questions. Janice sat next to him. "You did the right thing."

"I hope so. I still think we should have waited a couple of days, just in case things got resolved quickly."

The FBI director was detailing how every scientist in America who might have the capability to capture the micro black hole had been contacted. He believed none were implicated and that the specialist required to remove the micro black hole would have to be coming from

163

outside the country so all entries were being monitored.

Janice snorted. "Yeah, right. As if that's going to work. I wouldn't be surprised if the guy's from right here in Washington."

"Jay girl! What makes you say that?"

"Well, for example, my cabbie this morning was an emergency room doctor back in his home country. I wouldn't be surprised if there are hundreds of immigrants running around who have the know-how. And pretty well all of them would do it for the cash."

He thought about what she said. It was true. Professionals from all walks of life were constantly complaining how they couldn't practice their homeland-learned skills.

The NASA whiz kid stood and, explain what a micro black hole was. Questions were fired as to how dangerous it might be. He laughed off the doomsday people. *Smart kid, that one. Glad he's on our side.* "So Jay, let's say there's somebody out there with the know-how to capture this thing. They've still gotta get the equipment to do it. Don't they? That can't be stuff you pick up at your local Walmart."

"Actually, that's the sad part. You just about can. Aki told me that all one needs to do is create an electromagnetic field around it and it should stay inside. With enough batteries and copper wire, it could be done easily."

The news just keeps getting worse. "Then why haven't we done that already?"

"One small detail. Astronaut Jones has to be dead for it to work. The electrons in her brain have it captured and unless she dies, there's no way of getting past them."

"Shit! She could be dead already. Then we'll never get the blasted thing."

"It's quite possible."

Decisive action was needed. He rose from his chair and approached the microphones. Everyone went quiet as he gathered himself and stared down the room. "Ladies and gentlemen, this is s crisis unlike any other our nation has ever faced. I am going to break with protocol and offer a reward right now of one-hundred million dollars for astronaut Jones' return. I am also prepared to negotiate her ransom should the perpetrators of this crime be so inclined. Until Miss Jones is safe once more, I will not rest. God bless America."

He turned and headed out, the refrain of "Hail To The Chief" picking up again as he went. *Damned if I'm going to lose the whole friggin' planet on my watch!*

CHAPTER 38

Brooke contemplated the chains for the umpteenth time. Try as she might, she could not break them. *I guess there's a limit to how strong I can get.*

What she needed was a tool of some kind. Unfortunately, there was nothing in the room except her cot. The bathroom hadn't provided anything either. Outside of the standard kitchen implements, knives, forks and spoons, she couldn't recall anything in the main room to use. If only she could get her hands on a hammer or a crowbar.

She had stayed awake the entire night, listening through the door as the men came and went and the television played. It wasn't until *Good Morning America* came on that she had any idea what time it was. To her surprise, she was the top news story. They played back the comments from the president. The rustling in the next room told her someone was awake there as well.

"Hey, Mikey, wake up! You gotta hear this. The prez just offered a reward for this gal, a cool one-hundred mill!"

"Huh? What, Nick? A hundred mill? You gotta be kidding."

"Come on. Would I shit you? I'm telling you, one-hundred million, and he's even willing to talk to whoever has her. Says he's breaking policy or something to that effect."

"What's the diff? They're coming this morning to get her anyway. Steve told me they got the equipment they need set up. Once she's gone, we get the balance of the cash we're due and we're out of here."

"Mikey, you ain't thinking. What's a half million between us when we could be getting a hundred mill to split. I say we grab the girl and blow now. Contact the FBI and collect."

"Oh, yeah, sure. And don't you think they'll put the pinch on us once they get her?"

"We'll hire a go-between to do it, a lawyer or somebody. For fifty million bucks, are you telling me you don't want to take the chance?"

"What about Steve and Chuck? They were in this with us."

"You see Steve and Chuck here? It's you and me, man."

"Chuck's my friend, I trust him. He's in or we're out, take your pick."

"Okay, fine, but Chuck only. That Steve's a prick. Won't let us talk to that Barnaby guy. And who's to say that the original payoff is only one mill? Only Steve knows for sure. What if it was a whole lot more? And he's only paying us two-fifty each. I don't trust the bastard."

"Alright, I'm in. Let me chase Chuck down first. We need him with us before we pull this off."

"Make it quick. Who knows when Steve's going to show and ruin everything."

She heard the men rustling around. The idea that they would kidnap her from the other kidnappers seemed almost comical. Still, it appeared to be her best chance. Anything was better than waiting around for them to cut open her brain.

After a few minutes, the door opened, and Nick walked in. "Okay babe, time to go. Ya gotta use the can or anything?"

"Yes, if you don't mind. Where're we going?"

"That's none of your business. Just move along now and go do your thing. Time's a-wasting."

She shuffled into the main room.

Mike watched her pass. "Chuck said he'll be here in ten minutes."

Nick stopped her and turned toward Mike. "He's in?"

167

"Yeah, it took a bit of explaining, but he's in."

"Good." Nick prodded her. "Okay, keep going."

When she was finished in the bathroom, instead of putting her back in the makeshift cell, they sat her down at the table. "You want anything to eat while we're waiting?"

"A coffee would be nice. One cream and one sugar."

"Sure, give me a minute."

Mike made coffee for the three of them and she was just enjoying her first sip when Chuck entered. "Okay, I'm here. Hey, enough coffee left for me?"

Nick had been packing a gym bag. "No time for that. Now you're here, we have to go." He pointed at Brooke. "Finish that thing, lady."

Maybe I can use to this to my advantage. "You know if you're in a hurry you might want to at least undo the chains at my ankles, I can't move too fast with them on."

"No chance, sweetheart. I'll just drag you if I have to. Come on, Mikey, let's go."

Chuck sat down next to her. "Relax for a couple. I want to have a coffee before we go. Five minutes aren't going to make a difference."

Mike handed him a coffee. "Here you go."

Nick tossed his bag to the floor. "Are you guy's nuts? Stopping to drink coffee? We gotta blow!"

She glanced at Chuck and saw him spill a bit of his coffee as he lifted the cup. She wondered what he was thinking. *Stall for a couple of minutes, just a couple. He'll be here soon.*

She tensed. *Something's up.* She put her cup down and turned to look at the door. Nick was busy picking his bag back up. She wondered who would be there soon. As if in answer to her question, she heard the sound of running feet.

168

The door flew open, and in came Steve. "Going somewhere?"

Nick dropped the bag once again and looked to Mike. "He's my friend, he says. I trust him. Yeah, some trust. He ratted us out."

"He is my friend and I do trust him. It's you, I don't. I told him to get Steve. Sorry, Nick."

It happened fast. Nick pulled a gun before the other three could move. He got off a couple of shots, and she heard one zing by her ear followed by the "umph" of Steve, standing behind her, getting hit. As he dropped, the other two tackled Nick. She slipped to the floor and began to search through Steve's pockets. There was a lot of blood and it made her queasy as her fingers became slick with it.

It didn't take her long to find the key. As she undid the shackles, she kept an eye on the struggle across the floor. Mike had the gun, and Chuck was landing a number of punches to the head of the downed Nick. *If I'm going to make a run for it, I'd better go now.*

Chuck must have spotted her. "Quick, Mike, grab her before she gets away."

She grabbed the loose chains and tossed them at the oncoming Mike. *If only those chains would wrap him up, then I can get away.* As she watched, the chains encircled the man and she made out the distinguishable click as the shackles locked on him.

Mike keeled over. "What the hell?"

Startled for just the moment, she snapped out of it, jumped up and dashed out the door. A quick right, a few strides, another quick right, and she spotted the street exit.

As she had guessed, she was in an industrial district. She made for the next building and was stopped by a security man at the gate. "Hold it there, missy. Where you running to?"

"Quick, please, call the police. I'm Brooke Jones, and I just

169

escaped some men who kidnapped me."

The man looked over her shoulder. "Who kidnapped you? Where?"

She turned and pointed at the building she had just fled. "In there. Call the police before they get away."

The security guard pulled a cell phone and dialed 9-1-1. "Hello, police? Listen, this is security down at Pembrook Industries. There's a woman here claiming she was kidnapped." He covered the phone with his hand and looked at her. "What did you say your name was again?"

"Brooke Jones. Astronaut Brooke Jones."

The man's eyes widened, and he returned the phone to his face. "She says she's Brooke Jones, you know, the missing astronaut.... Yeah, she's here with me right now.... Okay, will do."

He put the phone away. "You'd better come with me, Miss Jones. I'm going to take you inside until the cops come."

She followed the man toward the building but before she stepped inside she watched two cars speed away from where she had just been.

CHAPTER 39

Bart smiled as Jesse entered his office. "Sit anywhere; I finally cleared all the files off the chairs."

Jesse picked the closest chair. "I never understood why you kept so many paper files in the first place. Everybody does everything online."

"Yes, well, now that it's over, I'll let you in on a little secret. It took a lot of book shuffling to cover over your trip to Mars and the Senate oversight committee never had the gumption to go through all those records. Of course, I'll categorically deny that, but bottom line, it worked. And I'm all about bottom lines."

His comment elicited a small smile from Jesse, and then his usual somber demeanor returned. "You wanted to see me?"

"Yes, I did. First of all, how's your health?"

"Doc says I'm fit as a fiddle and anytime you want me back up there I'm ready to go."

"And Mark? Brian?"

"Both the same. But I suspect you already know that."

He picked up and waved one of the few reports still on his desk. "Yes, I did. But I like to hear it from the man as well, not just his doctor." He tossed the reports back on his desk then pick up another, far larger one. "And I suspect you know whose file this is?"

Jesse sighed. "Brooke's."

He let that one drop on the desk from a foot above, getting the loud thump he wanted for effect. "Yes, astronaut Jones'. We just did another complete physical as a result of her ordeal over the past few days, and of course, she's in perfect health. In fact, even better than before. How's Robert, by the way?"

"He's okay, I think. He had a bit of a relapse while Brooke was gone but that might have been from the stress. In fact, I believe she's home with him right now. He'll be right as rain in no time."

"I'm aware. Our security has attached an officer to her, as have the Feds. I'm afraid she won't have any peace or privacy for quite a while."

"At least until whoever kidnapped her is caught."

"Yes, let's hope it's soon, but back to my files, Jesse. Have you wondered why I'm looking at your medical reports in hard copy? Never mind, I'll tell you, because just an hour ago the FBI came in and attempted to seize all of these. Of course I blamed the lost files on when Drumdat came in and swept our systems but there's more to it than information gathering."

Jesse leaned forward. "What? Am I missing something? What's going on?"

He opened Brooke's file and pulled out a report he had just re-read for the third time. "Take a peek at this, and you'll understand. I had Aki do another test on her special asset. It seems her zone of influence is continuing to grow. Rather than only a few centimeters as pointed out by the Drumdat Report, the distance is now expanding to as much as half a meter, depending on where you are measuring from. Aki can't predict exactly how large it will get but based on the new data he's thinking a complete sphere around her with a diameter of some four to five meters."

"So why is the FBI so interested?"

"Call it a gut feeling. I spoke with the president when she was first abducted, and he was pretty adamant that a solution be found resolving Brooke's continuance of hosting that thing. I have tried to placate him that she is of no risk, but he believes otherwise. Now, with this report showing a continued growth, I'm afraid that people will read this the wrong way."

Jesse flipped through the report, passed it back, then slumped into his chair. "Okay, I get your point but I don't know what it is you expect me to do."

Bartholomew opened his desk and produced a large manila envelope. "Here are your orders. You're cleared for the next mission to the moon in six months. Upon your arrival, you will take command of Moon Base Alpha for the length of your stay."

Jesse opened the envelope and scanned through the documents, glancing every now and then at him. "I see we're to expand the Helium 3 recovery program. But I don't see what this has to do with Brooke."

"You might have a change in your crew at the last moment."

"Then why not just change it now? Send her up with me."

"I want to give Aki and our people every chance to see if they can come up with a solution and I don't want the press jumping on it should they see she's on the list. The media circus has already started."

Jesse nodded. "You're telling me. I've had more requests for interviews in the past couple of days than I had when I got back from Mars. And you know they only want to talk about one thing. Brooke."

"Exactly. No, if she ends up going, it's going to be a last second insertion, but I need you to prep her on the sly. When you go over and visit with her, take her through the basics. I'm quite sure Robert will be of some use in that regard as well."

"If you say so." Jesse got up and turned the manila envelope over in his hands a few times as he started to leave. He stopped at the door and faced Bart once again. "Just one thing. What if she doesn't want to go?"

"Don't worry, she'll go. It's not anything one wants to lose her head over."

CHAPTER 40

Brooke looked out the window at the horde of media camped outside Robert's home. "When will they ever leave?"

The FBI woman, Grace Simpson, moved to stand beside her. "At least no one will try and kidnap you again with so many looking on. But if you like, I can get a restraining order to move them a certain distance away so you don't have to look at them on the front walk."

"No, that's okay. Sooner or later, they'll get bored and go away."

"I find that unlikely, Miss Jones. Excuse me for saying, but you're a freak show. The rumors out there say you can do all kinds of things— read minds, bend steel, fly. Personally, I have my own misgivings about all of this. How much of it is really true?"

"Pff! Nonsense. Fly? How I wish."

Robert, stretched out in front of the television, started to laugh. "It's like saying you're Supergirl. Faster than a speeding bullet, stronger than a locomotive, able to leap tall buildings with a single bound! Is it a bird, a plane, no, it's Brooke Jones!"

She sat by him and gave him a soft punch to the shoulder. "Laugh all you want. As long as I live here, you're going to have to put up with them as well."

Robert rubbed at the spot she punched. "Easy, remember I'm injured. I'm on your side. Maybe the order might not be such a bad idea. Perhaps when they catch those guys there will be an end to it." He turned to face Grace. "How goes the investigation?"

Grace picked up her comp pad from the table. "As you know, we did catch the one fellow, Mike, who was wrapped up in chains. At first he tried to claim he was a kidnap victim as well, but we were wise to that and he's since revised his position. So far, he's denying knowing any of the names you mentioned: Chuck, Nick, or Barnaby. The one you said was Steve was DOA at the hospital so we won't be getting anything out of him."

Brooke jumped up to look over the shoulder of Grace at the comp pad. "That Barnaby guy is the one you need to find. He's the mastermind behind the scenes. They all deferred to him."

"It's too bad you didn't get any last names. Right now we're tracing all known accomplices of Mike in hopes of finding the rest and going through all of his phone records, but it's going to take time. By the way, he claims you locked the chains on him just by throwing them at him. Out of curiosity, how did you manage that?"

Robert gave her a warning look and she recalled their last private conversation where he warned her against admitting to any special skill. "Just blind luck, I guess. I threw them and ran. Maybe he put them on to hide the fact he was a kidnapper."

"Hmm, we thought about that but it doesn't hold water. He had a chance to run for it when the others did. We'll leave that as a question mark for now."

"Perhaps it might be a good time to go over all the details you've given us so far. Maybe there's something you missed and you might remember as we review it."

They spent the next two hours rehashing all the details until Brooke put up a hand. "Agent Simpson, we're starting to go in circles. I've been through this four times now and I don't think I'm missing anything. Maybe, if you wouldn't mind, you could give Robert and I a little privacy for the evening."

Grace started packing up. "You're right, Miss Jones. I've got my own family to see. There are two agents outside keeping an eye on

176

things and there's that fellow from NASA out there as well. You're in good hands for the night. I'll see you tomorrow."

Agent Simpson left and Brooke headed into the kitchen to prepare a quick dinner for the two of them. "How does soup and sandwiches sound? I'm not up to making anything that requires too much work."

"Sounds fine. There's some Italian salami in the fridge and sliced Havarti cheese. Make mine with some mustard while you're at it."

She put together the sandwiches and heated up some canned chicken soup then brought everything out to the dining table. As she sat down she could see Robert watching her.

"Just curious. How did you wrap that guy up in chains?"

"I don't know how exactly. Like I said, I just threw the chains at him. I was thinking how I wished I could lock him up in them and they simply flew into place and locked tight. I tell you, I was as surprised as he was."

Robert reached for the salt and pepper, sprinkled some on his soup, stared at the shakers for a moment, and then placed them before her. "Why don't you try and can get these shakers to move toward you like you did that day we had lunch."

Some anxiety was building in her. Could she really do it? "You told me about that, but it seems that those kinds of things only happen when I'm not paying attention. As if only my subconscious can do it."

"Just…." Robert spaced the shakers a foot apart, "try."

She sat still for a moment and took a deep breath. Holding a hand out toward the salt, she concentrated on it floating toward her. A few seconds passed, nothing happened. "See? I can't seem to control it."

"Keep trying. Try for a little longer before giving up."

She furrowed her brows at him but reached out her hand again and tried once more. *Come on! Float over!* To her surprise, the salt shaker bolted toward her open hand. She wasn't able to catch it as it bounced off her palm and landed on the table before her. It spilled everywhere. "Oh my god!"

Robert chuckled. "Great job, Brooke, but spilled salt, that's bad luck. You'd better throw some over your left shoulder."

She picked up the salt and gave it a shake as instructed. "Okay, I did it. Now what? I just about broke my hand with how it hit it. What good is that?"

"Now try the pepper. Try and control the speed this time."

"*Okay.*" Holding out her hand once more she concentrated on the pepper shaker. Unlike the salt, this time it came almost right away and moved at a rate that she could grasp it easily. A sense of giddiness overtook her. "I did it!"

She changed her concentration to the plate before her and the sandwich on it. The sandwich drifted up to her waiting hand. She then tried the plate, and that worked, too. Once it was back down she concentrated on the entire table. The "whoa" of surprise from Robert brought a grin to her face. She let the table down and changed her target. Robert began to rise.

"Amazing, but if you don't mind, please put me down easy. I still have two casts on."

She lowered him down. "As you wish." She decided it was time for one more experiment. Brooke concentrated and slowly she began to rise toward the ceiling. "Look, Robert, I'm flying."

"You are indeed my Supergirl."

178

CHAPTER 41

Aki watched as the technicians completed setting up the equipment. Looking over his shoulder was Professor Francis from Drumdat. "It looks like you're ready for bear here, Aki."

"Let's hope it works. Setting up magnetic fields within magnetic fields is a tricky business. It's far too likely that somewhere the fields will merge, and we'll be back to square one."

"Most likely. I came as you requested, to assist you in this. I would like to help Brooke just as much as you would. When I saw your proposition on how to capture the micro black hole, I knew I had to see this thing firsthand."

"Your initial testing of her gave me the idea. Come on, the techs are just about finished. I want to inspect each station before we begin the test."

He and Francis approached each piece of equipment and chatted with the technician monitoring it. They also examined everyone to make sure they were in rubber shoes and gloves and reminded them of the minimal distance required to stand away so that their own bodily electrical currents wouldn't interact.

As they moved about the room, Francis proved to have a significant depth of knowledge on the machinery and its proper use. "When you've been doing lab work as long as I have, the theoretical part almost becomes second place to the practical application, including how to build all this stuff. I swear, I've learned more about electronics in the past couple of decades than anything else.

"When I was at CERN, I watched the technicians rebuild components on a regular basis, but I never got to use my hands while helping. Needless to say, I'm a little nervous about this venture and glad to have an extra set of eyes on it."

Francis chuckled. "Well, keep your hopes up that everything goes according to plan and there are no gremlins in the machinery."

"Gremlins?"

"Yeah, gremlins. Sheesh, nobody knows their history anymore. Back in the old days of aviation, when planes broke down the pilots would blame it on gremlins mucking up the works. There was an old classic episode of the Twilight Zone called *Nightmare at 20,000 Feet*. The lead character has a window seat, and he sees a gremlin fly onto the wing and start pulling the wiring out. No one believes him because every time they go to check, the gremlin hides. In the end, the guy grabs a gun from a cop, opens the emergency exit, and shoots the gremlin."

I don't believe in gremlins so let's just hope everything is going to be okay."

They completed their inspection. Aki stood by a monitor and gave the lead technician the signal to turn it all on. The readings showed the currents flowing as predicted. "It's looking good."

Francis put a hand up. "Just wait a bit. Let it run for at least however long you think you're going to need to ensure it's running properly."

After another dozen seconds or so, there was a sudden spike in one of the readings and from across the room, electrical charges zapped at one of the machines. "Shut it down, quick!"

The tech threw the switch and cut all the power. Aki and Francis walked over to the spent device, the smell of ozone filling the air. "The fields crossed. What went wrong?"

Francis knelt to peer into the machine. "I'm thinking it's the air.

Even in this white room, free of dust, there's still atmosphere to provide a conduit. Once the fields reached sufficient strength, they leapt across and merged. Just like a solar flare on the sun."

He left instructions for the technicians to tidy up and invited Francis to the cafeteria. "I'm sure you've heard the ramblings of some of our fellow scientists that Brooke's micro black hole poses a threat. What is your opinion?"

Francis smiled and clapped him on the back. "I like you, Aki. You're young, intelligent, forthright, and unfortunately, at times, stupid. You think about it while I grab us some coffee."

Stupid? Why am I stupid? What's he talking about? I'm not stupid.

They lined up for the coffee behind a couple of other NASA staff and when they reached the counter, Francis grabbed the pot to pour. "Cream? Sugar?"

"Double double please."

Francis handed Aki the coffee and led the way to a nearby table. By that time, Aki was so mad he was tempted to storm out and leave Francis sitting there, but he held it in check enough to sit down.

Francis smiled. "I can tell by the look on your face you still haven't figured it out. Politics, dear boy, politics."

I still don't understand. "What politics are you talking about? Are you saying because the president had me in Washington to discuss the details of her condition and what minimal threat a micro black hole poses? You don't think that was a cover up, do you?"

"No, though that probably had a small part. I'm talking about the scientific community. Look, you wrote a paper on this phenomenon and how it plays its part in quantum mechanics. And, to date, how does your theory stand?"

181

"Still not accepted by the scientific community. But it's just a matter of time. I mean, how long can they ignore the facts? We have the living proof inside astronaut Jones."

"Proof, smoof. Don't you see? If they acknowledge the micro black hole is not dangerous, that amounts to a tacit approval of your paper on quantum mechanics and how the universe works. You theory strikes at the very heart of everything they hold dear, all the way back to Einstein. The last thing they can do is concur with your assessment. No, it will be some time before your theories are considered proven. In the meantime, you're going to have to live with these false claims."

"You had me worried. I was beginning to think you were on their side, calling me stupid."

Francis laughed. "My apologies, I was trying to make a point. Maybe I used the wrong words but I needed to drive it home."

"Well if all we have to worry about is a few old farts unwilling to accept the new reality, I can live with that."

Francis sighed. "Let's hope that's all we have to live with. Remember, those old farts have the ear of those in power. Right now you have the inside track on this so make hay with it while the sun shines. Who knows, tomorrow you could find yourself on the outside looking in."

CHAPTER 42

Sammy stretched out on the sofa, comp pad in one hand, double scotch on the rocks in the other. *God, how I hate reading all of these damned reports. It's so much easier when someone just tells me what the hell is going on.*

He scanned them. "Boring…boring…read it…boring…know that one…that one, too…."

He paused to take a sip of his drink then returned his focus to the next on the list. Update on Brooke Jones' kidnapping. "Hmm, what happened to you, girl? What the hell am I going to do with you?" He opened the full report and scanned through it. When he read the names of the suspected kidnappers he sat up, spilling half of his drink on his lap in the process.

He hit the intercom. "Where's Janice? I need to see her."

The door opened right away, and Janice stepped in. "I'm here, Sammy. I was just next door. Where's the fire?"

He waved his comp pad in the air. "Did you read all these reports? More specifically, the one about the kidnapping?"

"I glanced through them, yes. Why, is there a problem?"

"It's just a hunch on my part. Some pieces are missing though. Help me figure it out."

"Sammy, what in heaven's name are you talking about?"

"The kidnapping, Jay baby, the kidnapping. Look, this report says that the one kidnapper she never met was some fellow named Barnaby. Now tell me, how many Barnabys do you know?"

"Well, none, but what does that matter?"

"Everything. I don't know any either. It can't be a very common

183

name."

"Perhaps, but there's still probably a whole mess of them, considering there are over four hundred million people in the United States. That's not counting the other eight billion in the world. Barnaby sounds English. I bet there's a whole mess of them over there."

"Work with me, Jay girl. The reason I'm saying this is because do you remember that day I visited Nate Drummond?"

"Yes, and he threw you out. What of it?"

He laughed. "Yeah, he did. But while I was in there, his flunky, Al, said something about a Barnaby."

Janice looked at his comp for a second then sat down and pulled out her pad. "Do you think this Barnaby involved in the kidnapping is the one Nate knows?"

"Yeah, but I need to figure out Nate's connection in all of this."

"What makes you think there is one? Let's assume you're right, and this is the same man. For all you know, he got inside information about astronaut Jones and did this on his own."

"Inside intel? What kind of inside intel?"

"Something I read." She worked her comp pad, and Sammy stood behind her to follow what was on the screen. Different reports flew past as she cycled through them, using her rating to override all the security blocks. After a few moments, she settled on one. "Here it is. This shows when Drumdat knew about the micro black hole. It's an email the FBI pulled from her computer. It was sent to her by a Professor Francis who was in charge of their bio lab."

Sammy read the email then clapped his hands. "We've got him!"

Janice turned to look up at him. "Got who?"

"Nate Drummond, don't you see? It all fits now." He did a little dance across the floor.

"Okay, Sammy. Enough with the theatrics. Tell me how we have Nate Drummond."

"Look, the people at Nate's science lab discover Miss Jones has this thing inside her. Everybody knows now its side effects have improved her health almost immeasurably but back then just Drumdat knew and maybe a few people at NASA. Hell, I should have figured it out myself when they came back. She damn near broke my fingers with that grip of hers."

Janice made a rolling motion with her hand. "Yes, okay, I know that. Go on."

"*So*...look at that email. The one thing they can't figure out is how to get it out of her without killing her. Now tell me, how far would you go to possess the one thing that could maybe let you live forever? What would you pay?" As her eyebrows rose, he knew he had hit home.

"So *you* think Nate Drummond hired this Barnaby guy to get it for him because he couldn't get it himself."

Sammy threw both arms into the air. "Touchdown! The lady scores." He pretended to spike a football into the floor. "Bam!"

"But that would be stupid. Sooner or later, we'd figure it out and then he'd go to jail. Would someone in his position risk all he has for that?"

"Why not. What's he got to lose? Say he does go to jail. Thirty years. What does thirty years mean if you can live forever? Nothing. Besides, he'd hire more lawyers than there are people in Washington. They'd find some way of clearing him. The worst we could get him with would probably be possession of stolen goods. What's that, a misdemeanor? No, he's got this all figured out."

Janice pulled out her cell phone. "Then we better get hold of the director of the FBI and tell him your theory. He'll want to investigate this right away."

He put a hand over hers. "No, don't."

She put the phone back in her purse. "Are you nuts, Sammy? Why not?"

Sammy went to his humidor and pulled out a big Cuban. He paused to look at her. "I feel like celebrating. Want one?"

"Pff, no! You know how I hate it when you smoke in the White House. And you still haven't answered my question."

He clipped the end, found his lighter, and lit up. After a few big puffs, he smiled at her. "Because, Jay girl, no harm, no foul. He didn't get want he wanted, and astronaut Jones is home, safe and sound. But in the meantime, my term of office is up in half a year, and I'm thinking of a nice sweet deal for you and me with the Drumdat Corporation. Once I let Nate know what we know, there's no way he can refuse me."

He took one long drag and let it blow out slow. "Man, don't you just love it when things come together like this?"

CHAPTER 43

Brooke pulled on her shoes while Agent Simpson stood nearby waiting. "Are you ready to go, Doctor Jones?"

"You bet. One week of being cooped up in this house while being constantly grilled by you would be enough to drive anyone crazy. No offense, but I'll be glad to get some fresh air and see the world again." Brooke gave Robert a kiss on the cheek. "I'm off to give NASA a chance to pull this thing out of me. Wish me luck."

"Let's hope it works. Then you can go back to a normal life."

"Yeah, a normal life. I've just about forgotten what that is. Now all I have to do is get past that bunch out there." Agent Simpson opened the door, and she stepped onto the threshold to see the throng of reporters rushing to the foot of the walk to meet her. She took a deep breath. *Here goes nothing.*

She wasn't more than three steps down the walk before the reporters broke ranks and crossed the property line to where she was. They all clamored with questions.

"Did you know who your kidnappers were?"

"Word is they caught another one. Have you heard anything new?"

"Is it true you have super powers?"

That last one caused her to pause and frown at the woman who had asked it. Before she could respond, Agent Simpson put up her hands. "Everyone, please. You have all been receiving the briefing reports and know just as much as Doctor Jones does. Yes, we caught a second kidnapper, the one identified as Chuck, but like the first one, he doesn't know anything more that could be useful to us. We're still searching for the fourth, known as Nick, and the mysterious intermediary known as Barnaby. Doctor Jones would like to get back to her life, so if you would excuse us, we need to get going."

The female reporter stepped in the way. "You still haven't answered my question."

Brooke glanced at Agent Simpson, who shrugged then returned her focus to the woman reporter. "It would be great to have super powers. I could fly around the world and right all the wrongs. But unfortunately, I'm just plain old me, Brooke Jones. If you don't mind, I'd like to go now."

The reporter stepped aside, and Brooke and Agent Simpson climbed into the backseat of the waiting car. Two other FBI agents waited in the front. The drive to NASA was a quiet one. When she got inside, a few of her close friends were quick to find her and wish her well. Once the pleasantries were over, she reported to the administrator's office. "Hello, Bart. I'm here. You cleaned your office, I see."

Bart came over and shook her hand "Glad you're okay, Brooke." He gestured toward Grace. "I hope these FBI types have been treating you well?"

Grace offered her hand. "Administrative Director Higginbottom, it's a pleasure to meet you. Agent Grace Simpson, at your service."

"Likewise." After accepting the handshake, he gave Brooke a wink. "Well? Are you ready for it? Aki has me convinced this is going to work."

Nervousness crept into her. "I guess as ready as I'll ever be. Let's get it over with."

"Outstanding. That's my trouper. I've got a shuttle waiting for us. Let's get going."

They exited the building and clambered aboard the shuttle. The last time Brooke had been in it was when she was on her way out to the launch pad to board EROS I. It brought back memories of the trip—her expectations. All of them seemed so distant.

At the science lab, she was surprised to see Francis beside an Asian man who she figured must be Aki. "Francis! I'm so glad to see you. How goes the project?"

"Everything's going well. The chemists are synthesizing the drug. In fact, they don't need me there nursemaiding them so I offered to come and help Aki here with this. It's the least I can do."

She turned to the Asian. "And you must be the Aki everyone is talking about. Have you really got this thing licked?"

He bowed. "I hope so. We had some difficulties to overcome but we think we've got it figured out. We're going to do it in the vacuum chamber, so you're going to have to don a spacesuit. We'll be communicating through your headset. Once you're ready to go, we should see results in a matter of minutes."

The nervousness she had felt back in Bart's office returned. "I'm as ready as I'll ever be. I don't think I can stand to wait any longer."

They led the way to a room where she could don a suit. The techs spend ten minutes testing the seals before leading her into the vacuum chamber and sealing the door. Pieces of equipment were arrayed everywhere. She was glad the faceplate gave her a wide range of vision as she could easily look up at the observation window. Even though they were up there and she wasn't, it gave her some piece of mind to keep an eye on them and their confident faces.

Everyone was gathered at the glass—Bart, Agent Simpson, Francis, and Aki holding a microphone "Hi, Brooke, can you hear me okay?"

189

"I hear you fine."

"Good. We'll be starting up everything in just a few minutes. We're only waiting for the room to be cleared of air. I want you to talk about how you feel and any symptoms you may be experiencing as it goes. We've got all of your health monitors showing on our screens up here, but if you start feeling ill, let us know immediately, and we can kill the power with one switch."

"Don't do that. I want this thing gone."

"I understand. Systems show a vacuum has been obtained. Are you ready?"

"Fire away."

Some of the equipment began to hum and other pieces glowed with flashing lights. "I see everything working. So far I don't feel anything."

"Keep talking. It takes a couple of moments for the magnetic fields to generate."

It started small, with a narrowing of her vision. "I can't see quite as well. Something's bothering my eyesight. Now my head is starting to feel heavy, as if I had a bad cold."

"You're heart rate has picked up considerably, and your blood pressure. If it gets too high, I'm going to stop this."

"No, don't stop. I can do this. I'm getting some muscle spasms. It's nothing I can't handle. Keep it going."

The room began to dim; colors flashed before her eyes.

"Your blood pressure is at a dangerous level. Brooke, can you hear me?"

A sudden jolt shot through her. In that same instant there was an intensely bright light, and then the room went dark.

"Holy cow! Every machine just blew! Brooke, answer me. Can

you talk? Somebody get some lights on."

The muscle spasms eased, and the pressure in her head subsided. "I'm…I'm fine. I'm okay. What happened?"

"Thank goodness. We don't know yet. Everything is fried. We're restoring an atmosphere to the room right now. We should have you out of there in a few."

She stood in near darkness, with only a small amount of light from the window to the control room to see her surroundings. She moved toward the door. When it finally opened, a rush of hands helped her through and then out of the suit. "Did it work?"

Francis shook his head. "Who knows? We need to check to be sure. They're going to take you over to the doctor's office for an MRI to check. Aki and I will examine the recorded results and hopefully we'll know soon enough what happened." *Something tells me it didn't work.*

Hearing Francis' thought told Brooke all she needed to know. She turned to face Aki, and his thoughts were all about what went wrong. Bart's held concern for her welfare. What an old softie.

When she turned to glance at Agent Simpson, she sensed a certain amount of hostility. *I'm going to have to report this. They may want to initiate Protocol Alpha.*

Protocol Alpha? What the heck is that?

CHAPTER 44

Nate buttoned his shirt. "Thanks for coming, Doctor. You're probably the only one left in the entire U. S. of A. who still makes house calls."

The doctor chuckled. "Only because you pay me so well. But all kidding aside, you had better start thinking about slowing down. Your body isn't able to keep up with the demands you put on it. Take a vacation. By gosh, at eighty-six, you've earned it enough times over. How many years do you think you have left?"

"I intend to see one hundred. Lots of people live that long nowadays."

"True, but how many of those retired and took it easy long before they reached your age."

"That's why I have you coming around. To make sure I keep going. Same time next month?"

The doctor fastened his bag closed and gave a salute. "See you then."

He went out the door, and Alban came in before it could close. "How was the check up?"

Putting on his jacket, he went over to the bar. "You know, the same old, same old. I work too hard. I need more rest. I won't last forever. Enjoy life while I can. I smoke too much. I drink too much." He pulled a bottle out. "Scotch?"

"Well, it's good to see you're following doctor's orders. Yes, please. Ice."

He poured two healthy drinks and handed one to Alban. "I've made it this far doing what I do. But I'll at least limit myself to just the one for now. What's new to report?"

"The expansion of the Helium 3 program on the moon is all set. Once it's in full production, we'll have more than enough to power every reactor in the country. Come the new year, Drumdat Energy Corporation is expecting profits to set a new record. It will be the highest valued stock in the world."

They clinked glasses. "As it should be. And the dividends will pay you handsomely, Alban. You've been with me a long time. Your twenty percent share in the company is well deserved."

"Yes, with my most recent stock option, I'm the largest shareholder next to your fifty-one percent."

"Which is exactly why we need to begin aggressively buying back stock. Tell our brokers to get on it."

"Certainly. How do you want to start? The preferred stock? It will be expensive."

"Of course, but worth it in the long run."

The intercom buzzed. "Mr. Drummond, it's President Davidson on the phone."

He sighed. "What does that jock fool want? Excuse me, Al. I'd better take this. No matter how much of a clown I think he is, he's still the president of the United States."

Alban headed for the door. "I'll be in the boardroom."

Nate retreated to his desk and turned on his vid phone. "I'm here, Sammy."

The toothy grin of the president showed on the screen. "Nate, baby, how ya keeping?"

"What is it this time? I thought it was understood our business dealings were at an end."

"Nate, ol' buddy, whatever gave you that idea?"

"Oh, perhaps how I threw you out."

"Yeah, that ya did. But I forgive you. After all, that's what friends are supposed to do."

His finger hovered over the disconnect. "Well, old friend, it's been a pleasure chatting with you, but I'm rather busy, so unless you have something really important to say, I'm going to have to let you go."

"I got one word for you. A name. Barnaby."

His finger froze in midair. *How does he know that name?* "Who's Barnaby?"

Sammy laughed. "Ya see, Nate? That's why you could never be a politician. You lie like shit. *You* know who I'm talking about. Don't you read the news? It's all over how a Barnaby was the mastermind behind the kidnapping of astronaut Brooke Jones."

"Yes, I know about it. Why would I want to have Doctor Jones taken hostage? She was already working for me at my research lab. What would I have to gain having my own employee kidnapped?"

"Because, Nate, budderroo, You found out about the micro black hole and you found out you couldn't get it out of her without killing her, so you got Barnaby to do it for you."

"If that is so, why isn't the FBI here, beating down my door and arresting me?"

Sammy looked away, looked back, and winked. "It's our secret for now. I haven't told them. In the meantime, I got to thinking about that position you promised me. You know the one, chairman of the board."

So, blackmail, is it? "I never promised you any such thing. If we're done with this nonsense, I'm going to hang up."

"Alrighty there, Nate. I'll give you some time to think about it.

But don't keep me waiting too long."

He hit the disconnect. *That toothy bastard! The last thing I'll let him do is pull a fast one on me. I need to figure a way out of this mess. Have him assassinated? No, too heavy handed. Besides, he's probably got other people in the know, like that chief of staff of his, Janice. Expose him for the back door deals we've done? That'll get him put away, but me with him.* He took a sip of his drink. *This is going to take some thinking, and I don't think I can do this alone.*

He went to the bar and grabbed the scotch then headed down to the boardroom. Alban was chatting on the vid screen with one of the department heads. "Shut that off. We need to talk."

Alban excused himself from the conversation and disconnected. "What's up Nate?"

"Al, I did something stupid, and now I don't know how to get out of it."

"If you're talking about the Jones kidnapping then I'm in agreement."

What the hell? "What do you know?"

"It wasn't that hard to figure out. I get the same reports you do. And when I heard a Barnaby was behind it, it didn't take a lot to put two and two together."

He sat down across from his longtime business associate and refilled their glasses. "Then help me figure things out."

"Alright, start at the beginning. Tell me everything. Remember, just like some of the seed money you needed way back when, I still have those friends."

CHAPTER 45

Brooke left the doctor's office with Bart at her side and Agent Simpson in tow. "It's like I figured. Nothing's changed. The micro black hole is still in there."

"The important thing is, you're okay. The extraction attempt didn't hurt you in any way."

"Thanks for the concern. I'm fine. The only discomfort was a slight headache and some blurry vision while the procedure lasted."

Agent Simpson chirped up from behind them. "Maybe for you. My eyes still hurt from that flash. What was that all about?"

"Who knows? Maybe it was the machinery. Some kind of electrical discharge."

"It didn't look like any kind of electrical discharge to me. It looked…different. Are you sure something different didn't happen in there?"

Bart put a hand on Brooke's arm and turned to face the FBI woman. "Whatever it was, we'll let the tech guys figure it out. In the meantime, let's not get into any incrimination. I was there as well, and it happened so fast I couldn't even begin to guess what it was. All I know is, up until that time, Brooke was standing calmly in the middle of all that stuff, not moving."

He turned and started walking again and Brooke, after a quick glance at Grace's scowl, quick-stepped to catch up with the administrative director and leaned close. "Thanks."

"Don't mention it. Now let's go see what those guys have done since we left."

They headed back to the lab to find Aki and Francis, along with a couple of the tech guys, crowded around a monitor. Francis looked up and he smiled when their eyes met. "Ah, Brooke, come and watch the replay of what happened. Give us your own play by play."

She took a seat in front of the screen. The voices were recorded as well and at the start she could hear Aki instructing the tech to turn everything on. A time counter was running across the bottom and at approximately the thirty-seven second mark, the screen went dark with only a faint amount of light showing her still standing in the middle of the room. She could still hear the voices and the clock was still running. "What happened to the flash?"

"That's what we were wondering. We all saw it. We took the one-second video clip from when we thought the flash could be. One of the cameras uses a specialized electronic charge-coupled device-imaging system which can achieve speeds of up to or in excess of twenty-five million frames per second. By constantly halving the segment, we were able to get it down to the thirty-two frames where the flash occurred."

Aki hit a key and the frames went by slowly so the flash was visible. "Watch closely." It wasn't uniform but went around the room in a circle with Brooke at the middle.

"That's it? That's incredibly short. And why is it like a spinning light?"

Aki hit another key and returned it to the start. "Let me show it to you again. Pay attention to the central point." He played it once more and then paused it in the middle. He pointed toward the part of the image where Brooke's head was. "There. This light beams out from…your head, or probably more specifically, the micro black hole within it."

"So what am I looking at? What is this light?"

"My best guess is we just saw an electromagnetic pulse of the

197

highest order. Until I do further analysis, I wouldn't be surprised to find both x-ray and gamma rays included in this emission. It's like the rotating beacon of an interstellar pulsar."

Glancing at everyone's faces, she could see the sudden consternation of many. *They're afraid they've been poisoned with radiation.*

Francis chuckled. "I've been belted by gamma rays. Will I turn into a big green monster?"

Aki shook his head. "No, I don't think so at all. Gamma rays are deadly. But the dose was probably small, so I doubt you suffered any effects."

Francis hit his forehead with the palm of his hand. "Geez! Doesn't anybody watch old cartoons anymore? Big green monster? The Incredible Hulk? None of this rings a bell?" He broke into song. *"Belted by gamma rays, turns into the Hulk, now he needs glamour rays...."*

Brooke smiled at how easily Francis had broken the ice in the room. "I remember the movies. I don't recall gamma rays being part of it though."

"Yeah, they changed it later. Too bad. It was a catchy tune."

She turned to Aki. "So what do you make of all of this?"

"My interpretation is that when your mind began to feel it was under attack from the magnetic field, it instinctively lashed out at the source. I'm afraid we're never going to get that thing out of you."

Agent Simpson got up and went to the door. "Excuse me. I'm going to step out to make a call. I need to report in."

Grace frowned at her before closing the door. *That woman doesn't like me.*

Francis stood up. "Well Aki, I guess this goes a long way toward

198

proving your theories on black holes. The scientific world can't deny you forever. Wait until they hear about this!"

Bartholomew rose as well. "I'd prefer they didn't hear about this right away. I'd like to keep a lid on this for a while. It's bad enough that Brooke is being hounded by reporters over the rumors already out there. I'm sure Aki and the rest of you will come up with some other solution. In the meantime, let's give her a chance to get some kind of a normal life back."

A grumble of agreement spread through everyone present and they all rose and began to vacate the room. Brooke followed them out the door and spotted Grace who hung up her phone when they made eye contact.

"Are you ready to go now, Doctor Jones?"

"Yes, I guess we've done all we can do today. I'd like to visit Drumdat's research lab tomorrow and see where they are on the methanogens." She turned to Francis. "Are you heading back there as well?"

"Yes, my dear. In fact, I'm returning tonight. I'll look forward to your arrival."

She gave him a kiss on the cheek and headed out. Agent Simpson called her partners, and the car was waiting outside the building. Climbing in the back, she overheard Grace make a quick call. "We're on our way." *We must have more security to deal with her.*

When they came to the turnoff to Robert's, the car continued on. "Hey, you missed the turn."

The driver didn't answer. She tapped him on the shoulder. "Are you not listening? You missed the turn to Robert's house."

Agent Simpson pulled Brooke's hand away. "Keep going."

Brooke turned to look at the FBI woman. "Keep going? Keep

going where?"

"Doctor Brooke Jones, I am exercising protocol Alpha in regards to your case. Until such time that *I* deem you safe, I am putting you in protective custody."

"But that's ridiculous. You've already caught most of the kidnappers. And with all the media around, no one is going to try again. I'm already safe."

Grace's eyes narrowed on her. "Yes, you're safe, but is everyone else safe from you?"

CHAPTER 46

Robert awoke to the sound of the alarm. He rubbed at his eyes, yawned, stretched, and then smacked his mouth a few times. *Well, I'm up.*

It took a few minutes to get dressed and move from the bed into the waiting wheelchair, struggling with both legs bandaged. He rolled out of the bedroom and down the hall. *That doggone medication puts me out like a light. I didn't hear Brooke come in. Maybe she didn't want to disturb me and she's asleep in the guest bedroom.*

The door was ajar and he peeked in—no Brooke. *Hmm. Maybe she went to work.*

After his morning hygiene routine, he went into the kitchen and put on a pot of coffee. While waiting for it to brew, he went into the living room and looked out the picture window to the front walk. Only one reporter was out there. He recognized her from the news the previous night. She'd asked Brooke, "Is it true you have super powers?" Maybe a little damage-control on his part might be in order. He opened the front door. "Hey! You want some coffee?"

The girl pointed a finger at herself. "Me?"

"Yeah. You. Would you like some coffee? I just put it on. It's fresh."

"Uh, okay. Sure." She stepped quickly toward the door.

He moved out of the entry to let her get in. "Close the door for me, will you? Kitchen's this way."

Her stilettos clicked on the ceramics as she followed him in. "Thank you, Mr. Tangler. I appreciate the hospitality. I'm Sue Fontaine, by the way."

"Pleased to meet you, Sue. Since you're here, perhaps you could lend a hand and grab a couple of coffee cups and the cream out of the fridge."

She did as he asked and sat in one of the kitchen chairs at the small table. He poured the coffee. "I'm glad for the company. Being in this wheelchair all day gets mighty boring. Brooke isn't here. What brings you by today?"

"I thought I'd check again. She's not at work so this seemed the most likely place. I think there's a real story and I want to make sure I get it all."

She's not at work? "It's good to be enthusiastic. Brooke's probably in transit. I'll give her a call on her cell in a bit. I thought perhaps we could chat first. Do you mind?"

"No, not at all. In fact, since I'm here, maybe you could corroborate a few facts for me."

He took a sip of coffee to give him a chance to gather his thoughts. "If you're alluding to whether she has super powers as in the question you posed yesterday, I'm afraid you're wasting your time. Yes, it's true she is hosting a micro black hole in her brain and yes, there have been some benefits from it. But nothing one would consider super. The way it was explained to me—and from what I have observed—she has been blessed with excellent health. Something about the sped up neurons in her brain leading to an overproduction of hemoglobin and stuff like that which gives her such health. She can run faster than she could before, is stronger, and has a better mental capacity resulting in total recall, but none of these are things to be considered super."

The corners of her mouth drooped a little. "Gee, that's too bad."

"Why the sad face? You should be happy that she's normal. It's better than being labeled a freak, as some people are doing to her."

"Freak? No, that was never my intention."

He became curious. "Then just what *was* your intention, Miss Fontaine?"

Sue sighed. "I wanted her to be super, to be a super woman, like Wonder Woman in the comics. Have you ever noticed how few comic characters are female, or for that matter, in the movies? It's always the man who's the hero, the man who has achieved super deeds, the man who gets all the recognition when it comes to this kind of thing. For a change, I was cheering for Brooke to break that mold. To be somebody special with super powers, someone other females can adore."

He'd misjudged her. "I tell you what, let's give Brooke a call and see if she can still be that heroine for you, but with regular human abilities. She was, after all, the first woman to step on the planet Mars. And she did discover the first extraterrestrial life, even if it was microbiological. That has to count for something."

"Oh, I suppose so. A personal interview would still be special."

He smiled, grabbed his cell, and hit the speed dial. Brooke's phone went to voice mail, so he left a message and hung up. "Maybe she's tied up. Let me try something else." He searched through his phone to find the number for Agent Simpson. After a few rings, she answered. "Good morning, Grace. I was trying to track Brooke down. Is she with you?"

"No, not at the moment."

That's odd. The girl has been Brooke's shadow for a week. "Do you know where she is?"

"I'm sorry; I'm not at liberty to discuss that with you."

"Not at liberty to discuss…what the hell are you talking about? Do you know where Brooke is or don't you?"

"This is a matter of national security. The whereabouts of Doctor Jones are confidential. She is in protective custody. When we feel it is appropriate, we will notify you. Good-bye, Mr. Tangler."

The line went dead. *Well isn't that a hoot. What am I to do? These aren't some two-bit criminals who've grabbed her. This is the FBI.* "They're not going to get away with this. This is America. People have rights."

"What happened?"

Robert calmed himself. "It appears our government has decided to—how did she put it?—put Brooke into protective custody. I guess I'm going to have to excuse myself for a bit. I have a bunch of calls to make."

Sue rose. "Thank you for the coffee. I think I'll go do the same. Maybe I'll find out the limits of the power of the press."

CHAPTER 47

Brooke sat on the cot, staring at Agent Simpson while the FBI woman tapped away at her comp pad. So far, Brooke had been subjected to a myriad of medical tests and peered at by a number of people, including the man with a large case standing nearby, supposedly being a quantum physicist. Two other FBI agents stood by the door. "Why does this seem so familiar?"

Agent Simpson looked up from her pad. "Pardon?"

"Oh yes, *now* I recall. It's identical to when I was kidnapped for a couple of days. The cot, the sterile room, the locked door. The only difference is who's done the kidnapping."

"You have not been kidnapped, Doctor Jones. You are in protective custody."

"I don't see any difference. I cannot come and go as I please. You've even taken my cell phone away from me."

"You are free to come and go as you like within the facility. There is an entertainment center, an exercise room, even a swimming pool. For the time being, you simply cannot leave the building. Consider it a vacation where you stay in the hotel."

"This vacation stinks. I want to go home."

"We've been over that before. Whether you agree or not, the danger of the micro black hole within you is real. Until it is determined you are no longer a threat, you are to remain with us. Stop wasting my time. This gentleman is here to try and understand what happened in the NASA lab the other day."

The fellow was looking everywhere but at her. Brooke concentrated to read the man's mind. *Even though she's an American hero and we shouldn't be treating her this way, I've got a job to do. I hope she cooperates.*

She decided to play ball. She just wanted to get out of there. "What do you want from me?"

"I want you to answer this man's questions, and the doctor's as well. For some strange reason, your medical files at NASA appear to be missing. I've spoken with the administrator, Mr. Higginbottom, and he seems most evasive on the missing documents. As it was, it took sending my own people to retrieve the files from your physicist Aki Fujiyoshi. They couldn't deny those existed because I was there."

Agent Simpson pointed to the waiting gentleman. "This is our own specialist in quantum mechanics. He has a few questions for you. Be a nice girl and give him the answers he needs. The sooner we can get through, this the better."

Brooke thought about Robert and what he would say. *Don't tell them anything.*

The man bowed. "I'm sorry about the circumstances under which we are meeting, Doctor Jones. I've had the chance to review the files from NASA and am astounded at the EMP you were able to produce. How you managed to survive such an event is also a curiosity but not my field. Have you done this before?"

"Done what before? I don't even know what happened. You tell me it was an EMP. The only thing I know is there was a flash and then everything went dark. The end."

The fellow produced a device from his case and held it up toward her. "Most impressive. The electromagnetic field you are generating extends some distance already." He took a couple of steps backward. "All...the...way...to...here!" He held the device close to the ground then back as high as he could reach, moving it closer to and farther from Brooke. "My lord, that's a sphere fifteen feet in diameter." The agent bowed again. "Thank you, Doctor Jones. I should be able to do my calculations from here and quantify the micro black hole based on its sphere of influence. From there, we'll see."

She looked to Agent Simpson. "Good, that means I'm done and I can go."

"No decision has been made for you to leave.."

"And who makes that decision? I want to speak to that person right now."

Agent Simpson stood up. "I decide. I want to know the limits of what abilities it has given you. Your refusal to cooperate so far is not acceptable. And I'm not satisfied." Agent Simpson waved dismissal to the man and started for the door. She paused in the doorway to look back. "You're going to be here for a while. If I were you, I'd make the best of it."

The temptation to throw something was tempered quickly. There was nothing within reach. She got up and headed down the hallway. The two security men followed her. *Twin shadows, how nice.*

She was still seething when she entered the entertainment center. The large television on the wall might suit as a temporary distraction. A couple of people seated on leather sofas were watching it. When she sat down on the end of one sofa, they looked at her, exchanged glances, got up, and left. She slumped into the vacated seat. "Fine, more room for me."

She grabbed the remote control and channel surfed, settling on CNN. After about fifteen minutes, the news switched to her.

"What has happened to astronaut Brooke Jones? We were all mesmerized by the news of her abduction a couple of weeks ago. It was with great relief we learned she was safely returned home. But news has it that government agents have whisked her away. Our field reporter Sue Fontaine brings us this report."

The blonde young reporter who had asked her about having super powers stood beside Robert in his wheelchair.

"I'm in front of the home of Lieutenant Brooke Jones' fellow astronaut and partner, Captain Robert Tangler, who spoke early yesterday with the FBI. Robert, tell us what happened."

"I was told that Brooke has been put into protective custody. They won't even tell me where she is or allow me to call her. My lawyer says that because we aren't legally married, I'm not entitled. That doesn't sound right to me. That can't be legal. I want to see Brooke and know she's okay."

"There you have it folks. An only child with her parents deceased, she has no immediate family. If not Mr. Tangler, then who else?"

The scene switched back to the news anchorman. "We contacted the FBI for a response earlier today, and here's what we were told."

The new image showed a man she did not know standing before a few microphones. "I assure you Doctor Jones is in perfect health. As you are aware, there are still two of her kidnappers unaccounted for. Until such time as we can be confident of her safety and these individuals are apprehended, it was decided to remove her from the public eye for her own protection."

The show went back again to the anchorman. "We'll keep an eye on this story as it develops. In other news—"

She switched the station before having to hear what was next. *They're lying. It's one thing to escape from those kidnappers, but how do I escape from the government?*

208

CHAPTER 48

David entered his apartment. Another day done, he changed out of his uniform into a sweatshirt and jeans.

He was irritable; work had required him to evict a terminated employee at Drumdat's headquarters. He never enjoyed hovering menacingly over a person, demanding his office keys, and waiting for him to clear out his desk. Company policy required they be out in fifteen minutes but he always let them say their good-byes for up to an hour. This one, though, had been belligerent. For the first time that he could recall, he'd had to strong-arm the guy out the door.

I need a drink.

He approached the counter where a three-quarters-empty forty of Canadian whisky sat from the night before. He took a swig from the bottle. "Brrr! Good stuff!"

Getting a large tumbler, he half filled it with ice then topped it off with the rest of the whisky. He tossed a frozen pizza in the oven then plopped in front of the television and turned on a game show.

He was halfway through the pizza when the news came on. After a couple of lead stories, the newscaster talked about the astronaut who got kidnapped. In the end, the anchorman explained that the mastermind behind it, known as Barnaby, was still at large.

It had been some weeks since he last saw his friend. Was he the Barnaby they were looking for? Why would he kidnap that woman? What was in it for him? Remembering that no ransom had been demanded, he felt more confused than ever. Did Mr. Drummond have anything to do with it? None of it made sense.

He finished the last of the whisky. The pizza was gone and

nothing looked good to watch on the set. He decided he'd go out, find his friend, and put his mind at ease.

Barnaby was a real secretive kind of guy. David tried to call him, but got voice mail. "Hey, it's your pal David. Give me a shout. You know the number." *Maybe he isn't answering. I'll drop by his house.*

He stopped at a liquor store and picked up a new bottle then drove to Barnaby's house. When he got there, the unkempt lawn and overflowing mailbox told him Barnaby probably hadn't been home in days, if not weeks. Now he was worried. Maybe his friend *was* mixed up in that kidnapping.

He had started for home when he remembered Barnaby kept a small bachelor unit downtown. The place was a dump off an alley, but his friend said he liked it and it had its uses.

He found a parking spot a block or so away, grabbed the bottle, and then made his way to the place. When he got there, a television played inside. He pounded on the door, and the noise stopped. He waited, but when he didn't hear anyone approaching, he knocked again. "Open up. It's me, David. I know you're in there."

The door opened, and his friend yanked him in. "David, what the hell are you doing here?"

A quick glance told him all he needed to know. Multiple empty food cartons and bottles were piled on the table. How long had he been there, anyway? "I was worried about you. I hadn't heard from you for some time and when I heard a Barnaby was behind that kidnapping I started to wonder. What have you gotten yourself into?"

Barnaby plopped down onto the sofa. "Do yourself a favor and get out of here. Don't get mixed up in this. It's over your head."

"Bullshit. You're my friend, and I'm going to help you out, no matter what." David pulled the bottle out of the brown paper bag. "I

210

brought some whisky. Let's have a drink, and you can tell me what's going on. I find it hard to believe you were involved in that thing."

"David, you're my friend, but you're also an idiot. Why the hell do you think I'm holed up like this? I got a tip from a friend at the Bureau they suspected it was me. You worked there, too. You know what would have happened. They would have grabbed me, and I'd be gone, maybe forever. I'm waiting for things to die down a bit then I'm going to make a run for Canada. After that, who knows?"

"Why'd you do it?"

"The money."

"The money? How much? Enough to make all of this worthwhile?"

"Fifty million dollars. Yeah, I would have been set for life."

Fifty million dollars? He gave his head a shake. What should he do next? "You need a good lawyer, and Drumdat's got plenty of them. I'll talk to Mr. Drummond on your behalf. He knows you. I'm sure he'll do it."

Barnaby sighed. "Drummond is the last guy who'll come to my defense. Trust me."

At a loud crash, David turned to see three men burst through the door with guns raised. "What the hell?"

Barnaby jumped off the sofa. "David, you moron. You led them right to me!"

The closest man waved his pistol at them. "Excellent deduction. A pleasure to finally meet you."

The man fired three bullets into Barnaby, the last into his forehead. Blood spattered David as he stumbled backward. "Jesus! Why'd you do that? He wasn't threatening you. He didn't even have a gun. What department are you from at the Bureau anyway?"

The man took aim at David. "Who said anything about us being from the Bureau?"

In that instant, he figured it all out. Barnaby *had* masterminded the kidnapping, and Mr. Drummond *had* paid him to do it. These men weren't FBI but hit men sent by Mr. Drummond to make sure Barnaby never told. David wanted to get out of there and tell somebody the truth but the only thing he could think about was the sudden searing pain as a bullet entered his skull.

CHAPTER 49

Brooke's day began the same way as her last several. Before she could even have a cup of coffee, the doctors from the FBI were running her through a battery of tests. From there, she managed to grab a bite to eat before spending the balance of the morning undergoing another intensive grilling by Agent Simpson and her team and then having to take another round of tests that were designed to figure out the level of her psychic abilities.

"Three wavy lines."

The tester marked the response then held up another card with the back facing Brooke. "And this one?"

"A picture of a cat."

The agent dropped the card. "Doctor Jones, there are no pictures of cats in this deck. You know that. Please concentrate." He held up another card. "This one?"

Brooke leaned back in her chair and looked at the man, or perhaps lad would be a better definition. The kid couldn't be much over nineteen. The images of the cards were easy to see in her mind with each one he picked up but Brooke had decided not to play along. "A checkmark."

The young man sighed then stacked up the cards and put them aside. "Doctor Jones, the reason I got this job is because I have a small measure of ESP myself. And the one thing my skill is telling me is you are lying. As it is, statistically you're way outside the boundaries of average, but in the wrong way. In three days of testing you should have at least guessed one right, if not several. The fact you've gotten every single one wrong tells me you know more than you are letting on. I'll have no choice but to report this behavior to Agent Simpson."

The guy was rocking his chair backward as he talked. His recent tone had upset her so she waited until he reached the apex of his backward tilt and used her skills to pull the chair out from under him. He landed with a crash. She covered her mouth to hide her smile as the agent jumped to his feet.

"You...you did that! I could have gotten seriously hurt." He stormed away, leaving her sitting with her two shadows standing behind her. "Well, boys, I guess this session's over. What say we go get lunch?"

The one on her left snickered. "Sounds like a good idea to me. After you, Doctor Jones." He pulled back her chair as she rose.

"Quite the gentleman, thank you."

They made their way down to the kitchen, grabbed some sandwiches, and headed into the common room to sit at a table. Halfway through their meal, Agent Simpson entered and scowled at the men. "Quit fraternizing with the subject and one of you get the car. We're going for a ride." She stared down at Brooke. "Come on, Doctor Jones. We've got somewhere to go."

Brooke ignored her. How she detested that woman. "Not until I finish my lunch." She took another bite and chewed slowly.

Agent Simpson sat down. "Hurry up, then. I'll wait."

What should have taken Brooke a couple of minutes to finish, she managed to drag out for nearly half an hour. "Okay, I'm ready."

Agent Simpson rose. "You continue to test me, Doctor Jones. I'll remember that. Let's get going. It's a long drive."

"Where we going?"

"I can't tell you. You'll see. Get in the car."

They headed to the garage and climbed into the waiting sedan.

Brooke sat in the back with Grace seated beside her so it was a quiet ride the whole way. After a couple of hours, they arrived at a three story office building she surmised to be another FBI facility because of the security at the entrance. When she went inside, Brooke was led to a large room with a board table big enough to seat sixteen. She was delighted to see Robert, Jesse, and Mark. "Guys! How wonderful you're all here. Robert, how are you? Feeling better?"

"It's up and down, but seeing you changes everything."

She kissed him then turned to give Jesse a hug. "Thanks for coming."

Jesse smiled and pointed at Robert. "When he got the call he could see you, he was going to drive here himself. Somebody with a little more common sense needed to take charge, I volunteered."

She hugged Mark. "And you came, too. How nice."

"Hey, somebody had to be the official wheel chair pusher. Jesse nominated me. How could I refuse?"

She stepped back to take in all three then turned to Agent Simpson. "So what's the occasion? How come I get to see them?"

"It's just for a few hours, Doctor Jones. I don't want it said the FBI is holding you hostage. Enjoy your visit. I'll be in the next room until it's time to leave."

Brooke sat down, but not before observing the large mirror on one wall. "They're watching us, no doubt."

Mark moved in front of the mirror. "And listening, I'd bet, as well. Maybe this is the time to try out my standup comedy routine. After all, I've got a captive audience."

Brooke couldn't help but laugh. "You're the funniest guy there is. So how did the three of you convince the FBI to agree to this meeting?"

Jesse pulled up a chair. "I'd like to say it was us, but, truth be told,

215

Bart threatened to go to the press if they didn't cooperate. The public outcry would put them in so much hot water; they wouldn't be able to show themselves for decades."

"Good old Bart. But that's only good for today. What about from here on?"

Robert reached and took her hand. "I can visit once a week. That's what they told me. When are you going to be able to come home?"

She nodded toward the mirror. "Once that agent, Grace Simpson, says I can go, not before. I have to convince her I'm not a threat to anyone. I've got a feeling that isn't ever going to happen."

"Listen, for now, pretend they're not listening. Think back to that dinner we had at my house. You know the one where I made the lake trout in the wine and tomato sauce. It was just the two of us then. When we're together like that, it's like we're one person. As if you can read my mind and I yours." He gave a small nod as he said it.

Oh my god, he wants me to communicate with his mind. "Yes, that was a lovely night, wasn't it?" She focused on Robert. Would it work?

"Yes, it was." *Bart says he doesn't have the clout to get you released.*

"Maybe next time they'll let you bring dinner. If they only knew how good a cook you are." *If Bart can't get me out, then who can?*

"I only cook for friends. The rest of them will have to order take out." *You'll have to convince Grace. I've hired a lawyer, but he doesn't think he can do anything either.*

"Don't forget to bring the chardonnay." *I don't know if I can. The woman hates me with a passion. She thinks I'm the devil incarnate.*

"I was thinking a Pinot grigio. Something with a little snap to it." *You have to try. We'll keep working on our end. The media pressure* might work, but people forget the news quickly.

"You're the chef. I'll leave the choice to you." *I don't know what to do. They know I'm lying on all the tests they're giving me.*

"Grigio it is then." *From the sound of it, you're never getting out anyway, so what have you got to lose?*

She pulled her hand slowly free and sat back. Tears wanted to come, but she managed to hold them off. *If I try and fail, I'll lose everything, including you.*

CHAPTER 50

"Sammy, you better have a look at this."

He put down his drink and cigar. "What's the crisis, Jay babe?"

She handed him her comp pad. "Looks like your friend Nate's one step ahead of you."

He read about a Barnaby Moore found dead along with a David Smithson. Both men had been shot in the head. "Son of a bitch! That bastard knocked his own man off."

"What do we do now? Your approval rating has hit the basement. The scandals during your second term have made you untouchable by the big corporations."

He picked up his drink and drained it. It gave him time to think. A plan came to mind. "Get hold of the director of the FBI. We implicate Drummond, quick. I'll tell the story of how I heard of this Moore fellow at one of my visits with Nate. Get them to seize his records, pronto. Track the money. Once the squeeze is on, we'll renegotiate."

"Don't you think they'll have covered those tracks by now? I mean, they've gone so far as to have the man killed. I don't think they'd leave any loose ends as to money trails."

Sammy smiled and turned Janice toward the door. "It's not Drummond's money we need traced. It's Mr. Moore's. All we need is proof he was on the Drumdat payroll. Don't worry, we'll prove it. Now, go get the director for me and tell him what I just said."

She dashed out, and he refilled his drink. *You're not getting away from me that easy, Nate ol' boy. I'm coming to getcha.* Hoisting his cigar once more, he turned on the television to watch the news. A story like this would get a lot of coverage once it hit.

It didn't take long before it came up.

"There's been a new development in the abduction story involving astronaut Brooke Jones. In the early hours today, the bodies of two men were found, both victims of an apparent assassination. The men were identified as Barnaby Moore and David Smithson. Mr. Moore was a private investigator while Smithson was head of security at Drumdat Energy Corporation's head office. Our investigative reporter has learned the men were friends and former employees of the FBI. When questioned, the FBI gave us this response—"

The scene switched to the media room in Langley and the FBI press officer at the microphones. "For some time we've had our suspicions about the involvement of former agent Barnaby Moore in the Brooke Jones case. The participation of former agent David Smithson has added to that theory a connection to the Drumdat Energy Corporation who first discovered the special circumstances involving Doctor Jones' infection by the micro black hole. We believe Mr. Smithson provided Mr. Moore with the intel that eventually led to the kidnapping of Doctor Jones. Just this morning, the CEO of Drumdat, Mr. Alban Moceri, provided the FBI with evidence they had been collecting over the past few weeks to confirm that theory. Apparently, he was part of their investigation into the matter. Our efforts are now focused on finding the remaining member of this group, a Mr. Nick Barbosa. From information provided by the others detained so far it is known Mr. Barbosa had a falling out with the gang and was the one to kill Steve Williams when Miss Jones made her escape. Ballistics have determined the bullets were from the same gun."

The image reverted back to the lead reporter. "Just moments ago, a statement was released by Mr. Moceri from the Drumdat Corporation. It reads, 'It is with great disappointment we have learned of the implication of one of our most trusted employees in the plot to kidnap Miss Jones. As head of security, Mr. Smithson had privileged access to all Drumdat data systems. Our suspicions were confirmed that sensitive emails regarding the status of Miss Jones had been accessed, but it wasn't until the horrifying news we heard this morning that we were forced to face the fact one of our own was tied to the crime.' It sounds like all the pieces are accounted for, and for Brooke Jones, this unfortunate event is coming to an end."

Janice re-entered the room. "Sammy, I've got the FBI director on the line."

He turned the television off. "Tell him to forget it. They've run a reverse on me, and I got caught with my guard down."

"Why, what happened?"

He told her what was in the news report. "They're never going to find that last guy. He's probably dog food by now. My guess is they caught up with him, iced him, took his gun, and finished off Barnaby to make it look like an in-fight. With Drumdat providing assistance to the Bureau, there's no way any fingers are going to be pointing at them."

"What now? You're back to square one."

"Never count Sammy out, especially when the goal line is in sight."

"But you've played all your cards. You threatened Nate, and he outmaneuvered you. You've got nothing left to negotiate with."

"Not true. I still have that astronaut, Brooke Jones. He wants that thing inside her—bad."

"Yes, but how are you going to get it to him? The reports state there's no way to get it out of her. Not while she's alive. Any serious attempt would kill her."

"Yeah, but what would be the case if something bad happened to her, a bad accident, for example. If she died, we would be able to hand it over based on the contract we made where Drumdat got everything that came back from Mars in exchange of their funding the trip."

Janice scowled at him. "I don't like where this is going."

"This is not the time to be squeamish, Jay girl. You know everybody here who's assigned by the Secret Service to protect me. Figure out which one you think can pull it off."

"Sammy, I'm not comfortable doing this. This is going way beyond anything you've done before. I don't think I'm up to it."

He felt a rush of anger but quickly gained control of it. "Listen, you're in this with me up to your eyeballs. Now quit arguing and go make an accident happen."

She gave him a sidelong look then slipped out of the Oval Office. *She'll do it. It might take her time, but she'll do it.*

He found his cigar and noted it was out. He got a fresh one and lit up. *Nobody stops me from scoring. Nobody.*

CHAPTER 51

On the long ride back, Brooke sat wedged in the corner by the door, giving her a view of both the driver and Agent Simpson beside her. She folded her arms across her chest and put her most dour pout on her face in hopes of them understanding her displeasure at not being able to go home with Robert. Neither looked her way. *They're ignoring me. They couldn't care less. What is it going to take to convince these people to let me go?*

The agent seated in front of her was the only one who was polite and seemed to care. Maybe he was the answer. She decided to take a peek at the man's mind. Random thoughts filtered through. The fellow was not concentrating on anything, just watching the road and everything that passed by.

She had only ever read surface thoughts but something inside told her maybe now was the time to try and go deeper. She focused on the man. Things became cloudy. It was as if thoughts were whizzing past but too fast for her to catch or even have any notion as to what they might be about. Nothing made sense.

She pulled back. A moment of disorientation passed. *That was confusing. Maybe I'd better take a different approach.*

She went back in. This time, instead of trying to make sense of the man's decision process, she decided to concentrate on changing it, to plant in the passing thoughts one of her own as strong as she could. *I need to go pee.*

The man tilted his head and looked at the driver. "Hey, pull over at the next stop. I gotta go to the bathroom."

Oh my god! It worked!

The driver glanced at the other man quickly. "Just hold it. It'll give you big balls."

"Screw you. Pull over. I gotta go bad."

"Alright, alright, there's a gas station up at the end of the block."

They pulled into the station and the man dashed out.

Boy, did that ever work. I wonder what would have happened if the driver hadn't stopped? What should I try next?

The man returned and climbed in. The driver smirked. "Better?"

"Just drive."

She decided the poor fellow had suffered enough and concentrated on the driver. *I'm hungry.*

They drove another couple of blocks until they reached a McDonald's. The driver swerved across to the inner lane and pulled into the drive through. Agent Simpson, who had been busy with her comp pad, put it down. "What are you doing?"

"Sorry, I'm starving. Just going to grab a bite. Won't be long. Anybody want anything?"

This is fun. Brooke decided to take the driver up on his offer. "If you wouldn't mind, I'll take a burger."

The driver pulled up to the order speaker. "Right, a burger and three Big Macs for me, plus a large fries and a coke."

The fellow in the passenger seat chuckled. "Three Macs? You *must* be hungry. I've never seen you eat more than one before."

The driver pulled up to the next window to receive the food. "I've had two plenty of times. I'm just feeling extra hungry tonight."

He pulled into a parking space and passed the small burger to Brooke. As he devoured his food, she took a bite of her own sandwich and spotted Grace eyeing her. *Maybe that's enough for now.* "Thanks for the burg."

It had been a week since her visit with Robert, and this time Brooke had practiced to be ready. During the past six days, she had worked on those around her, testing the limits of her skill, implanting thoughts into their minds.

The simple ones that dealt with basic human needs were easy. Just like on that day when she convinced the two shadows they needed to urinate and eat, commands like needing sleep, yawning, standing, sitting...all were achieved without difficulty.

But when she tried to be more constructive, to get someone to go get her something, go do something, believe in something, these were harder to attain with often mixed results. She tried to reason out why and figured the difference was people's memories. Attitudes were a result of a lifetime of collective actions that created them. Her onetime command was not enough to override such a conglomeration.

That morning, one thing had changed. She had a new second shadow. The one she instilled the hunger thought in was missing. When she asked, Brooke was told "Vacation time."

Throughout the trip, she focused on Agent Simpson. Rather than sending a straight command of *let her go*, Brooke found her best success was subtlety. She would pass on ideas that she was a nice person and deserving of better treatment. She sent ideas of how being locked up was hard on her, anything she could think of that would grease the wheels when the time came to try for freedom.

They arrived at the location where Brooke had been reunited with Robert before. The large chafing dish visible when she entered the room and the settings on the table along with the wine glasses told her

224

Robert had brought something special. She hugged and kissed him. "Robert, you shouldn't have."

"Are you kidding? After I described the meal, both Jesse and Mark here were after me to make sure I brought enough for them as well."

Mark grabbed a knife in one fist and a fork in the other then pounded the table in true caveman fashion. "And I'm ready to eat."

There were enough settings for Agent Simpson and her two cohorts as well. "Looks like you planned for everyone."

She sat and Robert motioned to the FBI people. "Sit. I made plenty. Let's enjoy a friendly meal."

The two men looked to Agent Simpson, who nodded and sat. "Thank you for this. It is unexpected."

"It's my hope you'll understand how fond my fellow astronauts and I are of Brooke and how dearly we would like her to come home."

"I'm still undecided on that. But I must admit, I've been having some misgivings lately as to maintaining her protective custody. I can see how much she means to you. You may find this hard to believe, but I have a husband at home who would miss me just as much." She lifted the lid of the chafing dish. "In the meantime, this smells absolutely delightful. Can we start?"

Robert and the others laughed. He waved his hand in Agent Simpson's direction. "Be my guest."

As the dinner was served, Brooke glanced at everyone digging in. It lifted her hopes to see Agent Simpson actually smiling, something missing from the woman's demeanor since Brooke had met her.

Glad faces were all around except for one, at the far end of the table. The new guy. She concentrated to try and catch the man's surface thoughts.

I need to act. If Grace lets her go, everything is screwed.

Act? What does he need to do?

She focused again.

This is going to be tricky. Lots of people here. Is it best to shoot Grace and the other FBI guy first? Or the woman?

Oh my god! What do I do?

She could sense the man reaching for his gun. She placed both hands on the edge of the table and shoved with all her might. To cries of dismay from everyone else gathered, food, plates, and stemware went flying everywhere but the table did what she wanted and rammed into the man just as he was pulling his gun above the table top. He managed to fire a couple of shots before he flew into the far wall. She felt a sting in her left shoulder. As the shooter collapsed, the table caught him at head level. The sickening thud was enough to tell Brooke the man had been severely hurt.

At a groan from beside her, Brooke spun around to find Robert on the floor, a bullet wound in his chest. Blood was flooding his shirt. "Robert!"

She dropped to her knees and lifted his head. His eyes rolled then focused on her. "What happened?"

"You've been shot. We've got to get you to the hospital."

Jesse and Mark dropped to their knees beside her. Jesse whipped out his cell and called 9-1-1. Mark straightened Robert out on the floor. "Boy, if he hated your cooking that bad, he should have ordered a pizza."

Jesse was pressing down on the wound. "Can it, Mark. This is no time for jokes. He's hemorrhaging badly. I don't know if I can save him."

Robert managed a weak smile then coughed up some blood. He

grasped Brooke's wrist. "I'll be...okay. I'm sorry...the meal...was spoiled."

She grabbed hold of his hand with both of hers. *Please, God, don't let him die.* "Never mind that. Just lie still until the medics get here."

She glanced over to where the shooter lay to make sure the man was still down. Agent Simpson was by him and when their eyes met, she shook her head.

"He's dead. His skull is crushed. Now I won't know what the hell he was up to."

"It's pretty obvious. He was trying to kill me."

Agent Simpson stared back, tight lipped.

Brooke returned her attention to Robert. His eyes were unfocused. "Stay with me. Stay with me!"

She felt the muscles in his hand relax. *Oh no!*

Jesse began to pump Robert's chest. "Come on, buddy. Stay alive. The paramedics will be here any minute."

Jesse continued working but nothing was happening. Brooke let go of Robert's hand and leaned closer to his ear. *This can't be happening. Not after he's been through so much.* "Robert, come back to me, please, come back."

Sirens announced the arrival of the ambulance. Jesse was doing whatever doctors do until the paramedics came and replaced him. The lead paramedic tried shocking him back but it was no use. He shook his head. "I'm sorry, he's gone."

Brooke clapped her hands to her face and cried. "No! It's not fair. That bullet was meant for me, not him."

The paramedic was looking at her shoulder. "What happened to you? Did you also get shot?"

Brooke glanced to where she had felt the sting. The clothing was ripped, and a small stain of blood tinged the tear. She pulled the fabric farther open. "It's just a small cut, nothing to worry about."

"Okay, get a bandage on it. I've got to go." He handed her one.

She glanced down at the cut again. It wasn't bleeding anymore and already looked better. It was then she noticed the spent bullet on the floor. *It didn't kill me.*

As they hoisted Robert onto the gurney and wheeled him out, Brooke found Agent Simpson beside her. "I think...I think you'd better go. I'm going to release you."

Tears came again as Brooke turned and gave the smaller woman a hug. "Find out why this happened."

She dashed off and jumped in the car with Jesse and Mark.

Agent Simpson followed her out of the building. "I will. I promise."

Brooke sat in the back, tears rolling down her face. The world was much lonelier now.

CHAPTER 52

The house was her only haven of peace. News of Robert's death and her attempted murder at the hands of an FBI agent had doubled the number of reporters looking to hear her story. They camped out front, waiting for her make an exit. NASA security people were making sure none of them crossed onto her property.

When Jesse's car pulled in the drive and Bart got out of the passenger side, she wondered what was going on. She beat them to the door and opened it. "Hi Jesse. Hi Bart. It's nice to see you. Come on in."

Jesse was very tight lipped. Bart looked sheepish. They said their greetings in a hushed manner as they entered.

It was late enough in the day. "Can I get either of you a drink? I think I'm going to have one. I'd appreciate the company."

Jesse nodded. "I'll have whatever you're having."

"Gin martini's. Bart, what about you?"

He craned his neck to look over her shoulder toward the kitchen. "You have any beer?"

"I think I've got a few bottles stashed in the back of the fridge. Let me get you one."

She returned with the drinks and joined the two men at the table. Jesse took a sip. "Whew! Strong!"

She sniffed hers and switched glasses. "Sorry Jesse. I got them mixed up. I need to make mine that way nowadays. The thing in my head is keeping me so healthy; it's hard to get a buzz on. So what brings the two of you out today?"

Jesse turned to look to Bart who was busy having a taste of his beer. "Ah, that's good. Thanks. Here's the story. Let me put it straight. They want you off planet, Brooke."

She looked back and forth to read their faces. Was he serious? "Who's they?"

"The president. He doesn't think it's safe while that micro black hole is still inside your head. He thinks it's best, until they come up with a way to get it out of you. He said something about not wanting you falling into the wrong hands in the meantime."

"But what if they don't figure it out?"

"He said we'll deal with that problem then."

"Off planet? Just where do they expect me to go? Back to Mars?"

Jesse leaned in. "No, Brooke. You'd be with me in the next rotation at Moon Base Alpha. It's for six months and while we're there, we're going to dedicate the base to Robert. You'll be the one doing the dedication."

She took a sip of her drink. "The moon? Six months?" She leaned back to give it some thought. Robert would think it was the right thing to do. "Alright, I'll go."

Bart finished his beer and stood. "It's decided then. The shuttle doesn't leave for a couple of months so keep this under your hat. We don't want the media knowing. Come on, Jesse, let's go. We've got work to do."

Jesses put down his drink and gave Brooke a kiss on the cheek. "It'll be okay. I promise."

"I'll hold you to it."

***

Bart sat drumming a pencil as he waited for everyone to arrive.

The boardroom filled up. When everyone was seated, he cleared his throat to gather their attention. "Thank you all for coming. This briefing is about the next team to be shuttled to Moon Base Alpha. As you are all aware, astronaut Jesse Cain will be in charge of this mission."

Jesse waved a hand in acknowledgement of the short round of applause that followed.

"There will be a change, though, in the science officer. I have decided to send Brooke Jones as a replacement."

A murmur rippled through the room. He waited for it to settle before continuing. "I want everyone to understand the circumstances that have led to this decision. First of all, the president of the United States has requested it in the interests of national security. If it wasn't for the upcoming national election, I suspect I would have been replaced as NASA Administrator by now. Aki, would you be kind enough to update everyone on this."

Aki rose from his chair. "Yes sir. As many of you know already, we made an attempt in the past to remove the black hole, with disastrous results. Not including the damage to the machinery, the short EMP she emitted did indeed include gamma rays. No one received a harmful dosage but there's no telling what might happen the second time around. I've been in touch with the FBI and their scientific appointee, Agent Paul Sweetman. The surprising result, which I have since had a chance to confirm, is an increase in the intensity and field of effect of the hole. In short, any future attempts to dislodge it will be at the risk of a higher intensity pulse."

"Thank you Aki. Doctor, now might be the time for you to update us on Doctor Jones' physical condition."

Aki sat and the doctor took his place as the center of attention.

"I've been monitoring Brooke continually since her return from Mars. Hers is an amazing story. Not only is she in perfect fitness, but her strengths have continued to improve as time goes by. She runs the mile like an athlete would run the hundred-yard dash. I don't even have enough weights on my machines to determine her upper limit. Her bone mass has become very dense and her musculature as well. Though still the same size, she has gained almost a hundred and fifty pounds. It takes considerable pressure to get a needle into her arm to retrieve a blood sample. I dare say, she's almost indestructible."

The doctor sat as a number of people started to ask questions. Bart held his hands up to get everyone to wait. "Listen, there's more. The Drumdat Corporation is still after us as well, claiming ownership of the micro black hole pursuant to their contract for funding the Mars mission. And get this, the army has contacted us. They want to study Brooke and see if the condition can be recreated in others to create super soldiers. I don't know how they know so much, but finding that leak is a different issue and not why we're here today. The big problem is public opinion. This must be kept quiet.

"At this time, unless there are any serious objections, this meeting is adjourned. I expect each and every one of you to get to work and make the necessary adjustments in your departments to accommodate this change. I also expect no one to breathe a word about this to anyone. That will be all."

Bart heard a couple of grumblings but no one challenged his decision. *Now I won't have anything to worry about until she's due to come back.*

***

Nate read in the news that astronaut Brooke Jones was on her way to the moon. Good riddance. *It's probably for the best she's gone.*

The intercom at his desk rang. "Mr. Drummond, your new chief of security is here."

"Send her in."

The woman who walked in surprise him with her small stature. He was expecting someone who would appear more formidable, as David did. "Good morning, Mr. Drummond. I'm reporting for duty."

She's awful small for a security head. He rose to greet her. "Yes, welcome. Sarah Cooper, isn't it? Glad to have you aboard. I'm told you're the best we have."

"David was, sir. I'll try my best to fill his shoes. He taught me everything I know. He was a good friend."

"A shame what happened to him. I guess he got mixed up with the wrong crowd. But I have high hopes for you." *Let's hope he didn't teach her how to drink.*

CHAPTER 53

Brooke walked beside the sifter, using the hand-held remote to steer it across the lunar landscape. The thing crawled at an incredibly slow speed but it still needed watching. There were cameras that would allow her to control it from inside Moon Base Alpha, but it always managed to get snagged on a rock or tilted, requiring someone to come out and manually correct it. She found it easier to simply walk along and keep an eye out for any protrusions under the regolith.

A green light flashed on her console, and the machine stopped moving. Brooke opened a panel in the sifter, disconnected a compression tube, and replaced it with an empty one. She hefted the full canister as the sifter started its crawl once more. *It's amazing. This small amount of Helium 3 is worth millions. To think, the crawler spits out almost three of these a day.*

She stowed the tube in a compartment attached to her suit. Her helmet communicator crackled to life. "Hey, Brooke, how's it going out there?"

"Hi Jesse, just changed the containment unit. I'll be bringing it in soon. Whoever's next on the monitor to steer this thing, tell them to be ready. I'll be switching control back to base in a moment."

"Already on it. Come on in and get your beauty rest. The big dedication is tomorrow."

The renaming of the base in honor of Robert. Brooke hadn't forgotten. She had been trying to keep herself busy so she wouldn't have to think about it. "I know. I only wish it was not because he is dead."

"I miss him, too. Oh, that reminds me. You've had a call while

234

you've been out there. It's that FBI woman, Grace Simpson."

She hit the switch killing the remote control. "I'm on my way in."

It took some time for her to get out of her space suit. *I wonder what Grace wants? If she's thinking she's going to put me back under protective custody when I get back, she's dreaming.*

A quick glance in the mirror confirmed she had helmet head. Brooke decided to take a shower and look refreshed when returning the call.

The shower was a recent installment at Moon Base Alpha. It had taken the complaints of a number of previous female astronauts to get it installed. She mentally thanked each and every one of them as the warm water washed over her. It calmed her, something Brooke needed before facing her old nemesis.

Dressed and ready, she sat before the monitor and sent out the connection request to the FBI agent's vid phone.

"Agent Simpson here."

"Hello, Grace. I got your message."

"Brooke, I'm fulfilling a promise as best I can. The agent who took a pot shot at you and inadvertently killed Mr. Tangler was previously assigned to protect the president. The orders to move him to my department were a result of a request from Janice Roberts, the president's chief of staff. When I tried to determine why the transfer occurred, I was stonewalled, both by my superiors and by Miss Roberts."

"Since the election, with a new president, there's a new FBI director. I had the opportunity to chat with him one-on-one at his swearing in party. I told him the story and he promised to look into it. He got back to me yesterday. He didn't tell me much but he did say one thing that had me thinking. Apparently Miss Roberts was most adamant

235

that the agent be your bodyguard. Her reasoning was the president wanted the man on the case. As it was a direct order from the commander in chief, they didn't want to say no. There's nothing else to be found out. President Davidson is out of office and with him, his chief of staff. I'm told that the file is to be considered closed and not to pursue it any further."

Brooke paused to take in everything she had just been told. "So why would the president or his chief of staff want me killed?"

"First of all, we don't know that's the case, but it is a possibility. Your guess is as good as mine. I do know that President Davidson has a close relationship with Drumdat Energy Corp. owner Nate Drummond. I read that the kidnappers had a connection with the chief of security at Drumdat, but he's dead as well, so that trail is cold, too. In the meantime, I've had a very interesting conversation with the current chief of security, a Sarah Cooper. She has provided some very interesting information to us that we are currently investigating."

"Thank you, Grace. I'll give the matter some thought."

"Good luck to you, Brooke. We won't be talking again."

She joined everyone in the common room for lunch. Try as she might, her appetite wasn't up to eating. She retired to her room and spent the afternoon searching through the Internet for answers.

A knock on the door broke her from her task. "Yes?"

"Brooke, you coming out? The dedication is in an hour. You still need to get suited. It's going to be a live feed but I don't think any of the major networks are picking it up."

"Sorry Jesse. I'll be out in a minute. I'm putting on some make-up."

"Okay, look your best. See you out there."

She shut down her comp pad and hurried to apply some lipstick and mascara. *I haven't used any since I've been here. For that matter, since Robert died. I miss you, Robert.*

She stepped out and headed for the airlock, where everyone was getting into their space suits. It took most of the crew fifteen minutes or more to put on their suits. Brooke was able to lift the heavy chest unit over her head and drop it on. She finished first and waited by the door.

They stepped out into the bright day. Brooke noted the camera already set up. The cloth-draped plaque rested on a stand about ten feet from the entrance. She had helped dig in the base some days before but she had yet to see the actual plaque. *I hope it's fitting.*

Jesse was calling for everyone's attention. "Brooke, move to the outside of the plaque, away from the building. That way it's between you and the building, like it's greeting you. Everyone else, over the other way. I'll be doing the intro. After the unveiling, we'll all meet in front of it for a photo op."

As everyone milled about, getting into place Brooke contemplated what Grace Simpson had told her. *I need to know why it happened. I need to know why Robert was killed.*

Jesse spoke toward the camera, but his words sounded garbled to her. She wasn't really paying that much attention but when he turned and looked at her, she knew her lines. She reached out to grasp the covering. "In memory of astronaut Captain Robert Tangler, we do hereby dedicate this base in your honor. May it forever be a testament to the effort and fortitude you devoted to establishing it."

She pulled the sheath away to see the plaque with an image of Robert sculpted in brass above the words THE MOON IS MY SISTER. IN HER CARE, I WILL NOT FALTER. A cheer went up, and they all converged on her.

Brooke had promised herself not to cry. Not on television. But the bronze image was more than she could stand. She backed away as the others neared. *I've got to find the answer to Robert's death.*

She continued to back away, and Jesse waved to her. "Brooke, come closer. We need you in the photo."

"I...I can't. I've got to go home. I *must* go."

"Go? Come on, let's get this over with, then you can go inside." He started toward her then stopped. "Brooke, what's going on? What's happening?"

Her vision was clouding, like someone pulling a dark veil over it with the veil growing ever darker. She held out a hand in warning for Jesse to stay back. "I must go!"

Everything went black.

CHAPTER 54

Bart had sat with a number of his senior staff in the conference room watching the proceedings from the moon along. He leapt to his feet and pointed at the screen. "What in heaven's name just happened? Can someone please tell me what the hell just happened? What in God's name did I just see?"

Bruce and Aki, to his left, engaged in a heated discussion. "Bruce? You have an opinion?"

Bruce stopped his debate and faced Bart. "Not me, but Aki here has a theory. I think it's crazy."

"Aki then, come on, let's hear it."

Aki stood up and gave a quick glance at everyone gathered before returning his attention to Bart. "She wormholed."

"She what?"

"Wormholed...teleported...whatever. She created a wormhole and went through it. It's a passage through the fabric of the universe. She could be...anywhere. This is incredibly exciting! Think of the possibilities."

"Yeah, I know what a wormhole is. Let's not get all googly over this. Is that even possible?"

Aki pointed at the screen. "Until today, I would have had my doubts, but see for yourself. There's the evidence. She did it."

Bruce also indicated the screen with a nod of his head. "By the way, it's still live. Maybe you should do something about that."

Bart looked back at it. Everyone was milling around, circling the spot where Brooke had been. But not getting too close. "You're right. Quick, somebody call down and kill the online feed to the media.

While you're at it, hook me up to Jesse Cain. I want a firsthand report of what's happening there."

After a few seconds passed, Jesse looked back at the camera. "I'm here, Bart. I don't know what to tell you. I was looking at her when the whole thing happened. She backed away from the group and then this large, dark globe enveloped her. Up until it went totally black, I could still make her out inside the sphere. Then it flashed intensely bright for the quickest of instants, and she and the sphere were gone."

"What is everybody looking at?"

Jesse looked over his shoulder at the others gathered where Brooke had been. "The ground. A circle of it is gone. It looks like a crater. Here, I'll show you."

Jesse stepped forward and pulled the camera free of its stand. The view moved toward the group who stepped aside to reveal a perfect circular hole shaped like a bowl. "It's about two feet deep in the middle and maybe six or seven feet wide."

"Get an exact measurement on that then report back to me. In the meantime, get everybody away from it. What if she was to suddenly pop back?"

"Will do." Jesse began to guide everyone away from the new crater.

Bart was still shocked. In his pocket, his phone was notifying him of requested vid connections. He called his receptionist. "I don't have time to talk to anyone right now. I've got to figure out this mess. Take all my calls and tell them I'll get back to them after I've had a chance to get some answers."

He signaled to Bruce and Aki. "You two with me. Let's go to my office. We need to discuss what we do from here."

Bart walked as quickly as he could despite the soreness of his bad back. As he entered the lobby, the receptionist gestured to him to hold up. "Administrator, an important call for you...."

"I told you, no calls right now."

"But, sir, it's the president."

He sighed. "Very well, put it through to my desk."

He sat down just as the vid screen came to life. Bruce and Aki followed him in and took the two chairs across from him. "Yes, President Pallabee. I know why you're calling. We are looking into the matter as we speak. I'm sitting with two of my top scientists right now, working on the problem."

"Bartholomew, this is a most unpleasant development. My predecessor seemed to be ambivalent about this woman, looking to buy her freedom one minute, arresting her, the next. In the end, he acceded to this temporary banishment, which left the ball in my court when his term of office expired. There are those of importance who are calling her an abomination and want her dealt with as all abominations are dealt with, if you get my meaning. Resolve this thing quickly, or I shall have to resolve it for you."

The screen went dark. He looked over at his two guests. "You heard the man. He wants this dealt with, pronto. Huh. Bartholomew. The last person to call me that name was my father, and that was forty years ago, when I was a child. I don't know who I like less. The old president, who called me Higgy, or this one who talks to me like a preacher. I wonder what it takes to get someone *normal* elected to office once in a while."

Aki chuckled, but Bruce sat stone faced. "What do you want us to do?"

Bart grabbed a pencil and started tapping on his desk. "First of all, I want to know for sure what happened, make sure this wormhole theory of yours is correct. Second, I want you to find astronaut Jones."

"How are we supposed to do that?"

"Isn't there some kind of energy trail you can trace? Some vector you can follow?"

Bruce chuckled. "I think you've been hanging with Francis from Drumdat too much, and watching old movies. If Aki is correct and it was a wormhole, there's no telling where she went."

He changed his focus to the younger man. "Aki, is this correct?"

"Uh, yes, sir. Absolutely. Bruce is one-hundred percent correct. Wormholes shortcut through space. Miss Jones could be anywhere, from the farthest reaches of the universe to the next room!"

"Fine. Get to work on your theory. I'll get the Feds to start a man…or in this case, woman hunt." Bart resisted the temptation to get up and look next door.

CHAPTER 55

Brooke knew *where* she was. She was still trying to figure out *why*.

She stood in the bedroom of her own house. Beneath her feet, a mound of moon regolith in the shape of a circle.

She struggled out of the spacesuit. With normal Earth gravity, it was much heavier. Since she was in her own home she picked out some comfortable clothes from her closet and got changed.

When she stepped into the living room, she caught her breath in surprise. Someone was sleeping on the couch. After catching her breath, she noticed the young man wore a NASA security outfit. She went over and gave him a gentle nudge. His eyes opened, and he jumped up. "Huh, what, uh, who are you?"

"I'm Brooke Jones. This is my house. The question should be who are you, and why are you sleeping on my sofa?"

"Oh, Doctor Jones. I thought you weren't supposed to be back for a couple of months. My apologies. I'm on night watch guarding your house. I figured I'd catch a few Zs before starting my shift. Since you've been gone, there've already been three break-in attempts. Headquarters decided it made a lot more sense to post someone inside." He held out his hand. "I'm Ben, by the way. I just started last month. You're not going to tell on me, are you?"

She held back a chuckle. She didn't want to embarrass him. "No, Ben, I'm not. And yes, you're correct. I'm not due back for a couple of months, so let's keep it our secret for now, shall we?"

He blinked several times and she smiled at his confusion. "Listen, I'm going into the kitchen to make coffee. Would you like one?"

"Um, yes, that sounds good. Cream and sugar."

"Do me a favor then, and turn on the television. Find the news. I want to know what's going on."

As Brooke made coffee, the sound of the different stations as Ben searched through carried to her. When the channel surfing stopped, the voice of a newscaster reporting on the stock market took over. She finished the coffees and brought them out. Ben was perched on the edge of a chair. She handed him his and took the sofa.

It didn't take long for the coverage to switch to what she wanted to see.

"It seems it's never a lot of time before there is something new to report about astronaut Brooke Jones. Only this time, it's gotten a lot weirder. What you're about to see is coverage from this morning's dedication of Moon Base Alpha in honor of Captain Robert Tangler, the first man on the moon since Apollo. Doctor Jones was doing the unveiling when things went strange."

The image cut to the ceremony. There she was, pulling the cover off the plaque, stepping backward and then being enveloped in a black sphere and vanishing. The camera focused on the spot she vanished with Jesse reporting then it went back to the anchor. We have yet to receive an official response from NASA as to what just happened but rumor has it they believe Doctor Jones created a wormhole and passed through it. To where, only heaven knows."

So that's what happened. I only remember this incredible desire to be at home.

She turned to look at Ben, who was staring at her, the coffee cup frozen midair. "Doctor Jones? What am I supposed to do now?"

She got up and patted his hand holding the cup. "Finish your coffee then go get NASA Administrator Bartholomew Higginbottom.

Don't talk to anyone else. Just go directly to him."

The young man gulped his coffee then dashed out the door.

She turned off the television. *I need to know if I can do it again. But what about that pile of moon dirt? If that came with me, I'd better not try it here in the house.*

Brooke went out into the backyard. She stood in the middle and concentrated. It came quicker this time. The blackness enclosed her and she next found herself back in her living room. This time there was a mound of grass from her back yard. *My own pitching mound. This won't do. I'm going to have to try and focus it so it's only me.*

She spent a couple of minutes and used her telekinesis to move the sod and dirt to repair the giant divot she had made. Standing on it once again, she made another attempt. As the sphere began to form, she willed it in close to her body. It worked. Once more she found herself in the same spot in the living room but this time only the tops of the grass that had been beneath her feet accompanied her. *I can live with that. The lawn needed cutting anyway.*

Feeling empowered, she grabbed her comp pad. "Now to find that Janice Roberts and get to the root of why Robert died." She located the woman's address. Concentrating, she tried to wormhole her way there. Nothing happened. *Hmm, I think I can only go where I can visualize. The woman is in Washington. I've been there plenty of times, including the White House. There's a great hot dog stand I've been to right downtown near this address.*

The sound of a car pulling into the drive brought her to the window. Ben was back with the head of security at NASA and Bart and Mark.

She opened the door and the four rushed in with Bart in the lead. "Brooke, what in heaven's name is going on? Why are you here? How are you here?"

"Relax Bart. That ticker of yours won't handle the stress. I'm home to get Robert's killer, end of story."

"Robert's killer? I thought the FBI agent who did it was dead. Killed by you, if I'm not mistaken."

"He was a lackey. I want whoever sent him."

"Brooke, the president wants me to take you in. I'll back you all the way, but you have to come with me."

"I don't think so. At least not until I've done what I've come to do. You can tell him that. Stand back."

"Why? What are you going to do?"

"I'm leaving. This is for Robert. Take care, Bart."

She focused and the black envelope came quickly. Before it went completely black, she had enough time to wave good-bye.

Mark waved back. "Looking good, girl!"

CHAPTER 56

When the blackness evaporated, Brooke found herself in front of the hot dog stand. It was still morning and there wasn't anyone near except the guy manning the stand. He held a number of dogs in one hand while the other was poised over the grill with a single one. His face was frozen in a look of surprise.

She chuckled. "Well, don't just stand there gawking. Get those dogs on. I'm hungry."

The fellow gave his head a shake and blinked several times. "Wha...wha...where did you come from?"

"My house, but before that, the moon. I'll take three dogs—loaded."

The guy looked to his left and right then returned his attention to the grill and put on the rest of the dogs in his hand. "Uh, it'll be a minute. Um, are you sure you want three dogs?"

"Absolutely. You've got the best dogs in the country. I'm in a hurry, so I'd appreciate if you'd focus on the food."

"Yeah, yeah, sure, right away."

Brooke glanced up and down the sidewalk. A few people across the street were staring and pointing. Obviously her arrival had not gone unnoticed but she didn't care. She was feeling empowered. She had a mission, and nothing was going to stop her. She waved at the people across the way who moved off while casting backward glances at her.

"Miss, your dogs are ready."

"Thanks." She paid the man and found a nearby bench to sit and enjoy her meal. As she polished off the last one, she stood just in time to flag down a cab. Jumping in, she gave the driver Janice Roberts' address.

It didn't take the cabbie long to get to the condominium tower a handful of blocks away. As she stepped out of the vehicle, Brooke scanned the outside of the building. She counted the stories, twenty in all, and noted the darkening sky. In the twilight, the moon glowed low on the horizon. *Hey, Jesse, do you miss me?*

At the security entrance, a guard opened the door for her. "Evening, miss. Who you looking for?"

"Good evening. I'm here to see Janice Roberts."

The guard stepped behind his desk to look at his comp pad. "Hmm, I'm sorry, miss. I don't have any scheduled visits for Miss Roberts. I'll have to check. Who should I say is calling?"

She stepped up to the desk. "Tell her it's Brooke Jones."

The guard's eyes went wide. "Hold on."

He hit a key on his comp pad and the face of a young black woman appeared. "Yes?"

"I'm sorry to bother you, Miss Roberts. There's a Brooke Jones here to see you. Shall I send her up?"

"No, don't send her. Haven't you seen the news? Call the police." The screen went black.

Brooke had made out the room behind Janice Roberts. She stepped back from the desk as the guard did as he was instructed and hit 9-1-1. "Never mind. I'll let myself up."

She concentrated, the black veil returned, and a moment later cleared to have Brooke find herself in the room she saw on the vid. She glanced around. *Where's the woman? Did she bolt in those few seconds it took me to get up here?*

A sound of a toilet flushing told her otherwise. The woman came out of the bathroom and, froze. "How'd you get in here? Get out, or I'll call the police!"

Brooke closed the gap, grabbed the woman by the front of her blouse, and lifted her in the air. "That doesn't matter. What does is you're going to tell me why you tried to have me killed, shooting my fiancé in the process." The woman struggled with both hands but Brooke held firm.

Her struggles ceased and she glared. "I don't know what you're talking about. Let me go."

The denial angered her. She tossed the woman onto the nearby sofa like a rag doll. "Yes you do, or so help me, I'm going to break every bone in your body."

Righting herself, the woman cringed into a corner of the sofa as Brooke move d in front of her. "I don't know anything. I don't. Really."

"Liar!" Brooke grabbed the woman below the chin and held her firm. She concentrated and entered the woman's mind. *I'll find the truth.*

As before, the thoughts blurred past. This time she intended to be as forceful as possible in the planting of her own thoughts. *Think of the attempt on my life by the FBI man you sent. Why did you do it? Why did you want me dead?*

The thoughts coalesced in the woman's mind. Brooke learned of the plan to bribe Nate Drummond with the micro black hole. She saw the Secret Service man as he was told to kill Brooke at all costs. And most importantly, she saw President Davidson telling the woman to get it done.

Her anger had a new target. But she wasn't finished with this one. *You will call Grace Simpson at the FBI and tell her absolutely everything. You will do this on fear of your life if you don't. You will do it right away.*

There began a banging at the door. "Miss Roberts, it's security. The police are on their way. Can you hear me?"

She let Janice Roberts drop. "Do what I told you. Call Grace."

"I...I will. But it won't do any good. He's an ex-president. There's no paper trail. No one will take my word over his."

She could make out the distinct sound of a key entering the lock. The man was going to come in. "Then I'll make him tell."

She summoned the black veil once more.

CHAPTER 57

Nate wasn't feeling well. He looked at the glass of water in his hand with disdain. The doctor had just been there and this time he had issued a very stern warning. No more cigars. No more alcohol.

Alban had joined him for their daily confab and agreed not to partake of any scotch as well. "Did you see the news this morning? It seems that Jones woman is popping in and out of the place all over the country."

"Yeah, I saw it. They ought to arrest that woman. She's a menace."

Alban chuckled. "They would, if they could. Apparently there's a nationwide warrant and manhunt for her. But every time there's a sighting, poof, she's gone.

Alban continued to chuckle and it was irking Nate. "What's so damned funny?"

"Oh, I was just thinking, if you had managed to get that thing out of her head, it would be you doing the poofing all around the country."

Despite his foul mood, Nate smiled. Alban had raised his spirits if not his health. "Yes, that would have been funny, wouldn't it?" He rose from behind his desk and made for the bar. "Come on, one scotch each. Just one. I'll be good tomorrow."

"Whatever you say. You're the boss."

He opened the bar and retrieved his favorite brand. After he poured liberal portions for him and Alban, they relaxed in the large wingbacks. No sooner did he get comfortable than his receptionist buzzed him. "What is it? You know I'm in my regular meeting."

"I'm sorry to disturb you, Mr. Drummond. But this is quite

251

urgent. The FBI is here to see you."

"The FBI? What do they want?"

"They say it's personal."

"Oh, alright, send them in."

Nate rose to greet the woman who led the charge of half-a-dozen agents into his office. "What is the meaning of this?"

The woman declined to shake his hand. "Nate Drummond, my name is Agent Grace Simpson. I am here to arrest you on behalf of the US government. You have the right to remain silent. Anything you say or do can and will be held against you in a court of law. You have the right to an attorney. If you cannot afford an attorney, one will be provided for you. Do you understand these rights I have just read to you?"

"What is this, some kind of joke? What's the charge?"

"The list is long, Mr. Drummond. You have been found complicit in the murder of Barnaby Moore and David Smithson. You have been found complicit in the kidnapping of astronaut Brooke Jones. You have engaged in business with organized crime. There are a number of lesser charges, but these will do for now."

Alban had risen as well and sidled away. "I'll go call your lawyer."

Grace Simpson signaled to the men by the door, and they stopped Alban from exiting. "Alban Moceri, I have a warrant for your arrest as well."

Nate couldn't take it any more and lost his temper. "This is preposterous! These charges are outlandish. You have no proof. Wait until I get President Pallabee on the phone. You'll all be out of a job."

"President Pallabee is aware of these proceedings and has endorsed our actions." The woman motioned two of the men forward.

"Handcuff them both."

As they began to put the cuffs on, panic rose in him. 'You can't do this. What about the company? Who's going to run things?"

"We are seizing Drumdat Energy Corporation and all its assets. It is against the law to profit from illegal activity. The funding you received from the mob way back when makes anything after the fact illegally gained."

"This is impossible. Alban, you're a lawyer. Say something."

Alban hung his head. "I'm sorry, Nate. This is beyond me. I can't say anything as I'm charged as well. We'll have our day in court, rest assured."

His hands firmly locked in place behind his back, Nate shrugged off the agent holding onto his arm. "I'm not going anywhere. You can't take my company. I built it. It's mine. You get these cuffs off me now. I'm not going–" A sharp pain raced through his chest. He couldn't breathe. He wanted to claw at his throat but his hands were immobilized. His vision blurred. His left leg gave way. He crumpled toward the floor. Blackness came.

***

"Someone call 9-1-1, quickly." Grace knelt and felt for a pulse. Nothing.

In a couple of minutes, a man entered, accompanied by a woman dressed in a Drumdat security outfit. "Make way. This man is Mr. Drummond's personal doctor. He was still in the building when I heard the news."

The doctor knelt next to the prone form and began CPR. After a few attempts, he checked for any signs and shook his head. "There's nothing I can do. It was probably a massive stroke. He died almost instantly."

The security woman helped the doctor to his feet. "What's going on here? Why is Mr. Drummond in handcuffs?"

Grace motioned to the agent who had put them on. "Take them off. My apologies. Mr. Drummond was in the process of being arrested. We had no idea his condition was such that this would happen."

"I'm head of security here. Why wasn't I notified of your coming?"

Grace recognized the woman as Sarah Cooper, her informant. "It's not our business to warn perpetrators of our arrival. After we clear this up, I'd appreciate a few words with you in private."

The paramedics arrived, and the doctor informed them of the situation. They wheeled Nate Drummond out. Grace had the rest of her agents head back to headquarters, taking Moceri with them.

Alone with Sarah, she offered a handshake. "I want to thank you for the information. Your identity, of course, will be protected under the whistle blowing act. It was an amazing piece of investigation on your part to obtain those records."

"I didn't do it. My predecessor did. It was in his personal files. He had collected that information a long time ago. I was surprised he still had it."

"Hmm, I wonder why he never reported it then."

"David was a long time employee of Nate Drummond. He couldn't turn in the boss who had saved his career. He was a devotedly loyal man."

"I see. Then why did you turn it in? Not as devout?"

"Actually, I am. I take my job very seriously. But when David was killed, I had my suspicions. When I took over as head of security I discovered the ten million Nate had paid to Barnaby. I have a forensic auditor at my disposal to ensure against in-house stealing. He found the questionable money transfer and reported it to me. Knowing of Mr. Moceri's connection to organized crime, it didn't take a lot of math to add up what had happened. I accessed Mr. Drummond's and Mr. Moceri's private phone messages and discovered the plot to have Barnaby killed. They used David and then killed him. He was my friend. I wasn't going to be satisfied with just a murder charge. I wanted Mr. Drummond to lose everything."

The woman started to cry. Grace hugged her. "You did right. Be strong now. This entire sordid tale is almost at an end."

Sarah sniffed and wiped her eyes. Once she appeared to have regained her composure, Sarah opened the door and held it for Grace to exit. "What else is there left to do?"

Grace sighed. "I've got to catch up with Brooke Jones before she does anything she might regret."

CHAPTER 58

Brooke's decision to return home was a bad one. As soon as she materialized in her bedroom, she was tackled by a man. She hadn't expected anyone to be there. As they struggled, the man called for help and tried to put some handcuffs on her. Some of her self-defense lessons played in her mind, and she managed to reverse the grips on who held who. She tossed the man across the floor.

As she stood, a second man entered the room and pulled a Taser from his hip. "Stop where you are."

"Who are you and what are you doing in my house?"

"FBI, Doctor Jones. We're here to take you in. Come peaceably."

"I don't think so." She walked past him. He fired the weapon, and the electrodes bounced off her, unable to penetrate her skin. Still, for the briefest of moments she had felt the electrical shock and staggered one step. Regaining her senses, she continued on into the living room with the two men in pursuit. There was no sign of her comp pad. She turned and faced them, holding out her hand in a gesture to stop. "I'm not going with you and I don't want to hurt you. I just came to grab a couple of things and I'll be out of your way."

The one with the Taser had dropped it to pull out a hand gun. "I need you to surrender, Doctor. I don't want to shoot. My orders are to take you alive if I can, but to take you one way or the other, dead or alive."

A shock at what the agent had just said angered her. "Are you nuts? This isn't the Wild West. I'm unarmed. You'd shoot an unarmed woman? Who gave this crazy order?"

"If I have to, I will shoot. The president has ordered your

apprehension at all costs. Your ability to pop in and out of places has panicked the country. Our orders are to stop you, no matter what."

Forgetting what she came for—it wasn't that important—she summoned the wormhole. "Good luck with that."

As the blackness enclosed her, the man fired his gun. The second man took a run at her, and then they were gone.

***

As she materialized in her new locale, she saw Francis look up from his desk, a surprised look on his face. "Brooke, is that really you? I've been hearing about your teleporting everywhere but seeing it happen in front of me, it's still hard to take in. Why have you come here?"

The sound of two spent bullets landing on the floor at her feet had Brooke glancing down to see them. *What else is that beside them?* She shook it off and returned her focus to Francis.

"I need your help. They're guarding my home and, I suspect, the houses of all my friends. The people I know at NASA will be the same." She grabbed a chair and pulled it close to him and sat down. She couldn't help but note his slight withdrawal. She reached slowly and took his hand in hers. "Please, don't be frightened of me. I'm not some monster. I'm still the same girl. Brooke."

Francis smiled and grasped her hands and patted them. "I'm sorry. I know better. The damned media have everybody jumping at shadows. What is it you want? How can I help?"

"I don't have a lot of time. The FBI has orders of shoot to kill. Look on the floor here. That's from the last attempt on my life in my living room. My own living room!"

Francis bent and picked up the two bullets and the other item as well. He turned it carefully in his hand. A drop of blood leaked from it. "Two bullets, yes, and I daresay, that's a fingertip. Look, part of the nail is there. It's a clean cut. What did you say happened?"

She took a deep loud breath. "As I was leaving, one of the men was shooting at me and the other was lunging for me. His finger must have got caught inside my wormhole and come with me."

"Ha! Did you get the ring?"

"The ring?"

Lord Sauron's one ring. The one that ruled them all. In the movies. *Lord Of The Rings*. You must have seen those. It like how Gollum bit off the finger of Frodo to get the ring."

"Yes, I did see them as a child." She smiled and almost succeeded in holding off the tears but a couple squeaked out. She freed a hand to wipe at them. "I'm sorry. This has been hard. I found out who killed Robert and why. I'm trying to set things straight. There's only one left to bring to justice."

Francis produced a kerchief and handed it to her. "There, there, dry those tears. If you know who it was, why not just turn him over to the police? I'm sure they can handle it."

"No, they won't. They won't, because this person without absolute solid evidence is beyond their reach. And I don't have that. Telling the courts I read it in someone's mind is not going to hold up. It's Samuel Davidson."

"The ex-president? You're serious? What do you intend to do?"

"I intend to make him confess, but I have to find him first. That's why I need your assistance. Help me find him, Francis. Help me find him."

"You promise me that's all you're going to do?"

"I promise."

He turned and picked up his comp pad. "Alright, let's start searching. It's not like they post his itinerary on the net. This might take some work."

She stood and gave him a kiss on the cheek. "Thank you, Francis. I hoped you would understand."

"I feel like Humphrey Bogart as Rick Blaine helping Ingrid Bergman as Ilsa Lund in *Casablanca*."

She hugged his arm as he worked. "You and your old movies. It's what makes you…you."

CHAPTER 59

Brooke materialized in two feet of water. She was supposed to be standing on a sandy beach but the moon must have brought the tide in. She glanced quickly around. The beach was deserted.

Probably not more than a hundred feet away were the numerous cabanas that dotted the shoreline near the high-end resort where former President Davidson was vacationing.

It had taken Francis a few hours to finally find the man. The unflattering paparazzi photo of the president in swim trunks and loose belly had been their best clue. Using only the photograph, Brooke had been able to teleport there. Now the only job left was to find Davidson.

She glanced up and down the long line of private beach huts behind the cabanas in an attempt to figure out which one was the president's. The two men sitting outside a larger unit some distance away offered a clue. *Guards.*

Until that moment, she still had had no idea on what she was going to do next. She only knew what she wanted to accomplish at the end of it all. *Do I try and sneak by them? Or do I try the frontal approach? The likelihood of sneaking by is pretty small.*

She stepped out of the water and started toward them. When she was halfway there, she noticed two more men strolling along the water's edge in her direction. *How many guards does a past president get?*

The two men must have noticed her because their pace picked up. She stopped walking and they slowed as they neared. The one closest stopped in front of her while the other circled a bit to her right. Both wore small headsets. "Hello there, lady. This part of the beach is off limits right now. You're going to have to leave."

"I'm afraid that's not possible. I'm here to see someone."

The man to her right pulled his gun out. "Hey, wait a second. You're that astronaut, Brooke Jones!"

The first man followed suit. "Doctor Jones, I don't know what you think you're doing. But I need you not to try anything stupid. Turn around and start walking."

"I told you. I need to see somebody." She used her telekinesis and lifted the man in the air and out over the water. The other one stepped closer, the gun pointed at her chest. "I don't know how you're doing that, but put him down. Right now!"

She willed the man out to her maximum distance, fifteen feet, and dropped him in the ocean. "Whatever you want."

She turned and started toward the large hut. The two men in front of it turned toward her. She noted they were wearing headsets as well. One guard was still holding a gun on her as he followed her across the sand. "It's Brooke Jones. What do I do?"

The other man by the hut pulled his gun. "Shoot her, you idiot! Shoot her!"

She heard the bangs and felt the stings where the bullets hit. She trudged forward and hit the fellow in front of her with the flat of her hand, sending him flying across the beach. The other one stepped back and brought a hand to the mouthpiece of his headset. "Intruder alert. Brooke Jones is headed in. Gunfire is ineffective, please advise."

The door to the hut burst open and two more men charged at her. She managed to evade the first but the second caught her square. There was no choice left but to fight. She swung a fist that the man tried to block but that connected regardless. He crumpled to the ground. The other tried to grab her from behind and put her in a nelson. As she pulled her arms forward to break free, the fellow screamed and let go. She glanced back to see him holding his shoulder.

The sound of the door opening again regained her attention. Bolting away down the beach was Samuel Davidson. She took off after him. It took her a hundred yards or so, but she caught up with him and grabbed him by the collar. She remembered how he liked to be called by his nickname. "Looks like you're out of shape, Sammy."

"Please, let me go. I didn't do nothing."

The remaining FBI men caught up, guns raised. "Let him go!"

"I'm afraid not. The former president and I have a little talking to do."

She pulled him close and summoned the wormhole to encompass them both. As the last of the blackness closed in, Sammy screamed.

***

Brooke materialized with Sammy still in her grip on the observation deck of the Empire State Building. She had visited it as a child. It was late but there was still a small crowd who were gawking at her and commenting on who she was and on President Davidson being with her. It was what she needed, an audience.

She used her telekinesis to lift herself and Sammy up and over the guard rail. He ceased his struggling and clung to her. "What are you doing? Are you crazy?"

"What I'm doing is asking from you a confession for all those people to hear. If I don't get one, I let you go."

"Are you nuts? I'm not confessing to anything. I ain't done nothing wrong."

People thronged at the rail, gawking. She heard one yell to go ahead and drop the bum; he was a criminal. That remark brought a round of similar calls.

She shook him. "Think again, Sammy. Think about it carefully. I don't want the people here to believe I put words in your mouth so you'd parrot whatever I say to get free. Think about your plans to get on the board at Drumdat. Think about your last attempt to get on it."

She could see the memories of his directions to Janice to make an accident happen. They were at the top of his mind. But also was a thought on how he would never tell, no matter what. This wasn't working. She needed another plan.

A police officer appeared at the rail, Taser in hand. "Miss, it's time you put the president down."

"He hasn't confessed yet. I want everyone to hear his confession."

The crowd was pressing closer to see. She had to get Sammy to talk. She stretched her arm out in hopes that if he dangled away from her body, his fear might make him acquiesce. "Talk, Sammy. Now, or I let you go!"

Someone jostled the cop and he fired the Taser.

The electrodes bounced off her like they had before. But just like the last time, she felt the momentary shock. She released the president. By the time she had regained her senses, he was too far below to reach with her mind.

She watched him fall. His screams carried back to her and everyone gathered. There was nothing she could do. She could hear the people on the deck shouting that she had killed President Davidson and demanding the police officer shoot her.

Panic rose in her. *This is not what I wanted to happen. I wanted him to confess.*

She summoned the wormhole.

CHAPTER 60

President Pallabee sat at the Resolute Desk in the Oval Office listening to the report from his chief of staff. What an ugly mess. The whole situation with Brooke Jones had gotten way out of hand. And the antics of his predecessor were no less worrisome. "What else do you have to tell me?"

"Just one last report, sir, from an Agent Grace Simpson. She's waiting outside right now."

"Bring her in."

He decided to make things less formal and moved from behind the desk to a settee where the agent could sit across from him. She was brought in and, after formal introductions, took the seat indicated. "Thank you for seeing me, Mr. President, at this late hour. I know how valuable your time is but, though they are not entirely complete, I thought it best to present my findings to you as soon as possible."

"If there is any new light that you can shed on this debacle, I am most receptive to hearing it."

"Yes, sir. First of all, we've retrieved video footage of what happened when President Davidson fell."

"You mean when he was thrown to his death."

"No sir, that's just it. Doctor Jones dropped him when she was hit by a Taser gun."

"What of it? I understand the woman is invulnerable to even gunfire. I don't think a tap from a Taser would have any effect. The officer involved reported that the projectiles failed to pierce her skin and fell away."

"Yes, but I believe she still suffered an electric shock for just a

264

moment. I have it from one of our men in Florida that when he tried to Taser Doctor Jones in her home, the woman stumbled. Clearly, she's not immune to electrical shock. She may never have intended to drop him. It was an accident."

"Accidents don't happen when you hold a man twelve hundred feet up in the open air. Whether intentional or not, she brought about the death of a former president of the United States."

"Yes, sir, I understand. But further to her motives. Everyone heard her last night demanding President Davidson to confess. I now possess sworn testimony from his chief of staff, Janice Roberts, that President Davidson ordered the attempt on the life of Doctor Jones when she was in my custody."

This was troubling news. If word got out about Samuel Davidson ordering a hit on a citizen by security agents, the sanctity of the Office of the President would forever be tarnished. The quick public opinion polls that day had many people touting Miss Jones as a hero, not a criminal. Not just a hero, but a superhero. He needed to bring things to an end. "Thank you, Agent Simpson. Submit your report to the director."

"But, Mr. President, don't you see? Brooke Jones may be—"

"I said thank you, Mrs. Simpson. Now please leave me to cogitate on the matter."

"Yes, Mr. President."

As his chief of staff escorted her out, he told the man to give him a few minutes of solitude. Why did that buffoon of a football player have to be the man who held the office before him? Although this was the worst of all his offenses, Davidson had left a trail of deceit and corruption throughout his two terms.

He sighed, got up, and returned to his desk. He still had a couple of calls to make before calling it a night. One that he had been postponing was to the NASA Administrator, Bartholomew Higginbottom. In his mind, the problem with Brooke Jones had begun with that man sending her to Mars in the first place.

He liked to be hands on and called the man's private line. It took almost no time to connect. The fellow must have been waiting for his call. "Bartholomew, I've had a trying day. Tell me you have some good news for a change."

"Mr. President, how good it is depends on your point of view. My staff and I have come up with a plan where, during your term, we can be the first to visit the stars."

"What are you talking about? I haven't time for games."

"No games, Mr. President. It's quite simple, really. All we need to do is design a capsule that could serve as a self-contained living unit for one person. Brooke Jones. Using her ability to create wormholes, she could explore the galaxy on our behalf. Not only would we learn of all that is out there, Brooke Jones would be out of your hair for good. Think of the possibilities."

"Right now, I'm thinking of nothing more than catching Doctor Jones and putting her in the deepest, darkest prison in the country. Besides, what makes you think she would agree to such a cockamamie idea?"

"No prison could hold her. You know that. She's still an astronaut at heart, and whether you believe it or not, an honest and faithful American. She knows she has no place here at home right now. With Robert gone and that incident last night, there's nowhere she can go. And, after all, this is her idea."

"Hers? Are you saying you've been in contact with Doctor Jones? Where is she? I'll send the FBI to bring her in right away."

266

"I'm afraid that would be impossible because right now…she's on Mars."

He was flabbergasted. It was ludicrous, yet it had potential. Bartholomew was right. No prison would hold her. His only choice would be to have her killed somehow. He thought again of what the polls would show if he had to do that.

"Mr. President?"

In his stupor, he had forgotten about the NASA Administrator. "I'm sorry, Bartholomew. I was lost in thought for a moment."

"I can appreciate that. So… do we have a deal?"

***

Brooke examined the new samples she had retrieved from the cave. Unlike the methanogens she had recovered on that first trip, these were multi-celled. Life on Mars had progressed further than they had originally thought. It was believed the transition from single-celled to multi-celled organisms was a process that took many millions, if not hundreds of millions of years. The distance from multi-celled to complex animals was a comparatively short hop.

She was thankful there was still one working space suit in the Mars habitat. Exploring the planet had been a great thing to keep her mind occupied. After all, she had been there almost ten months since that horrible night at the Empire State Building. Brooke still suffered the odd pang of guilt, but, all in all, she was mostly over it.

When the bell rang, she knew a new message from Earth was waiting for her. She hit the key, and Bart's smiling face showed up. "Brooke…it's time to come in. It's ready."

She took the time to gather up a few small mementos and a sealed container with the multi-celled organisms. She was a little nervous but, deep down, she knew it was time. It only took an instant to call the wormhole.

***

She appeared in Bart's office. "I'm here."

Bart rose from his seat and came around his desk. He held out his hand palm up for her to take. "Are you ready?"

She dropped her hand into his. "I'm ready."

It felt like some kind of royal procession. Everyone they passed wished her well, some even applauded or cheered. They took the short ride to the hanger and when she got out of the vehicle, she was greeted by all her friends. Jesse was back from his tour on the moon. Mark and Brian were there as well. She hugged them all and gave each of them a stone from Mars with obvious fossil markings.

Francis was there, too. To him, she gave the sealed canister. "Open with care."

He was crying. "Stay with us, Brooke. Don't go." He wiped at the tears. "I feel like the Tin Man."

She kissed him on the cheek. "Don't worry. I'll be fine."

Behind them stood the habitat. It was round, like a ball, but with a flat bottom. Through a large window in the front, she could see a chair and a headrest that looked to be dead center. She went to the hatch, stopped, and turned back to face everyone. "Well, I guess I'd best be on my way."

Bart handed her a bundle. It was a jacket with an insignia showing the planet Earth and the name Earth I emblazoned on it. "We had this made for you. Our hope is you'll have the chance to wear it proudly should you encounter another intelligent species."

She put it on and gave the little man a long hug. "I'll miss you, Bart, perhaps most of all. You were always in my corner."

She stepped into the machine and took the seat. Aki poked his head into the still-open hatch. "Everything is done as the designs I've been sending you. It's nuclear-powered and should have a life of fifty years."

He closed the hatch and joined the others standing out in front of her. They all waved. She could hear their calls of encouragement. Mark was the last. "You go, girl!"

She concentrated to bring the wormhole to envelope the entire ship. She thought of it that way now. A ship, to pilot to the stars.

Everything went black.

***

Brooke stepped out onto the surface of the moon. The first wormholing of the ship had gone without a hitch. This was her first stop. She walked over to the memorial and placed her hand on the brass image. "Good-bye, dear Robert. Perhaps, in my travels, I'll find heaven out there. I know you'll be waiting."

She re-entered the ship, summoned the wormhole once again, and concentrated on the stars above.

EPILOGUE

The Voyager 2 spaceship woke up. Systems were coming back on. Its internal clock had stopped so it had no idea how long it had been lifeless. The nuclear engine that fed it had run out but energies surrounding it had recharged it somehow but only just enough for a short time.

It began to take readings once more. The flow of photons around it ebbed and swirled. It was at the Heliosheath. As it pierced through, hundreds of blank readings flashed past its sensors.

There was only enough energy to send one last message home.

OTHER NOVELS by MICHAEL DRAKICH

GRAVE IS THE DAY

In October of 1957, more than Sputnik fell to Earth...

Set against the back drop of the Space Race and the Cold War, both the United States and the Soviet Union have a new issue to deal with, aliens from outer space. Both the Braannoo and the Muurgu are at war with each other and Earth becomes the newest battleground in their struggle. Spanning time from the launch of Sputnik to the near future, the interplay of historical events from a new light make you ask the question, could this all be true? The capture of aliens near small town USA unites three players from different quarters, Commander Kraanox of the Braannoo, First Lieutenant Wayne Bucknell as his captor and seven year old Justin Spencer, the first to make alien contact.

Grave Is The Day is a superb read! This story is a must read for all the science fiction, extraterrestrial lovers on Earth. Grave Is The Day has earned my rating of 5 stars! --Ramsey's Reviews

I have read books that meld fantasy with historical events before, but never one that takes such minute details and blends them so thoroughly. This is a great read and an exceptional rewrite of history for all ages. – Bitten By Books

He created each character with amazing attention to detail and development. I thoroughly enjoyed this book and found myself identifying with more than one of the delightful characters. --Paranormal Romance Guild - Beth Price

271

THE BROTHERHOOD OF PIAXIA

Years have passed since the overthrow of the monarchy by the Brotherhood of Warlocks and they rule Piaxia in peaceful accord. But now forces are at work to disrupt this rule from outside the Brotherhood as well as within! In the border town of Rok, a young warlock acolyte, Tarlok and his older brother, Savan, captain of the guard, become embroiled in the machinations of dominance. While in the capital city, Tessia, the daughter of Piaxia's most influential merchant, begins a journey of survival. Follow the three as their paths intertwine, with members of the Brotherhood in pursuit and the powerful merchant's guild manipulating the populace for their own ends.

Great, well-rounded characters? Magic running rampant? A lost princess? Yes, this book has it all. – tHe crooked WorD

If you love fantasy that mixes magic, lost royalty, sacrifices, heroes, and strong characters, I would suggest The Brotherhood of Piaxia. – Captivated Reading

The Brotherhood of Piaxia is what it wants to be - a real entertaining fantasy story. It comes along with more characters than you normally get but a lot less then you meet in a famous series you can watch at HBO. It has definitely more magic than a famous fantasy trilogy you could see in cinemas. There is less blood and gore than in a book with a title how to serve a drink. It is also a book which does not drown in romance. For me is a book which you like to read when you want to have a well dosed mix of well-known books. Or in simple words The Brotherhood of Piaxia is like the espresso you enjoy after a good meal. – Edi's Book Lighthouse

LEST THE DEW RUST THEM

Terrorism in America has a new game…decapitations!

Homeland Security Director Robert Grimmson faces the task of catching five men in New York City. They call themselves the Sword Masters with a single minded plan of terror through decapitations.

Barely has the task begun when a new arrival at JFK is a man importing thousands of swords! Alexander Suten-Mdjai is a trainer in the deadly art of swordsmanship and Robert cannot help but believe there is a connection between him and the Sword Masters.

As he goes about the task, each step in his search is made more difficult through the interference of politicians, the media and his own government.

Robert's examination constantly draws him back to Alexander who regales him with a tale of swordsmanship from his lineage featuring events of mankind's bloody past and often oddly having a connection to the case before him.

With the clock ticking as New York collapses into a deep panic, he must catch the Sword Masters before it is too late!

This one of the best suspense thrillers I have read in a long time. – Voracious Reader

This book was really, really good. It was action packed from beginning to end. I could hardly wait to finish and see what would happen. – The Book Worm

This entire book was nothing but entertaining. I have never read a crime-type book that I liked and this book was so good that it's going on my favorite's shelf. – Angels In The Underworld

DEMON STONES

It's been almost a hundred years since warlock meddling freed the demons from their underground domain. Their eventual capture has encased them in large stones across all the lands. They became known as the *demon stones*.

Over time, the truth of their imprisonment devolved into legend and tales to frighten children.

Now, the seven kingdoms are in upheaval. The demon stones are being opened and the vile creatures once more roam the land. War has broken open between realms as the fingers of accusation are pointed.

Caught in the middle is Gar Murdach, a farm boy who recently passed the age of ascension of sixteen marking him as a man, and his younger sister, Darlee, as they both struggle in their separate ways to escape the horrors wrought by the demons and the war that swarms round them.

Sometimes a trip into a fantasy world, filled with the magic of the mind is a good place to go, add the intense story line, the detailed world and a young hero who clearly started out WAY out of his league and it becomes clear that sometimes fantasy characters mirror reality. – Diane at Tome Tender (Amazon Top 500 Reviewer)

Die-hard fantasy fans, particularly those who like a bit of high fantasy, will adore this book just as I did. – Kyra – The Review List

I would recommend this book to those who enjoy a good fantasy which is well-written and easy to follow. Well done, Mr. Drakich! – S. A. Molteni – And So It Begins…